Peggy **Chernow**

SECRETS

Other novels by Peggy Chernow

Despicable Lies

Second Chances

Trapped

Dangerous Attraction

Destiny

Monkedia Publishing dates: 09/2021

To families everywhere and especially to my own:

First and foremost,
to my loving and always supportive husband, Bart.

To our older daughter Anne and her wonderful husband
Woody - the parents of our two eldest and deeply cherished
grandchildren, Hunter and Logan.

To our youngest daughter Shandee and her two adorable
boys, our rambunctious and lovable grandsons,
Chase and Charlie.

To my precious sister,
Kay and her devoted husband, Dudley (Bun).

And to my brother-in-law, Ron -
a much better author than myself.

May you always know how much you are loved.

PART ONE

THE

ROMANCE

CHAPTER 1

Mattie Cartwright was always early. This evening she sat alone at one of the many high-top tables at *The Pelican Bar* in Ft. Lauderdale. She was expecting her on-again, off-again boyfriend Chad and a few friends from work and from her University of Florida years to join her in celebrating her 35th birthday. Slowly sipping an ice-cold apple martini, she was enjoying a delicious selection of happy hour appetizers while she waited for them. The shrimp, calamari and fried clams were wonderfully spicy, and she enjoyed every tasty bite.

Looking around the crowded room, she searched for familiar faces. She knew many people in town, having been born and raised here. She was popular and had a wide circle of friends and business connections. Her college friends were usually late, and tonight was no exception. Tardiness was a habit she deplored. She felt it showed disrespect and therefore she consciously strove to be on time.

Men and women of all ages were milling around, chatting, and flirting with each other, while trying to show themselves off to their best advantage. She usually never allowed herself the luxury of time to enjoy the lively bar scenes. She was too much of a workaholic, but tonight she was content to sit back, relax, and people-watch.

She noticed an attractive young woman, probably a college student, sitting by herself at a table, self-consciously dusting cracker crumbs off of her blouse and pretending to be fascinated by the happy hour drink menu. She was drinking a soda so probably she was under twenty-one, the legal drinking age in Florida. The sight of the girl's obvious discomfort triggered memories of Mattie's own, often lonely, adolescence.

She had been raised by a hard-working, loving, mother who had been widowed when Mattie was barely three years of age. Mattie did not remember her father, but as a child, her mother told her exciting stories about his life as a young Marine. He had been killed in the war and died a hero. His picture had always sat prominently on the living room mantle and still did. As a child, Mattie had envied her friends' large families. She yearned for her own brothers and sisters, but that never happened. She had to settle for a close relationship with her mother, Brenda, who over the years had become her confidant and best friend.

Living with her mother in a comfortable townhouse near *Victoria Park*, she endured the awkward teenage years when she was impatiently waiting to grow into her body, praying that her skimpy breasts and slim hips would fill out like those of her friends had. Her mother assured her they would, however, Mattie's boobs remained the same small mounds of soft flesh throughout her entire teenage years, no matter how much she pushed and massaged them, coaxing, and pleading with them to grow.

In college, her breasts had barely filled an 'AA' cup. Her roommates teased her when she regularly stuffed her *Playtex* padded bras with wads of Kleenex to make them appear bigger. She was tall and statuesque with a beautiful face, mesmerizing, wide, green eyes, and twin dimples. Everyone told her that she was lovely, but she had hated her body back then and had been desperate to improve it. From the gorgeous young woman, she had become today, no one would ever have guessed that she had once considered herself an ugly duckling. She suspected the young girl she'd been observing felt the same way about herself.

Mattie kept watching her with curiosity and shook her head. Something about her dejected, slumped posture tugged at Mattie's heart and reminded her of how she had felt as a young girl before she gained self-confidence from her breast implants. The successful cosmetic operation, a college graduation gift from her mother, had changed the way Mattie felt about herself and her body, and altered the way men looked at her. She had never regretted undergoing the surgery and was a vocal advocate for it to anyone who would listen. She would forever be grateful to her mother. She remembered gushing, "Mom most girls get bracelets or watches for graduation, but I got boobs. You are the best mother in the world."

Mattie felt instant empathy for the sad-looking, young woman. She was slim and pretty with large wide eyes and brown wavy hair. Aside from her shapeless top, she was a knockout. Had she been stood up by an inconsiderate date? Or was she hoping that some attractive man would miraculously stop by her table and offer to buy her a drink? Mattie continued sipping her martini. She remembered all too clearly how it felt to consider yourself unattractive and to feel the need to blend into the background, bringing no attention to oneself. She wished she could boldly march up to the young woman and suggest consulting a surgeon about gel implants. It could be life-changing for her. But of course, Mattie could not and would not do that. The young woman would be mortified. Mattie was bold, but not that brazen and especially not on her birthday.

Tonight, Mattie felt especially happy. She had taken extra time with her clothing selection and makeup application. In her Ralph Lauren mini dress, and red Louboutin heels, she appeared provocative and sexy. The delicate cut of her outfit showed off her shapely legs and accentuated her narrow waist, while enticingly displaying her perky breasts. A waiter approached. Mattie signaled for another drink. She noticed the girl she'd been watching had been joined by another girl and the two had left together. "Casey, this place sucks," she heard the girl's friend say, "Everyone's way too old. There's no action here."

Mattie bit back a smile. *Oh, to be that young again!* She put the young girl out of her mind and was ready to celebrate her birthday. She could not wait to get the party started.

CHAPTER 2

Happy Birthday," six of Mattie's friends shouted from across the room. They joyfully entered the bar carrying balloons and made their way to her. Mattie stood up and waved happily at them. Chad came up behind her, gave her a pinch on her butt and a wet, tongue tickling kiss. "You look fabulous," he gushed. "I swear, you get better every day."

Mattie disliked wet, messy kisses and wiped her lips in disgust with a cocktail napkin. She deliberately turned away from Chad to greet the rest of her friends. They all ordered drinks and more appetizers and began to laugh and chat amicably. Mattie stole a look at Chad and wondered once again why she was still dating him. He was attractive and well-dress, but a narcissist, only interested in his own pleasure. She should have tossed him to the curb months ago but had been too busy at work to make the effort. There at the bar table, she had a sudden epiphany and swore, as her birthday present to herself, that she would dump him tonight. Life was too short to waste on the likes of him.

As she laughed and talked with her friends, she glanced around the room, half expecting her mother to walk in with a birthday cake. Brenda was traditional in that way and Mattie's friend's adored that and would welcome her. She was almost as young in spirit and certainly as beautiful as her daughter. Mattie was a little disappointed that she did not see her mother, but she did spot her boss, Charles Cord, sitting by himself at a corner table. He was nursing a tall exotic looking drink and munching on a plate of nachos. She left Chad and her friends momentarily and went to say hello. "Are you here by yourself?" she asked. "Come join me and my friends. We're celebrating my birthday. There's no need for you to drink alone."

Charles looked up at her and grinned. He was always astonished at how beautiful she was. Tonight, as he sat, she towered over him in her four-inch stilettos and looked very sexy in her low-cut mini dress. He noticed men around the room turning to gaze appreciatively at her. She was a remarkably attractive woman and reminded him of the famous actress Lynda Carter, who starred in the *Wonder Woman* movies - statuesque and breathtakingly gorgeous.

"Thanks, Mattie. I'd really like to join you but I'm waiting for a friend. We're trying to wrap up a deal before we enjoy dinner together. Can we celebrate later in the week? I have a birthday gift for you back at the office."

"Okay, of course. If you're sure?" She kissed him lightly on his cheek and wondered who his lucky date was that evening and why she was keeping him waiting. He was so special and deserved to have a nice woman in his life, but for the ten years she had known and worked for him, he had not been with anyone seriously. He dated often, and always lovely, cultured women, but he explained that he had not connected with "the right one." He had been married briefly in his thirties, but soon realized the union was a mistake. The two had separated amicably and although long divorced, were still friends to this day. Mattie admired that.

She returned to her friends and in a few minutes, a waiter came over to the table carrying a tray holding two chilled bottles of Dom Perignon and champagne flutes. "Compliments of Mr. Cord," he announced with a broad smile. "The gentleman said to enjoy yourself, and he's taking care of your party's dinner tab. He left his credit card number with me."

Mattie looked gratefully back at where Charles had been sitting, planning to thank him, but he was gone. She did not have time to worry if he had been stood up or simply left on his own accord. Her friends were anxious to have fun and in spite of the expensive champagne, they were already downing shots.

Mattie's best friend Linda, who worked with her at Lux Charters, handed Mattie a small gift bag containing a card and a bottle of Chanel # 5 perfume. "Your favorite, right?" she said. "Don't waste it on that obnoxious Chad."

"I most certainly won't," Mattie hugged her friend affectionately. "I'm going to handle that situation later tonight. Thank you, Linda. You're the best."

Chad barged in between the two girlfriends. "Let's really get this party started." He squeezed Mattie tightly, letting his fingers drift and linger a few seconds too long on her breasts before he snickered. "The birthday girl's already two drinks ahead of us. We all need to catch up."

CHAPTER 3

Mattie and her friends partied, ate dinner, and danced until after 1:00 a.m., when she yawned politely and announced that she needed to go home. "Tomorrow's still a workday for me and I have two potential clients to meet."

"I understand," Linda said, a conspiratorial smile forming on her lips. "I think Mattie wants a private nightcap with Chad. Let's leave the lovebirds alone." She winked at Mattie and mouthed 'good luck', as she led their friends away.

"You couldn't wait to get me alone," Chad's face lit up with anticipation. "Is it going to be my lucky night? Can I get a birthday bang?"

"Not exactly. That's so crude, Chad. I just think it's time we had a serious talk."

"Oh really. What about?" His smile faded a little. Her expression had grown serious.

"Frankly. I think it's time you and I parted ways. We've been together on and off for over a year, and I honestly don't know why. We're still with each other. We've never had any real communication or the same goals. We come from such different backgrounds. You have been given everything you need and more, by rich, indulgent parents who worship you and seem to expect nothing from you. At thirty-six, you don't even have a job, for God's sake. How long are you going to let your folks support you?" She looked at him with disgust.

"My mother and I have always had to work hard for everything we have, and we appreciate what we have achieved. I told you on our first date, that I was not desperate to find a man. I do not need or expect someone else to support me, but were I to get into a relationship, I do want stability and to know there is the possibility of a future."

"A future?" he interrupted caustically. "How can anyone have a future with you? All you do is work. You are as good as married to Lux Charters.

"I don't want to argue Chad. Things are not working between us and I'd rather we part as friends. There's no need to hurl accusations around. Let's just decide this is over and go our separate ways."

He seemed dumbstruck by the absurdity that she would actually want to break up with him. The ridiculous thought had never crossed his mind. He considered himself quite a catch and believed any woman would be happy to be on his arm. He shook his head at her in utter disbelief. "I'll give you one chance to apologize Mattie and to change your mind. Get a grip. There are not too many guys around like me." His temper was about to boil over. "Well? What's your decision going to be?"

She shot him a quizzical glance. He could not possibly be that dense. What had she been thinking staying with him all this time? "I thought I made myself perfectly clear, Chad. We are done!"

Her reply was met with his stony silence. "Have it your way, Bitch." He sullenly gathered up his glass and a few remaining greasy fried shrimps before stalking off.

CHAPTER 4

Mattie returned to her oceanfront condo and although she was tired and had a little too much to drink, she was overwrought and too annoyed at Chad to sleep. Kicking off her heels, she curled up on the sofa and gazed around the living room that she loved.

Her one-bedroom apartment with its large balcony overlooking the ocean was decorated with sophisticated beachy furniture designed for comfort and relaxation. It was her private retreat from the world, and she had carefully selected every item in it. Against the backdrop of the blue Atlantic Ocean, the furniture, white and overstuffed, was covered in a soft white fabric with colorful throw pillows scattered everywhere. A large square, glass-topped coffee table held nautical coasters, and a collection of conch shells that she had found on her walks on the beach over the years. A tall glass bookcase stood in one corner, holding her favorite novels, a few pictures in decorative frames and books on famous yachts, and yachting capitals around the world. Glass triangular trophies from the last three consecutive years, touted her achievement as the Lux Charters salesperson of the year. They were prominently displayed. The trophies made Mattie happy. She had worked long and hard to become successful at her craft and her accomplishments made her proud. When she had earned enough in commissions for a substantial down payment, she had made an offer on the condo unit and become a proud property owner. She accepted no help from her mother, or Charles, both of whom offered to loan her the money. As always, she was determined to do things herself. Maybe that determination was one reason she wanted to distance herself from Chad. He had no aspirations, no remarkable achievements to his credit, and he didn't seem to have any motivation to better himself. He was content to party, smoke a little weed, and spend his daddy's money. Mattie could not respect that…or him.

Growing sleepy, she nestled into the comfort of the sofa, grabbed an Afghan, and closed her eyes. She began remembering how and when she had first met Charles Cord. He was her boss and the man who had made her present financial circumstances possible.

On a cool evening in early May when she was twenty-five, she was invited to a pool party at the palatial home of one of her friend's parents. There was a large crowd of Mattie's peers in attendance and an even larger number of guests invited by the host and hostess. Wine and liquor bars were stationed next to a small calypso band on the dock of the property which overlooked the intracoastal waterway. An enormous buffet table was set up to serve food poolside. It was a festive evening of good food and stimulating conversation. A few guests swam in the pool, but most stayed on dry land and enjoyed themselves with food and drinks.

Early in the evening someone introduced Mattie to Charles Cord. He was the handsome and dynamic, much talked about and admired, middle-aged CEO of Lux Charters. His reputation was well known in yachting circles and the international boating community. His picture had graced many boating magazine covers over the years. He was considered quite the eligible bachelor and a sought-after dinner party guest.

Charles had started his company with less than one thousand dollars and, in a short period of time, he had built it into one of the most prestigious yacht chartering companies in the United States. He was anxious to expand its reach to Europe and beyond. To him, the chartering business had endless possibilities. He had been a boat enthusiast since he was a young child and he loved life on the open seas. He nurtured his company's growth as a father would a child's…with complete single-minded attention and devotion.

That night, Charles had taken one look at Mattie and was immediately impressed by her beauty and poise. She was a striking woman, tall and elegant. As soon as he had the chance, he led her away from the crowd, so they could talk privately. They started chatting and spent the rest of the evening huddled together as he asked questions about her life, interests, and hobbies. He explained his business to her in great depth. She was fascinated by the story of how he grew his business from a small, one-man operation into the massive enterprise Lux Charters was today. She appreciated his hard work and that he had made his success happen by his own initiative and grit.

She willingly remained by Charlies' side all evening, feeling an immediate connection to him. He was old enough to be her father, but she was inexplicably drawn to him…not in a sexual way, but by his magnetism and vision. He was as dynamic as his reputation and as handsome as any movie star. The combination was awesome. His athletic build and golden tan indicated that he spent a lot of time outdoors, mostly on yacht decks or on their swim platforms.

"Mattie," he'd said earnestly after several hours of speaking with her, "I am successful because I operate on instinct and don't overthink everything. I genuinely believe that you and I were destined to meet and that you will become my lucky charm, if you believe in such things. I am not superstitious, but I do believe in first impressions, and you've made a damn good one on me."

"Thank you," she smiled warmly, a little startled by his effusiveness.

To his astute business eye, she projected the "perfect look," and the "perfect image" for the face of his company. He had been searching for such a person to represent Lux in person, and in print ads, as well as on the sales floor. From first appearances, Mattie had the magnetic personality to do it effortlessly...to entice wealthy clients to charter mega yachts with little regard for the costs. Although young by industry standards, she was mature, sophisticated, and carried herself with an air of self-confidence. In his mind, she was nearly perfect, and he became obsessed with convincing her to come work for him. He would settle for nothing less.

Without hesitation, he offered her a job. "What would you think about coming to work for me? I will make it financially worth your while and, believe me, you'll have the time of your life. In my opinion, there's no better job in the world."

"That is very flattering Mr. Cord, but I don't know anything about yachts and even less about the chartering business. The biggest boat I've ever been on is a twelve-foot sailboat," she answered somewhat embarrassed.

He chuckled, liking her honesty. "First, start by calling me Charles, and second, you let me worry about your lack of experience. I'll teach you everything you need to know. I can tell from talking with you that you'll be a quick learner. And I'll personally mentor you. That's how strongly I feel about you joining the Lux Charter family. I will not take 'no' for an answer. You'll soon learn that I'm persistent and usually get what I want...and I want you."

Mattie met his gaze directly and was intrigued, however, she was a little intimidated by his proposition. He was very intense, and she could see that he was determined to have his way. She stalled, asked many more questions until she was satisfied that his offer was legitimate - that he was not simply hitting on her. Then she made him incredibly happy by accepting the job.

"I'd be thrilled to give it a try," she smiled innocently. "I know I can sell almost anything, so why not charters?"

They spoke some more, and Charles agreed to pay her a generous base salary, much more than she was making at Macy's selling cosmetics, and with a good commission schedule, and a special bonus for every charter she procured for over a million dollars. He enticed her further by saying that Lux would pay her salary while she took all the courses necessary to obtain her sales license and then eventually her broker's license. He explained that brokers made more in commissions than regular salespeople. Charles promised to personally tutor her in all the intricacies and complexities of the business. He even offered to take her with him and to pay her expenses to visit the international boat shows in Monaco and Dubai that year and to introduce her to the local boating community. He emphasized that getting known in the right circles was necessary if she hoped to create a stream of ongoing referrals.

Mattie had thanked Charles profusely and left the party feeling energized and more excited than she could ever remember. Mr. Cord had given her the way to use her sales abilities and turn her skills into an exhilarating and lucrative career.

Mattie remembered that she had been too excited to keep the news to herself, so she woke up her mother, telling her about the meeting with the fabulous Charles Cord and his unbelievable job offer.

Brenda had been stunned by her daughter's good fortune. As a good catholic, Brenda looked up to the heavens, made the sign of the cross over her chest and silently thanked God for Mr. Cord and the wonderful opportunity he was giving Mattie. "I knew the good Lord would provide," she said gratefully to her daughter. "He always does."

As a mother, Brenda had worried that Mattie might never find a job with a decent salary and good benefits. Mattie's degree in English literature had not opened any career doors, and her job selling Bobbie Brown and Chanel makeup at Macy's was not a career Brenda had envisioned for her daughter. Tonight, as if by magic, a once in a lifetime opportunity had presented itself. Brenda felt certain that Mattie's financial future would now take care of itself. Her daughter was one of those people who could sell ice cream to the *Good Humor Man*, and now she would have a chance to show off her skills to everyone. Meeting Charles Cord might turn out to be the best thing that ever happened to Mattie. Brenda could not wait to meet and personally thank the man for his generosity.

"This deserves a celebration." Brenda smiled affectionately at her daughter. "How about a glass of wine and a piece of homemade chocolate cake? I just baked it this afternoon."

"I'll skip the wine," Mattie had grinned. "I'm high enough on life right now. But I will definitely take a piece of cake…and a *very big* one at that."

Before she could reminisce any further, Mattie gave into her weariness and fell into a sound sleep.

CHAPTER 5

Mattie had learned about budgeting and fiscal responsibility at an early age from her mother's example. As a young child, she methodically saved her weekly allowance, allocating a few dollars for herself and a small tithe for the church. She saved the rest in an old-fashioned piggy bank. The habit of saving had stayed with her. She was generous but not a spendthrift.

At seventeen, she graduated from high school and before attending The University of Florida on a full scholarship, she began waiting tables for the breakfast and lunch shifts at the *Grand Floridian Diner*. She also sold trendy, one-of-a-kind pieces of clothing in the afternoons that summer at an upscale ladies' boutique on Las Olas Boulevard.

Mattie was a born saleswoman. She could convince customers that they needed whatever it was that she was selling, whether it was eggs benedict, or an expensive cashmere scarf. She earned the most tips at the diner, and she collected the largest commissions at the boutique. She knew selling was her forte… but had not yet found her special niche. Hopefully college would point her in the right direction.

Her University of Florida years were fun-filled, and she studied hard to make good grades. She worked at a part- time job in the afternoons and some evenings in the University bookstore for extra spending money. Her mother was widowed and there was not much spare cash in the household. Brenda, a senior department head at a branch office of the *Bank of America*, did her best to support her daughter, giving her most of what she wanted and all of what she needed. The expenses for Mattie's breast implants had taken a large bite out of her savings, but she gladly sacrificed her nest egg for her daughter's happiness.

After college, Mattie floundered for a few months, but finally took a job at Macy's, selling Bobby Brown and Chanel makeup. Quickly becoming extremely successful at moving huge amounts of inventory and convincing women of all ages that they could not live another day without those makeup and skin care lines, she rediscovered her sales abilities and realized that selling of some sort was to be her vocation.

Mattie became excellent at reassuring the ladies who visited the cosmetic counter that the colors she'd chosen for them made them appear more youthful. She showed the women application tips and taught them how to apply false eyelashes. Her reputation grew and many socialites in town made appointments and came to Macy's for Mattie to do their makeup before important social events. She gained a reputation for honesty and was well-liked and trusted by her fellow colleagues, as well as her customers. In two years, her success was noticed and rewarded by management. She was promoted to head the entire cosmetic division… the youngest woman ever to hold that title. It was a major achievement for her. Neiman's and Saks tried unsuccessfully to entice her away from Macy's, but Mattie was loyal and appreciated how well she had been treated there. She had no desire to change stores, although the idea of selling something other than makeup was beginning to intrigue her more and more. She knew she wanted a career in sales but had not yet found the right product … until she met Charles Cord. When he convinced her to join him as a saleswoman at his yacht chartering company, her future was set, and she soon became their leading saleswoman.

With help from Charles, she submitted her application and the necessary fee to obtain a license to sell or charter boats. Several weeks later, after passing the rigorous test, she was finally ready to begin her chartering career. Florida law required her to work for three years as a saleswoman before she could apply for her broker's license, but that was not a hardship. Because of Charles' generosity and guidance, she felt ready to start earning commissions right away.

From the first day on the job, Mattie fell in love with the gorgeous mega yachts she represented and with the exciting itineraries she could provide for her clients. She quickly learned nautical terms, toured numerous yachts of all sizes, and met personally with the crews. She willingly turned down socializing with her friends, instead, immersing herself completely in her job. That commitment left little time for anything else. However, she did not feel deprived. She was completely focused on Lux and spent all her free time studying and learning about the different kinds of rental agreements, bare boat charters, and the complexities of the business. She became thoroughly acquainted with Coast Guard requirements and general maritime rules. By the end of her first six months in the business, she knew almost as much as most captains about charters and their complexities.

Every morning, after her daily run with Linda, she looked forward to the office. She loved working for Charles. He was a delightful, fifty-five-year-old man, who lived and breathed mega yachts and the cruising business. He shared his enthusiasm for the company with Mattie in their tutoring sessions and whenever she was free to listen to him. Every time he went to check out a new yacht or one that had been recently refurbished, he took her with him so she could see for herself why one boat was a better fit than another for a particular customer's needs. She found the business as exciting and glamorous as he did. It was hard for her to realize that she had grown up in Ft. Lauderdale, (nicknamed the Venice of America), and yet this was her first exposure to the luxurious and glamorous yachting world.

Charles assured her that there was no limit to how much money she could earn if she worked hard. He explained that many of his ultra-rich clients preferred to charter rather than to purchase their own yachts because it was simpler, more cost effective, and convenient. They could enjoy their vacation at sea with no worries about the boat's maintenance or hiring staff. If anything went wrong, it was the responsibility of the first mate or the captain.

Most who chartered were wealthy men and women, who could easily afford to rent the mega yachts and they did not worry about what it cost. It was their way of stroking their egos and showing off to friends and acquaintances. Mattie quickly learned to flatter her clients, but to keep her distance and fend off their advances. Her one rule was that she never dated or became emotionally involved with customers. Many persisted in flirting with her, but she always politely refused their invitations and advances.

In the ten years Mattie had worked for Lux, she had become Charles's most successful and trusted salesperson. She also acted as the office manager and supervised the other fifteen brokers and sales associates. He treated her and all the others with fairness and kindness, but Mattie was his favorite, and she was like a daughter to him. He was extremely proud of her achievements. Compared to the other salespeople and brokers in his company, and in the industry as a whole, she was incredibly young. However, she was smart, quick-witted and knew exactly how to comport herself with the mostly male, often entitled, and spoiled clientele that the company served. He never regretted his decision to hire her.

The chartering business was very lucrative, and Mattie enjoyed the financial rewards. She continued to save, and after three years bought herself a beachfront condominium and she purchased two new Mercedes cars for herself and her mother. She loved giving back to Brenda in recognition of everything her mother had sacrificed to raise her.

Mattie had hoped that Charles and her mother would become romantically involved, because she loved them both so much and did not want them to be alone as they grew older, but romantic sparks had never flown between them. They were great friends, admired and like each other immensely, but treated each other like brother and sister, not like lovers. Mattie refused to give up hope and kept thinking of reasons to bring the two together. Brenda would have been receptive, Mattie thought, but Charles appeared to be a confirmed bachelor, at lease so he said.

When she purchased her own condominium, Mattie had been sad to be leaving her mother and her childhood home. She and Brenda were extremely close and kept no secrets from each other. Most of her friends had been desperate to escape the watchful eyes of their parents, but not Mattie. She enjoyed her mother's company and Charles was a frequent and welcome guest in their home. Charles and Brenda were busy people, but when they discovered their mutual interest in the performing arts, they began to spend more and more evenings together attending concerts and plays at the Broward Center for the Performing Arts or venturing to Miami to the Adrienne Arsht Center to see a performance.

Charles dated a lot of other women, and was frequently seen around town, but he liked Brenda the most. She was a strong willed and a beautifully independent woman, like her daughter. He was impressed by what a resourceful and caring person she was. The fact that she made the best Bolognese sauce he'd ever tasted, didn't hurt.

With little or no spare time, Brenda still managed to volunteer regularly in the community and was active in her church. She seemed tireless and was fiercely loyal to her daughter…a trait Charles admired. Over time, the three had become almost like a family. They often spent the holidays together and had traveled to Aruba together last winter. Mattie continued to hope that in time, and with the right "push" from her, that would become romantically involved.

CHAPTER 6

Mattie was at her desk. Everyone else had left the office for the day. She preferred the peace and quiet of after "business hours" to get her paperwork done. Sitting in front of stacks of glossy yacht brochures, she leafed through the lists of crew members trying to come up with the right match for her latest client.

Some yachts maintained the same crews for years and others changed seasonally. Some crews were specialists in watersports and handling families with children, teaching them snorkeling, scuba diving, and riding wave runners or tubing behind a speed boat. Others were trained in elegant, white glove service for the most demanding and discriminating clients. Those crews went about their daily chores in silence, unobtrusive and discrete, affording the client complete privacy and autonomy. They even signed privacy non-disclosure agreements, when asked to do so.

Mattie only matched a boat with a potential client if she had personally been on board the vessel, interviewed the crew, the captain, and the customer. Because of her diligence, she had never had a disgruntled client and most returned time and again to her for other charters. Other less diligent brokers relied on word-of-mouth recommendations and often experienced major melt downs when their clients voiced angry displeasure and demanded refunds. Mattie believed a good synergy between the crew and the client was imperative for a successful charter. In her mind, that was the hardest part of arranging a memorable cruise. It was easy to suggest a beautiful yacht for the client, but if there was friction or discord between the crew and the client, the cruise would be a disaster, and no one would be happy.

In her ten years with Lux, Mattie made it a point to attend as many major boat shows as possible. She went to the ones in Ft. Lauderdale, Miami, and Palm Beach every year. If her schedule permitted, she also visited the international shows in Monaco, Dubai, and Antigua, sometimes with Charles and sometimes by herself or with her friend and co-worker, Linda. There she interfaced with the crews and personally toured the new yachts coming into service for charter. She took the time to meet the captains, the chief stewardess, the first mates, the chefs, and the engineers. Mattie always took pictures and copious notes so as not to forget a single detail.

She had met her present client at the Palm Beach show last March. He was coming into her office in the morning to finalize arrangements and she was still struggling, trying to match his needs with the right crew. She had selected everyone except the chef.

The yacht's captain always had the final say on his crew members, but Mattie felt obligated to make suggestions on behalf of her customers and they were usually accepted. She had an extraordinary ability to connect the right personalities with the most appropriate crew. Tomorrow's client was a bit of a problem. He was a famous physician with his own medical television show, and he was used to preferential service and had very particular nutritional requirements. He also had two sets of children by two different wives. The ship's crew had to be able to entertain and supervise the younger children, ages five and seven, as well as provide adult events for the doctor, his second wife, and their older kids, ages 19 and 15. He was also bringing along two other prominent couples as his guests, a world-renowned heart transplant surgeon with his wife, and another physician who was the editor of a prestigious medical journal and his wife, a famous neurologist.

The chef Mattie hired had to be willing to serve grilled cheese or peanut butter and jelly sandwiches as well as lobster salad and cold cantaloupe soup at the same meal. It was a challenge, and some chefs were too temperamental and thought preparing child-friendly food was beneath them.

Mattie checked her lists one more time and finally decided upon Chef Jeff Gunner as her first choice. She called the yacht's captain to be sure her selection was acceptable to him. He agreed. After placing a call to Chef Gunner, describing her famous client and his needs, she offered him the job to prepare the meals on a three-week Caribbean cruise in February on *Lady Denise*, a 210-foot mega yacht. Jeff had worked on the boat previously and readily agreed. Mattie e-mailed the contract to him. When it was returned, she smiled contentedly, turned off the lights and locked the office door. She felt confident that her client would be pleased with her efforts and would have an enjoyable cruise.

It would be a real coup, Mattie thought, *if she could get him to agree to let her use his name as a reference. The Doctor Tony* television show was popular and a huge, Emmy winning hit. Almost everyone knew the program and the doctor's face was recognized wherever he went. His recommendation would mean a lot to Mattie professionally. If he agreed, Charles would be proud and pleased to add Dr. Tony Grant to the list of endorsements and to Lux's client list.

CHAPTER 7

A silver Mercedes-Benz Maybach convertible pulled into the reserved parking space in front of the Lux Charters in Bahia Mar. Dr. Tony Grant swung open his car door and strolled casually towards the office, stopping to glance at the pictures of the many mega-yachts artfully displayed in the front windows. He ran his fingers through his wind-blown blond hair and took off his sunglasses. Mattie recognized her famous client immediately and went outside to greet him.

"Good morning, Dr. Tony. Nice to see you again."

"Hi, Mattie. I hope you have everything ready. I'm in a bit of a rush today. We're filming a segment on hip replacements in two hours, and I need to be at Holy Cross Hospital for makeup and the taping. It seems my life is always in a rush these days."

"Well, that's the price of success," she grinned. "And that explains why you're here in person. I had presumed you would be sending one of your assistants to handle this paperwork for you."

"Normally yes, I would, but since I had to be in Ft. Lauderdale today anyway, I thought I'd like to see firsthand what you've selected and get reacquainted. It's been a few months since we talked." He could not help but admire how beautiful she was, although he was happily married to his young second wife and was not looking for any romantic complications. One expensive divorce had been one too many.

"I have everything right there." Mattie brought him inside and pointed to a long table on the side of the room where she had placed all the materials for him to view. "*My Lady Denise* is the yacht I selected for you. She is a gorgeous, white hulled, 210-foot mega yacht with the capacity for 14 guests and carries a crew of 12. She boasts an overly spacious owner's suite/office, two deluxe VIP suites, and four additional queen size guest staterooms, each with their own private bathroom. Among the many amenities on board are an outdoor hot tub, a massage room, a gym, two outdoor dining venues aft and an interior elegant dining room off the main salon seating 14. There is also a media room, an elevator and even a helicopter pad. Numerous toys are on board for all age levels…wave runners, a ski boat, innertubes and even an inflatable slide that can be attached to the side of the boat. The boat also carries fishing, snorkeling, and diving gear. Every one of your family and guests will find plenty to entertain themselves.

"I've laid out pictures and detailed bios of the crew, our standard charter agreement and preference sheets that you will need to complete with everything you and your guests will require to eat and drink, the type of wines and liquors you like, the specialty cuisines you favor - Sushi, French, Italian etc. and how many meals you want each day, either served or buffet style. The crew wants to know as much as possible about your likes and dislikes, so the cruise will be entirely to your specifications. The only thing I cannot control is the weather. But you will have a wonderful captain, and he will be able to maneuver the boat to avoid most storms or rough seas. Actually, in my experience, a day at sea in a gentle rain can be quite fun and relaxing.

"Then there's the preliminary itinerary," she continued. There were so many details to go over. "You can change your destinations daily, if necessary, depending on the weather and the seas. I will also need your preferences for the younger children's activities: DVDs and games they like to play. And finally, the names and passport numbers of your guests, and, very important, any food allergies you or they may have. You can actually dictate all the menus for every meal if you're so inclined, or after telling the chef your preferences, leave it to him to surprise you."

"I see you've been very thorough," he smiled, admiring her attention to detail. He wished his own assistants were half as efficient.

He began looking through the assorted paperwork. "I like the looks of this yacht. You are right. She's a real beauty. As I told you in Palm Beach, I have done extensive traveling around the world, but this cruise will be my first private charter. My wife and I are very excited about this opportunity, and if we don't get seasick or lose a child overboard, I'm sure this will be the first of many charters for us."

"I hope so," Mattie smiled. "I haven't lost a passenger yet. And there's nothing on earth, in my opinion, as fabulous as a vacation on a chartered mega yacht where all you have to worry about is what to eat or drink next or when to take a nap."

He continued looking through the pictures. "The crew's credentials appear very professional. I'll leave the menus and the rest of the other details to my wife, Laura. Like most husbands, I just say, 'yes dear' and sign the checks," he laughed good humoredly. "You know…happy wife, happy life. Can she scan these preference sheets back to you in a few days?"

"Of course. We need them thirty days before departure, so the crew can do the necessary provisioning. Today, I'll need a deposit for 1/3 the total amount of the charter and then the balance is due thirty days before sailing. The sum total for the charter, exclusive of food, wine, fuel, and other extras, will be $1,049,100. So that is $350,000 a week as we agreed upon. The gratuities should be paid to the captain at the conclusion of the charter, and twenty percent of the total, minus the provisioning is standard. But tipping is completely at your discretion. Pay a little more or a little less, depending on your satisfaction with the cruise."

"Yes, I understand," he answered and admitted, "I'm familiar with that tipping procedure because I am an avid fan of *Below Deck* with Captain Lee and his crew, which I watch faithfully on Bravo T.V."

"So am I," she laughed. "Captain Lee lives in Ft. Lauderdale. I some-times run into him at *Publix* or at places like *Shooters*. He's very friendly and always happy to chat with fans."

Dr. Tony looked at his watch. "Thanks again for your help, Mattie. I know we'll have a wonderful vacation, thanks to you. So, I'll write the check now and then please show me where to sign the charter agreement."

Mattie pointed out the places on the application where he needed to sign and initial. She carefully placed all the pictures and yacht informa-tion in a soft leather carry-on bag with the Lux Charters logo embossed in gold on one side and handed it to him. "If you or your wife think of anything else, please don't hesitate to call. I'm always available on my cell." She shook his hand.

"It's been a pleasure doing business with you Mattie. I hate to rush off, but duty calls."

She wanted to ask if she could use his name as a reference, but then thought better of it. It was probably smarter to wait until the cruise was over in the unlikely event anything went wrong.

As Dr. Tony pulled away in his expensive car, she gleefully pulled out her calculator and totaled her commission for his charter…over $52,000, but she would not get paid until he made the final payment. It was certainly something to look forward to.

"Linda," she spoke to her friend sitting at a desk close by. "Can you get out of here a little early this evening? Dinner's on me. I just closed Dr. Tony Grant for a three-week charter in the Caribbean."

"No kidding. That's great. I thought I recognized him when he came in. And yes, I can leave here anytime now. Where should we meet?"

CHAPTER 8

Mattie and Linda were seated at the bar in one of the prettiest restaurants in Ft. Lauderdale, *Grille 66*. It was located at the base of the Seventeenth Street bridge, on the Intracoastal waterway and at the entrance to Port Everglades. Many of the major cruise lines loaded and unloaded their passengers at the terminals there and one beautiful yacht after another passed by the restaurant, many tying up there for dinner in the evenings. Floor to ceiling windows afforded the diners seated inside great views and there was a lovely outside patio next to the dock. The bar was lively with personable bartenders who hosted nightly happy hours with specialty cocktails and pleasant banter.

"Tell me about Dr. Tony." Linda sipped her Cosmo. "Is he as nice as he appears on TV?"

"Yes, and more so," Mattie exclaimed. "He's a really down to earth guy. I think he'll be very happy with the charter I've arranged for him and his family."

"You always do a good job putting the right client on the right boat," Linda smiled warmly. She admired her friend tremendously. "But now spill the beans. Tell me what's really going on in your personal life. It's time for some honest girl talk. I haven't had a long conversation with you in ages. You're always running off to meet clients. How is it going with Chad, the cad?"

"It isn't going anywhere." Mattie looked disgusted and took a sip of her martini. "As you saw, he made an ass out of himself at my birthday celebration, and I told him we didn't have a future together. He was unbelievably arrogant and I'm glad we are over." She sighed heavily and looked around the restaurant, full of attractive people enjoying their food and having fun. "I don't know what's wrong with me, but I seem to attract all the dysfunctional men. Aren't there any nice ones around…men who think about something besides getting into a woman's pants all the time?"

"I'm sure they are out there somewhere, but I guess they are few and far between at our age. Most are already married or someone's rejects."

"I know you're right. You are so lucky that you found Ted. He's a great guy."

Linda smiled broadly, and proudly thrust her left hand towards Mattie. "Look what he gave me last night. I was going to tell you about it at the office, but then when you invited me to dinner, I decided to wait and tell you here."

"Is that gorgeous rock what I think it is? … an engagement ring?"

"Yes, it is, and we've set a date for a year from September. Of course, I want you to be my maid of honor."

Mattie jumped off the bar stool and hugged Linda. "I am so happy for you…and Ted's a lucky man. Tell me everything – every detail. How did he propose and what are your plans?"

They ordered fresh Florida red snapper with asparagus and beet salads and happily chatted throughout dinner. Mattie was thrilled for her friend and secretly a little envious. She was thirty-five with no love interest of her own and none in sight. She was not panicked, but she did want children someday in her future and her biological clock was ticking. She did not have much time for dating, and she had wasted so much of it on Chad. She felt ashamed and foolish.

"The right man will come along when you least expect him," Linda said confidently. "You have to be patient."

"Easier said than done," Mattie rolled her eyes. She and Linda had been friends since third grade and often discussed wanting to have big families, the house with the white picket fence, and the whole marriage scene. "Just don't settle for anyone who doesn't measure up to your standards. You can't afford to waste any more time on the likes of Chad."

"I know," Mattie sighed. "Let's order a nightcap to celebrate your engagement. The night is young, and dinner is on me…or rather, it's thanks to Dr. Tony Grant."

"Maybe Dr. Tony can introduce you to one of his friends?" Linda suggested hopefully. "He must know a million people, maybe a nice doctor?"

"It's a possibility, I suppose, but I don't know him well enough to ask." She smiled at her friend warmly. "The good news is - at least one of us is off the market."

CHAPTER 9

Mattie looked at her desk calendar in utter disbelief. Where had the year gone? She was momentarily stunned when she realized that the Fort Lauderdale Boat Show was only a few days away…the busiest week of the year for her. She had been preparing for it for months, and now it was almost here.

The show occurred annually over Halloween weekend and was one of the year's biggest events in the boating industry. Tens of millions of dollars were spent by the public purchasing all sizes and kinds of boats or chartering yachts for the next season. It was a happening…like the Super Bowl for yachts.

Under Charles watchful eye, every year Lux Charters always put together the largest and most extravagant display pavilion at the show. It was located under a huge, white, billowing tent situated near the specially constructed floating docks where the mega yachts were tied up, side-by-side, and could be visited by invitation only. Guests wanting to go onboard had to be financially qualified beforehand and had to be accompanied by a yacht broker or someone in the yachting industry. The multi-million-dollar yachts were not available to be boarded by the simply curious, although many tried and were politely, and sometimes not so politely, turned away.

Old and new prospective customers gathered in the Lux's tent-like booth, sitting on the comfortable sofa and chairs during the four days of the show. The pavilion was a place to relax, to get out of the sun for a while, and in some years, to dodge the rain. Guests were served refreshments, given brochures, and introduced to the Lux staff. Prospective clients spoke to the yacht brokers about their specific needs and budgets. As part of her job, Mattie was expected to man the information desk a few hours every day during the show. It was the place where she would meet new potential customers and connect with the clients who had preregistered in advance for her to take them onboard the various yachts. She had lined up several good prospects and could potentially earn as much as two hundred thousand dollars in commissions from this year's show alone. It was a real pay day for the industry and no broker serious about the business, would dare miss the event.

Thursday, the first day of the show, was the VIP Day. Special guests, known to be serious about purchasing a yacht or chartering one, were given special invitations and invited onboard the yachts for intimate parties. They were served appetizers and champagne in the hope they would make an early commitment and secure it with a hefty deposit check.

Friday through Sunday were the days when the general public was admitted. They meandered along the docks on specially constructed boardwalks, shopping for boats and accessories and admiring the mega yachts. The cost of an admission ticket to the show was steep enough to preclude most casual "lookers" and attracted only the serious-minded boating enthusiasts.

Mattie was expecting to host several out-of-town clients who were flying into Ft. Lauderdale specifically for the VIP night, and she hoped to make more contacts from her hours spent networking in the booth. This show was a lucrative opportunity, and she could hardly wait for it to begin. Her adrenalin was rushing, and she felt almost breathless. It would all begin in three days.

The phone on her desk rang, jarring her from her daydreaming. "Lux Charters, Mattie Cartwright speaking. How may I help you?"

"Ms. Cartwright, my name is Evan Stone. My close friend, Dr. Tony Grant suggested I call you. No that is not entirely true. He *insisted* that I call you. I am the producer of his television show, and I'm looking to charter a large yacht for a month, or maybe two, next summer in the Med when filming is in hiatus. Tony was emphatic that I should speak to you and *only* to you."

"That was very nice of him." His name sounded familiar…Evan Stone…but she could not place him. She was, however, thrilled because she had not expected a referral from Dr. Tony so soon. It was flattering. "I'd be happy to help you. Would you like to meet me in person, or if you tell me what you have in mind, I can e-mail you some recommendations, and then we can speak again. A month or two on a yacht can be glorious, but you have to be sure the boat and the crew are the right fit for you and your guests."

"Yes, I figured that. I want to tell you my ideas and get your input. I am planning to be in Miami for a television shoot in the next few days and I believe the dates coincide with the Ft. Lauderdale boat show. I would like to meet you in person and have a look around at what's available for charter. I know it's a busy time in your profession, and this is last minute, but I'm hoping you can squeeze me in somehow."

"I will definitely make time," she said eagerly. *Two months, OMG*, she thought. *That would be my longest charter ever.* "Can we meet Friday morning at 10: 00 a.m. at the Lux booth? I'll text you a location map. You'll have to enter the show from the parking lot off A1A and come through Gate B. If you tell me what you are looking for now, I'll arrange to show you yachts that might be of interest, and you can meet the captains and crews too."

Mattie took down all his information and promised to e-mail him pictures of the yachts that met his specifications and would be on display at the boat show. She had to be sure which yachts would also be available for such a long charter in the summer and had not been promised elsewhere. If he did not like any of them, she would show him pictures of other yachts presently at sea or in dry dock that would be available for his timeframe in the Mediterranean. However, she did not think that would be necessary. A greater than usual number of mega yachts had registered to be part of this year's show. It was being advertised as the biggest and most elaborate boating extravaganza ever to be held in Ft. Lauderdale.

It took her several hours to research and go through the specs of the yachts that Evan Stone required in terms of size, number of bedrooms, and entertaining spaces. He wanted an affable, experienced crew, one not overly impressed with celebrities. He planned to host important people onboard during his weeks at sea. She compiled the information after excluding yachts she did not feel were right, or ships with crews that would not be a good fit with Evan Stone's lavish lifestyle. She carefully scanned everything to his office e-mail address in Los Angeles and entered the day and time of their upcoming meeting into her phone's calendar. She would devote the whole morning or the entire day to him if necessary. He was an excellent prospect and she wanted to provide exceptional service. She jotted off a quick note to Dr. Tony Grant thanking him for his referral and promising to do her best for him.

Then she could not resist. She sat in front of her computer with a cold *Diet Coke* and *Googled* "Evan Stone," the Hollywood producer. As soon as she typed in his name, his picture flashed up on the screen and then there were dozens of candid shots of him with various Hollywood actresses and sports personalities. In one photo, his arm was draped protectively around Jennifer Lopez and in another he was golfing with Tiger Woods and Phil Mickelson. He obviously traveled with the elite "A" crowd all around the world.

The text under his photo stated that he was forty-five, divorced for over a decade with no children. Mattie thought he looked younger though and found him instantly appealing. He had a mischievous grin and twinkling eyes that reminded her of Tom Cruise in his early films, *Top Gun* and *Cocktail.* There were several pages of information about his career accomplishments as a producer, and a as frequent late night talk show guest. He had appeared as a contestant on several television game shows and had developed a following after almost winning the jackpot on *How To be a Millionaire.*" His most successful show to date was *The Doctor Tony* Show. Evan was currently working on an untitled show for Netflix, set in Miami and reputed to be a new kind of drama series.

Mattie shut off the computer and took a deep breath. Wow, what had she gotten herself into? She was a little apprehensive and intimidated about working with the famous and incredibly attractive Evan Stone. But she was eagerly anticipating meeting him and could hardly wait for Friday.

CHAPTER 10

Sky Cooper was twelve years older than his kid sister, Casey, and had always been very protective of her. If she had a problem anywhere - with anyone - Sky always took her side. Casey was pretty, a free spirit, impulsive and uninhibited. She was extremely intelligent but sometimes lacked common sense and acted hastily, finding herself in trouble - nothing too serious, but misbehavior that required an intervention from Sky on her behalf. In spite of her mischievous nature, she was mature for her age. People often thought her to be in her mid-twenties and she easily passed for that with her fake I.D. which she used at bars and night spots in the area. (Unbeknownst to her parents).

At thirty, Sky was tall and lean, with dirty blond hair, twin dimples, and eyes as green as a deep forest moss. All of his sister's girlfriends thought he was "beyond" handsome and had wild crushes on him. When she was in high school, they begged her to invite them to "sleep-overs" at her house in Tampa, so they could be around if Sky happened to drop by. The best treat of all was for them to watch him swim laps in the Cooper's backyard pool. They drooled over his abs and muscular arms and legs. Casey paid no attention to his body and laughed at her girlfriends hysterically. Sky was just her older brother, nothing, and nobody special…except that she adored him.

Sky was a physician. After he completed all his medical training, he took a job as a hospital-based internist at Tampa General Hospital. He shared an apartment nearby with two medical residents, a typical bachelor pad. Cooking was not his specialty, so he often came unannounced to their parent's house for meals. His mother, Mary, was a fabulous cook and enjoyed preparing meals for her family and their friends. She was of Italian heritage and firmly believed anything could be settled over a plate of pasta.

Whenever Sky was home, the house took on a party atmosphere with him teasing his little sister and her friends. He told jokes and stories that made everyone laugh. Even his mother and father seemed more light-hearted and relaxed when he was around.

Their parents, Cam and Mary, were both recovering alcoholics who had been sober for over two decades. They had met at an AA (*Alcoholics Anonymous*) meeting and had been together ever since. Even now, after all those years, they took the twelve-step, self-help program very seriously and forbid any kind of alcohol in their home. Excessive drinking had caused them both to suffer terrible heartaches in their pasts and to be filled with regrets. They secretly feared that Sky or Casey might follow in their footsteps. Mary prayed every night that her two children would be spared from that horrible addiction. She was pleased that Sky seemed to have avoided the alcohol temptation, but she worried about Casey and kept her on a tight leash.

Casey was standing on the blistering street corner waiting for her brother to pick her up after her last day of high school. She was perspiring heavily in the Florida humidity and about to dump her heavy bookbag and purse on the curb when Sky peeled around the corner in his red Honda convertible with music blasting from the radio. "Sorry I'm late," he apologized and grinned sheepishly. "You know, doctors always keep people waiting."

"No worries," Casey smiled at him warmly. Sky could do no wrong in her eyes. "I'm just happy you're here. I'm wilting."

He helped Casey put her belongings safely on the car's back seat and hung her graduation gown on a hook so it would not wrinkle. "Go ahead, Ducky, I'm all ears. I know you're dying to tell me what's been going on at home."

By the time they arrived at their house, Casey had repeatedly complained to him about her problems with her parents and the strict curfews they enforced. "I feel like a fucking prisoner, excuse my French," she blurted out angrily. "They treat me like I'm a baby and it's driving me berserk."

"You only have to hang on a little while longer, Ducky," he tried to soothe her. "Your classes start at UM in a few weeks, and you'll be living on campus in a dorm with other summer students. Freedom at last," he grinned. "What Mom and Dad don't know then won't hurt them, and I'll be around to keep you out of trouble."

In less than a month, Casey would be transitioning from her high school graduation to her freshman orientation week at the University of Miami in Coral Gables. And afterwards, she would stay on campus to take two courses to lighten her freshman fall schedule. Although she had been accepted at Baylor, the University of Texas and Alabama, she chose the University of Miami because Sky would be working nearby.

He was taking a position in a private practice group in the Miami area and would be moving there two weeks after Casey.

As independent and grown up as she was, Casey felt a little apprehensive about moving from Tampa to Miami - leaving her strict, but loving parents and all her childhood friends behind. Having her older brother living and working nearby would be reassuring, and a safety net if she became too rambunctious once she was out on her own.

CHAPTER 11

It was a sunny, very warm day in late October, and the Ft. Lauderdale Boat Show was in full swing. Mattie waved at Charles who was entertaining clients on the one side of the pavilion. Nervously, she checked her watch, waiting for Evan Stone to arrive. He was twenty minutes late and she was getting antsy. Sitting behind the information desk, she politely answered questions from other guests and directed them to speak with their various brokers or boat captains.

Mattie was wearing a navy blue and white striped sundress with a wide brim white straw hat to protect her face from the sun, and her signature stiletto heels. When it was time to go visit the boats, she would change into white canvas rubber soled shoes. No footwear of any kind was allowed on the yachts. Everyone going on board had to place their shoes in a wicker basket at the end of each gangplank and reclaim them at the end of the tour.

"Excuse me, Miss," an attractive man tapped Mattie gently on her shoulder, trying to get her attention. "I'm here with my kid sister Casey. I promised her that that I'd bring her to this year's boat show so she could see how the really rich and famous live." He smiled broadly, revealing a perfect set of bright white teeth and a dimple on each cheek. There was something vaguely familiar about him. She was sure that she had never seen him before. As handsome as he was, she would have remembered. Yet, something about his amazing emerald green eyes drew her attention and made her feel that she should know him from somewhere. He stood casually by the information desk; his arm protectively draped around his younger sister. She too looked familiar, but Mattie had no idea where she might have seen the young woman before. As she watched the young girl, she suddenly remembered…the flat chested, unhappy looking girl at the Pelican Bar on the night of Mattie's birthday. Mattie was about to say something but the man spoke first.

"I didn't realize that our admission tickets only entitled us to walk around these docks. We've been doing that for a while, but Casey's dying to actually get on board one of the big boats. Can you help us with that, please? It would mean so much to my sister, and to me." He allowed himself a faint smile. "I've always wanted to see one of these mega yachts up close and personal."

"I'm sorry, but I can't," Mattie spoke honestly, regretting that she could not do as he asked. He seemed nice and was certainly handsome. She wished she was able to accommodate him, but her schedule was fully booked.

"My name is Sky, and this is my sister Casey. She's a freshman at UM and this is her one and only chance to get on one of these super yachts. She's been pestering me for weeks to bring her here. She read about the show in her campus newspaper and I kind of bragged that I'd get her onto one of the big boats as her birthday present. Now she's holding me to it. Please don't make me look bad in front of her. I have a reputation to maintain," he grinned sheepishly.

Mattie chuckled. "Sky, I'm sorry but as I started to say, for permission to visit the yachts, one must make an appointment in advance and be accompanied by an official broker or salesperson. I'm afraid everyone here at Lux Charters is already tied up today with previous commitments. This is serious business for us all. I might be able to find someone to take you and Casey around tomorrow afternoon, but strictly speaking, "lookers" are frowned upon. This show is primarily for serious buyers or charterers."

"I understand but I can't bring her back another day. I'm a physician and I have to be back at work this evening and I'm on call for the rest of the weekend." He made an exaggerated woeful face, trying to play on her sympathy. "Please, isn't there something you can do?"

"Oh, you're a doctor?" She was surprised. He hardly looked old enough to drive, much less practice medicine. "What kind of doctor?"

"I'm an internist, and I recently joined a private practice group in North Miami. Since I'm the new guy, my free time is extremely limited at the moment. Please, can you make an exception for us? I really want to do this for my sister, and quite honestly, I'm a little curious myself. We are both new to Ft. Lauderdale, having moved from Tampa, and we've been looking forward to this."

Could you lay it on any thicker? she chuckled to herself. He was very persuasive.

Mattie walked around to the front of the booth. Sky's eyes traced her every step as she moved gracefully towards him. She looked stunning, like a runway fashion magazine model. He had dated beautiful women in the past, but no one as gorgeous as she was.

"My name's Mattie Cartwright and here's my business card." She was struck again with the feeling that she knew him from somewhere. "I'm afraid, much as I'd like to, I cannot help you today. Everyone on our staff is fully booked. Maybe if you go to another booth, they might have a cancellation. Try the *Frazier* or *Lazarre* ones. They are right down the docks to your left."

Sky could not make himself move away from her. He was mesmerized by her gorgeous emerald, green eyes and shapely legs that went on forever. She stood almost as tall as he, and he was well over six feet. "Do you model?" He was curious, wanting to keep the conversation going. "I think I've seen your face somewhere, maybe in an ad or television commercial?"

"I do some print ads for the company I work for, but I doubt you would have seen them. They are mostly for the trade. But it's funny though," she grinned. "I was just thinking that you look so familiar too." She was enjoying their mild flirtation and wanted to continue their banter, but she could see that Casey was getting restless and moving around impatiently.

"Come on, big brother," Casey tugged at her brother's arm. "Let's try another booth. We're not getting anywhere here. Maybe someone else will help us." She started to drag him away and shot Mattie a frustrated look. "Thanks for nothing," she mumbled under her breath, but Mattie heard every syllable.

"I'm so sorry that I can't help you," Mattie repeated once again, pretending not to have overheard Casey's cutting remark. "I'm expecting my next client any minute. He is already late. If you can hang around for a little while and he doesn't show up, I'll make an exception and take you onboard a boat, although it's against regulations and my boss will have my head."

There was something so appealing about Sky that she, for a moment, actually hoped Evan Stone would not keep his appointment. He was disarming and intriguing and she loved the way he obviously felt about his sister. Being an only child, Mattie had often wished for an older brother. She thought Casey was very lucky to have such a nice and caring one. She hoped she appreciated him.

"That would be terrific. We'll walk around some more and come back in a few," he said gratefully. "Selfishly, I hope luck is on our side, and your client is a 'no show,' but I don't want you to lose a prospect. Just so you understand, we are not in the position to charter anything. It's only plain curiosity and my sister's birthday wish."

"I understand," Mattie fidgeted with some papers on her clipboard. Sky was adorable, and Casey had the potential to be a real beauty once she grew into her lanky body. She thought she would enjoy their company, but it wasn't possible today.

Sky reluctantly led Casey away, and they started walking down the floating docks past one spectacular yacht after another looking for the Frazier tent but hoping to be able to double back and find Mattie again. He rarely reacted so positively to a woman, but she had captured his imagination, and he wanted to spend more time with her…under any pretext.

Mattie soon lost sight of them as they blended into the milling crowd. She heard a stirring in the tent and realized why. Evan Stone had strolled nonchalantly into the pavilion like he owned it. There was a general murmur in the crowd as people began to recognize him, or at least admire his good looks.

"Mattie Cartwright, I presume?" He spoke in a smooth, polished voice. "I'm Evan, Evan Stone."

"Yes, Mr. Stone. I know who you are. I was afraid you were standing me up." She spoke a little too curtly. Mattie was always punctual and did not like to be kept waiting. "I have the whole morning reserved for you. We're going to visit four yachts that I think you should seriously consider." She was anxious to move towards the boats before the crowd grew larger and became emboldened enough to surround Evan seeking his autograph or a selfie. "Shall we go?" She walked around to the side of the desk, removed her heels, and put on her boat shoes.

"Please call me Evan." He oozed charm. "I look forward to spending the morning with you and not just to look at boats." He winked seductively and was obviously trying to flirt with her.

Evan Stone was accustomed to getting his way and was comfortable being around starlets and beautiful women. They usually fawned all over him, but not Mattie. She was strictly business. He could see that she was intelligent and efficient…a rarity in most of the women he had known. So many of the Hollywood set were shallow and self-absorbed. He took another close look at her gorgeous face and figure and knew that he was going to enjoy his morning with her immensely. Indeed, he was a lucky man, and he silently thanked Tony Grant for putting him in touch with the beautiful and efficient Ms. Cartwright.

Mattie was flattered that a famous television producer was hitting on her, but she did not take his flirting seriously and was not swayed by his charms. She had dealt with men like him often over the years and had learned how to politely squash their unwanted advances. She remained aloof but professional. A large commission was at stake here and she wanted to earn every dollar of it.

She momentarily thought of Sky and his sister and hoped they had found someone to help them out. If time permitted, she would try to track them down later. Right now, Evan Stone was her priority.

Sky and Casey wandered around the docks. Casey was especially intrigued by the multi-tiered yacht, *Liquidity,* and she stood hopefully at the base of the gangplank, trying to catch the attention of someone on board, but to no avail. The crew were busy helping brokers entertain their clients. When no one paid attention to her, she gave up in disgust and dragged Sky back to the Lux pavilion.

"Mattie's client must have shown up because there's someone else in the booth," Sky said regretfully to his sister. "I guess we're out of luck, Ducky."

"Damn." Casey was disappointed. "I really wanted to get on board *Liquidity*. Did you see how enormous she was? I've never seen a private boat that big. She looks like a small cruise ship."

"Maybe next year. We can try again." Sky tried to console her. "Let's go get some lunch, and I'll drive you back to campus."

"I'll take you up on the lunch, but I want to stay in Ft. Lauderdale this afternoon. Some friends from school are coming to shop at the Galleria Mall, and I told them that I'd meet them there. They'll bring me back to campus later."

"Are you sure? I don't feel right leaving you here, Casey. You don't know your way around this town. Let me drive you back to school."

"I've been here many times with my friends, and I'll be fine. I don't need a babysitter," she huffed. "Don't worry so much, big brother. I'm all grown up now in case you haven't noticed."

"Oh, I've noticed," he grinned. She was beginning to fill out in all the right places. She had their mother's curvy figure and pouty lips. "You are really pretty, Ducky. However, that doesn't mean I won't always be looking out for you…and heaven help any boy that tries to take advantage of you. They'll have me to contend with."

"Enough, enough," she lifted her slim shoulders in a nonchalant shrug.

"Okay, but here's a fifty-dollar bill, just in case." He handed her the money. "If your friends don't show up, take an Uber back to campus and text me when you get back there."

"All right, all right," she agreed but turned wistfully around to take one more lingering look at the gleaming back deck of *Liquidity*. "I'm starved. Let's go eat."

CHAPTER 12

Mattie walked up the gangplank onto the gorgeous yacht *Jasmine*. Evan followed closely behind her. She felt his eyes sizing up her butt, and it made her uncomfortable. She hurried onto the aft deck and turned around to confront him. She was dying to call him out but was too professional. Why did so many men feel compelled to ogle women, as if it were their right?

She moved aside and introduced Evan to Alan Rite, *Jasmine's* Captain, and allowed him to lead them on a tour around the spacious yacht. He showed off the boat's amenities and answered Evan's questions succinctly. Evan did not seem comfortable or appear to be enamored with the Scandinavian yacht. He whispered to Mattie that he did not care for the décor or the layout of the boat. But to be polite, he feigned moderate interest. He then turned to the captain and asked some pointed questions about the boat's maintenance and inspection timetables. Captain Rite braced himself. He was not used to being questioned about the physical condition of *Jasmine*, of which he was quite proud, and was offended by Evan's veiled insinuations. He stated emphatically that his ship was completely seaworthy, and everything was up to Coast Guard standards.

He guaranteed that no inspections had been postponed or cancelled.

"I didn't mean to insult you, Captain," Evan frowned slightly. "I'm afraid I know nothing about yachts and want to be sure my guests and myself are onboard the safest possible vessel. I would ask the same kind of questions if I were to rent a car for a cross country trip. I am super cautious. I'm afraid we got off to the wrong start. My fault, my apologies."

Captain Rite was not a forgiving or understanding man. "I don't believe *Jasmine* is a good fit for you, Mr. Stone," he said plainly. "I suggest you look elsewhere for another charter."

He turned his back on Mattie and Evan, pretending to inspect something or another. The conversation and the visit ended abruptly. Evan stalked off to find the gangplank and his shoes. Mattie followed quietly behind her client and off the boat.

"I guess that didn't go too well," she said, in a sarcastic understatement. "In my experience, I find captains to be very protective of their crew and their vessels, but he should always be open to questions about routine maintenance and such. His rudeness was unforgiveable, especially when you consider how much you might have paid to charter the yacht. I'll speak with him about it at another time. In the meantime, we have more yachts for you to consider and the morning is still young."

Evan was instantly mollified. He thought the arrogant captain needed a lesson in humility and manners, but it was none of his concern. He instantly dismissed Captain Rite from his thoughts. In other circumstances he might have said more to the man. In his business and personal life, he was accustomed to being treated courteously and with respect, but he didn't want to look churlish in front of Mattie. He bit his lips and kept his thoughts to himself.

"Can we see the next boat, please?" he grinned sheepishly. "I promise to be a good boy." Something about being around Mattie made him want to impress her.

"Let's go see *Liquidity*. She's one of my favorite yachts and her Captain, Mercer Llanos, is very accommodating and always makes sure his guests are happy and having a great cruise. I'm sure you will get along well with him?" She suppressed a snicker and led him down the dock.

They boarded the magnificent, blue hulled, 256-foot yacht with six decks and a diving platform. It slept 20 guests and carried a crew of 25. Captain Llanos was gracious and pleased that another famous celebrity might be interested in chartering his yacht. In the past, Oprah, Ellen DeGeneres, Sir Paul McCartney, Tom Brady and Peyton Manning had been among the many famous stars and athletes who had spent time onboard with him. He was used to famous people and knew how to handle them and their idiosyncrasies. However, he would never name drop or discuss his previous guests. He respected their privacy and knew exactly what to do to accommodate the rich and famous and their sometimes, outrageous or quirky demands.

Liquidity was Captain Llanos' pride and joy, and he did everything he could to show the boat off in the best way. He even took Evan to the crew's quarters and the engine room, which were kept as immaculate as the rest of the ship. "You can literally eat off the floor," he bragged.

Liquidity boasted extravagant features like a sunken onyx bar in the main salon, a three hundred bottle wine cellar, a disco on the top deck, a full-size gym, a heated small oval swimming pool, and hot tub. The yacht regularly boasted one of the few Michelin chefs that worked on boats. The food was exquisitely prepared, elegantly served, and always drew raves. In Mattie's opinion, there was no better yacht to charter than

Liquidity, no better captain than Mercer Llanos, and no better cuisine at sea. It was clearly her favorite boat.

Evan enthusiastically took pictures of almost every room with his cell phone camera and announced that *Liquidity* was definitely the yacht he wanted to charter. He told Mattie that she did not have to show him any others. Sitting down at the dining room table, he made himself comfortable while making extensive notes. He and Captain Llanos shared beers and discussed possible itineraries for the coming summer in the Med. Evan said that he was open to suggestions but especially wanted to visit the French Riviera. He explained how many guests would be arriving and departing the yacht in each of the different ports. His cruise would be a revolving door of celebrities and colleagues with special demands, but Captain Llanos assured him that his crew was up to the challenge.

When they were finished, Evan rose and agreed to go back to the pavilion to sign a two-month lease agreement with Lux Charters and Mattie. The captain and Evan exchanged cell phone numbers and shook hands. What a different experience than earlier with Captain Rite.

Everyone was happy, especially Mattie. Now she could inform Dr. Tony that she had successfully found the right charter for his friend and ask him if she could use his name as a reference in the future.

She and Evan walked leisurely back to the Lux pavilion, chatting, and admiring the other yachts along the way. Conversation was easy and Mattie found Evan to be interesting and charming. He continued to flirt and asked her to dinner. She smiled but graciously declined, citing paperwork she had to complete by morning. She did pour him a glass of champagne at the pavilion and had a few sips herself while they reviewed the charter agreement. She had thoroughly enjoyed her time with him and was sorry it was ending so soon.

"All right." He reluctantly accepted her rejection of his dinner invitation graciously. "But I won't be put off that easily. Dinner another night, perhaps?" He was a man determined to get what he wanted, and for the moment, at least, he wanted Mattie.

"Perhaps," she grinned just to get him to change the subject. She had no intention of breaking her rule about dating clients. But she was sorely tempted.

They attended to the necessary paperwork and continued to chat. Mattie kept glancing through the crowds, hoping to catch a glimpse of Sky and his sister, Casey. They must have returned to the pavilion, seen that she had gone and left the show. Such a shame. She would have liked to spend time with Sky, but Evan had taken up her whole morning and she did not regret it. She started to shake Evan's hand and wish him well when he suddenly drew her into his arms and kissed her boldly…right in front of everyone in the tent. She gasped in surprise and tried to pull away from his grip.

"You'll be hearing from me again," he whispered seductively. "And soon." He winked and walked nonchalantly away. Someone in the crowd applauded and Mattie blushed with embarrassment. She felt like she'd just been in a scene from a movie.

Breathless, she tried to compose herself. When she felt steadier, she returned to the booth and picked up her clipboard. She approached her next client, the junior Senator from Wisconsin who was patiently waiting for her and had observed the bizarre kissing scene.

"I see you have quite a fan in Evan Stone," the Senator teased. "Of course, I recognized him from late night TV. Do all your clients kiss you like that? Do I have that to look forward to?""

"No never," she blushed. "That was quite a surprise. Senator, I assure you. That has never happened before. Are you ready to visit some boats?"

By the end of that day, she had secured three definite charters and a couple of "maybes" that she would follow up on in a few days. She left the show and drove back to her office to drop off her paperwork for the assistants to handle in the morning, and to pick up her next day's schedule. Charles was in his office chatting with an attractive woman. When Charles looked up and saw her in the outer offices, he motioned for her to come in.

"You look mighty pleased with yourself," he chuckled. "Another successful day, I guess. Come have a drink with us. This is Candice. She's thinking about becoming a yacht broker and I was giving her some pointers," he said sheepishly, silently begging Mattie not to make a sarcastic comment. Mattie was protective of her mother, Brenda, and not pleased when she found Charles with other women.

I bet you were, Mattie thought and rolled her eyes. She again wished her mother was the woman who brought out Charles' flirtatious side. He pulled a bottle of fifteen-year-old scotch out from his bottom desk drawer and three short glasses.

"You wouldn't believe it. After Evan Stone, the producer and television personality, signed a charter agreement for two months in the Med, he grabbed and kissed me right in front of everyone in the pavilion. I was mortified," she blushed. "But it was unbelievably exciting."

"And?" Charles looked at her in anticipation.

"And I think I liked it," she joked. "I liked it a lot."

Before she could take a sip of the scotch, the office phone rang. Mattie automatically reached for it. "Lux Charters, Mattie Cartwright speaking. How may I help you?" she answered pleasantly still thinking of Evan's unexpected kiss.

"Mattie, hi, it's Evan Stone. I'm afraid I left my cell phone on *Liquidity*, in the dining room, I think. I'm desperate without it. Would it be too much trouble for you to send someone to go over there and retrieve it? I attempted to call Captain Llanos, but his phone went right to voicemail."

"No problem at all," she answered, happy to hear his voice again so soon. "I'll go back to *Liquidity* now myself. If I find it, how can I reach you?"

"I'm having drinks with a friend at the *Wharf*. Here's his cell number. If for any reason you cannot reach him, I'll call you back later or first thing in the morning. I can't leave town without it."

"No, of course not." Mattie smiled apologetically at Charles and Candice. "I hate to waste good scotch but duty calls." She grabbed her things and ran out the door. Her long day was suddenly becoming much longer.

CHAPTER 13

Mattie parked her car in the nearly deserted exhibitor's parking lot and showed her official boat show credentials to Martin, the security guard posted at gate B. She did not need to. He knew her well, but it was standard policy. He had to log in anyone that went onto the docks after the official closing time.

The yachts, each one more beautiful than the next, were brightly lit with hundreds of twinkling bulbs. The sight always reminded her of Christmas. Mattie had seen this night view of the boats many times, but it always took her breath away. She pulled out her cell and snapped a few photos. The pictures would make good advertising material. And, she thought, as long as I'm here, I'll take a picture of *Liquidity* and e-mail it to Evan once she recovered and returned his phone.

Many of the crews had taken Ubers or walked to the numerous local watering holes to relax after a long day, but a few remained behind, tasked with washing down the decks, polishing and dusting the furniture, and preparing the boat for a new parade of potential customers in the morning. Fresh flowers had been delivered by local florists and placed on the aft deck dining tables. Recently washed champagne and beverage glasses were returned to the bars awaiting the next day's libations. On some of the yachts Mattie could hear soft music streaming through the high-tech sound systems or see the flickering lights from televisions in the interior rooms. After the hustle and bustle of the day's activities, the scene was tranquil and enchanting. Mattie wished she could sit on one of the deck chairs with a cocktail and enjoy the beautiful warm evening in peace.

"What brings you back here so late, Mattie?" The guard asked as he wrote her name in the log and noted the time. "Can't get enough of us during the day?"

"My customer left his cell phone on *Liquidity*, and I'm here to retrieve it," she answered politely. Many of the security guards knew her after ten years of working the show. They liked her because she was always pleasant...not like some of the other brokers who were brash and demanding, filled with a sense of self-importance.

"Go on in," he opened the gate for her. "Hope you find it. Some of the crews are back. I did my hourly check a while ago and saw people standing on the aft deck of *Liquidity*."

"Okay, thanks." Mattie smiled and started walking slowly down the floating dock, past the empty Lux pavilion towards *Liquidity*. When she was in clear sight of the magnificent yacht, she gasped and stopped short. *It can't be*, she thought, but she was certain that Casey, Sky's little sister was standing casually on the aft deck with a beer bottle in her hand. She was talking and flirting with one of the crew. *How in the world did she get past security? What is she doing on that boat?*

Mattie took off her shoes and silently moved towards the gangplank, straining to hear Casey's conversation. She knew most of Captain Llanos' crew, but this young man was not familiar.

"I admire your spunk," she heard him say. "I noticed you hanging around the boat earlier today, didn't I? I wanted to invite you onboard then, but the captain would have thrown a fit. How did you get in here tonight anyway? It's not easy to slip by the guards. If they find you here, they'll haul your pretty ass off to jail. Believe me, they do not mess around."

Casey started to explain that she had climbed over a fence about thirty yards from the gate, but the man kept talking.

"Security will be back again within the hour," he said. "We need to go below now so you won't be seen. These floating hotels are worth a bloody fortune, and everyone is anal around here about protecting them from vandalism and graffiti. One of my main jobs as the first mate is to ensure the boat is safe and secure at all times. This is my first gig on this yacht, and I do not want to screw it up. Captain Llanos is out for dinner, and he won't be back for a while. If you stay hidden, I can sneak you back through the crew gate later tonight after he goes to bed. It would be too risky for you to leave now. There are still too many people around."

"But that's no fun," she giggled, a little tipsy. She was not much of a drinker. "I didn't go to all this trouble to sneak in here just to hide out. I want to see this whole gorgeous boat and maybe take a turn in the hot tub. Are you game?" She put her beer down and pulled up her blouse revealing a sexy red bathing suit underneath it. The sales price tag from *Dillard's* was still attached. "I bought it at the mall just this afternoon and I need to break it in. How about it? Will you take me? Please," she coaxed. "Pretty please."

"I don't want to be fired. And while I'm enjoying having you here to keep me company, we have to be smart." He stood up nervously and grabbed her beer and his and started moving towards the main salon sliding glass doors. "Follow me. Come inside where it's safe. I never should have let you talk me into this craziness. I'm old enough and should have known better. Come on Casey. Work with me here." Beads of nervous perspiration formed over his thick eyebrows. He knew the danger they were in, even if she did not. Having uninvited guests onboard was a major infraction of the captain's rules.

"Old enough to know better, you say. Just exactly how ancient are you?" Casey stumbled and held onto a chair back to steady herself.

"Twenty-four," he answered, still trying to coax her inside. "So, I guess that makes me a dirty old man. And you are?"

"Twenty-two," she lied with a straight face. She knew she could pass for that easily and had many times in the local bars. If he knew her real age – just nineteen, he might think himself too old for her and order her off the boat immediately. She did not want that to happen. This was more fun than she'd had in ages. "Oh, all right…spoil sport." She pouted. "At least let me see the hot tub and get my toes wet." She followed behind him sullenly and they disappeared inside.

Mattie stood on the dock, perplexed. *What should she do?* This was none of her business and she barely knew Casey. The teenager was not her responsibility, and the first mate was a stranger.

Casey was old enough to be held accountable if she was caught on the boat without permission, but she was inadvertently putting the crew member's job at risk. Mattie had too much respect for Captain Llanos and the way he ran his ship to allow that to happen. She needed to get Casey safely off the premises and the first mate out of harm's way. Taking a deep breath, she dropped her shoes in the basket at the base of the gang-plank and crept silently onto the boat, one slow step at a time.

As she approached the door to the main salon, she could hear the two laughing and joking inside. They seemed to be getting along nicely and enjoying themselves. She slowly slid the heavy, glass door aside and stepped into the main salon. The time for fun was over. She had to put a stop to this before captain Llanos returned.

CHAPTER 14

Finding Casey on *Liquidity* was startling, but how she got there was none of Mattie's concern. She was, however, certain that Sky did not know that his little sister had returned to the show and somehow talked her way onto the yacht. If Casey were to be discovered, both she and the first mate would be in big trouble. Mattie assumed that Sky would be devastated if his sister ended up being arrested for such a childish prank. She moved cautiously on the plush beige carpeting, determined to rescue Casey from her own foolishness.

Knowing the yacht as well as she did, Mattie made her way directly to the uppermost deck to the hot tub area where she suspected she would find Casey and her new friend. As soon as she was in sight of the spa, she heard Casey's lilting laughter. She was having an animated conversation and the first mate was laughing with her while working on his next bottle of *Bud Light*.

"I've always wanted to travel on a mega yacht. It seems so glamorous. Now that I know you, maybe that can happen in the future." She looked at him hopefully trying her best to appear sultry and seductive.

"I'm sure it can be arranged," he smiled confidently. He was not above bragging a little to impress her. "I have been an engineer on another boat in the Keys for the past three years but when the chance came along to join the crew of *Liquidity*, I jumped at it. I couldn't afford to go to college, so my life experience has been at sea. I've sailed through hurricanes and even a typhoon. I wouldn't trade the exciting life on a ship for anything else." He was emphatic. Casey looked at him carefully. She wished she felt so strongly about something ...anything actually. She felt trapped at college with nothing to look forward to except endless classes and exams.

He was intrigued that Casey seemed fearless. She was apparently not worried in the least about being caught trespassing on private property. Maybe she had a rich father who would bail her out of trouble? But she didn't seem spoiled or entitled, only willful. And a little silly.

"I'm very pleased that you were bold enough to come back to the show and ask me to let you come onboard. However, I should have listened to my common sense and done things properly. Once you are safely off this boat, I'll approach Captain Llanos and ask if I can bring a friend onboard for a visit sometime soon. He's a good guy and I'm sure he'll say 'yes'. That's all I can promise for now. I'm too new here to know all the ins and outs of how he runs things, but I've been told he's fair but a no-nonsense guy."

"I guess that will have to be enough," Casey grinned. "But I'm here now, and *he isn't*...so let's enjoy the evening. Can I have another beer?"

Mattie crept closer and closer to the hot tub, and the moment Casey caught sight of her, she panicked, took a deep breath, and slid sound-lessly beneath the water. Ned stood frozen in place, not knowing what he should say or do.

Mattie walked calmly over to the rim of the hot tub and reached down to tap Casey gently on the top of her head. "I hope you can explain yourself, young lady," she said sternly. "I have to get you off this yacht before someone sees and reports you." She looked disapprovingly at the first mate standing guiltily on the side of the tub. "And you, young man, had better hope that Captain Llanos doesn't find out about your shenanigans. What's your name?"

He could not look Mattie directly in her eyes and instead stared at his feet as if they were the most interesting thing in the world. "Ned," he mumbled softly. "Ned Sigler. I'm the new first mate. Please Miss, please, don't tell Captain Llanos about this. I really need to keep this job. We meant no harm. We were just letting off a little steam."

"Well, Ned. I'll do my part and will keep this little escapade of yours between the three of us. I did not come here to spy on you or get you in trouble. I'm a yacht broker here in town and my client from earlier today thinks he left his phone on the dining room table, so I came to retrieve it. Would you please go and bring it to me now, while Casey dries herself off and puts her clothes back on? We'll meet you at the bottom of the gangplank in a few minutes. And you'd better hope security isn't anywhere nearby." She rolled her eye at his foolishness, only matched by Casey's.

"Yes Ma'am," Ned replied gratefully and went running to fetch the phone, casting a guilty look at Casey. It was a shame the pretty broker had caught them, he thought ruefully. He was having a good time. In the short time they'd been together, he'd come to like Casey and found her very attractive, if a little too flat chested for his taste. Too bad the evening had to end so abruptly. It was a damn shame. He didn't get many chances to hook up with pretty girls. He was usually on the ocean somewhere or on land provisioning the boat for another charter.

Mattie reached for a beach towel that had been meticulously rolled up and placed neatly on the bottom of a nearby lounge chair. She flung it at Casey haphazardly. "Hurry up, Casey. Put on your clothes and follow me."

Casey quickly dried herself off and pulled her shorts on over her wet swimsuit bottom. She flung off the red top and covered herself with a tee shirt. She glanced apprehensively at the lady boat broker who she remembered from earlier in the day when Sky had asked her to take them onboard *Liquidity*. Casey had thought she was pretty at the time, but now she looked upset and angry, probably not finding the hot tub incident amusing. Casey was smart enough not to provoke her further. "Coming," she said solemnly as she followed Mattie sullenly to the yacht's elevator, holding her dripping bathing suit top in her hands. She felt like a naughty child being summoned to the school principal's office. It was humiliating.

At the bottom of the gangplank Mattie spoke grimly to Ned. "I suggest you clean up the hot tub area and get a fresh towel for the lounge chair." She looked at her watch. It was ten past ten. "Captain Llanos should be back anytime now. You'd better hurry. And did you find my client's phone?" She asked, suddenly remembering the real reason for her mission there.

Ned nodded and handed the phone to her. "Yes Ma'am. And I'm sorry about tonight." He sounded sincere. "I guess letting Casey on board was a dumb thing to do, but I didn't really think there would be any harm. Thanks for not turning us in. The captain would fire me for sure if he knew she was here. I know he's a stickler for the rules, and he expects perfection from his crew, especially from me. You know the saying, last hired, first fired."

"I think that expression refers to office situations, not mischievous pranks." She suppressed a grin.

Casey looked hopelessly at Ned and rolled her eyes. She had been acting like such an adult and could tell he liked her, but now, she was being hauled off the boat like a misbehaving teenager. It was revolting.

Ned was the nicest guy she had met in years, and she liked him a lot. They had not had enough time to exchange phone numbers. All Ned knew was her first name and her phony age. She tried to talk to him again, but Mattie grabbed her by her arm and tugged her away.

"There's no time for that now," she said firmly. "We have to get out of here."

"Sorry Casey," Ned winced, sounding remorseful. "I had a great time, and I really didn't think we'd get caught. I hope you're not going to be in trouble because of this. Just so you know, after this boat show, *Liquidity* is heading to the Bahamas for a two-week charter, but we'll be back in Ft. Lauderdale for Thanksgiving week. We usually return here in between charters unless we have to reposition the boat elsewhere. Maybe we could get together then? Can you text me your number?"

"Sure, but I'll probably not be here then. I'll be at home in Tampa for Thanksgiving break." She was disappointed.

"Enough of this chatter, please." Mattie was becoming more and more frustrated. "You two don't seem to realize the seriousness of what you've done. Casey, hurry. Write down your phone number for Ned and come with me right now. Not another word until we are safely in my car. Understood?"

"Yes Ma'am." She rolled her eyes helplessly at Ned, jotted her number on a used cocktail napkin she picked up from a nearby table, and handed it to him. Ned stared into her eyes as if trying to memorize all her features. Emotions played on his face. "I'll see you again soon, Casey, I promise."

Out of patience, Mattie took her arm and led Cassie away. As they approached the security guard station, Mattie bent over and whispered something to him. He nodded, smiled, and then opened the gate so they could exit.

"Now then Casey," Mattie said trying to sound annoyed, although she actually thought the whole situation was pretty amusing now that Casey and Ned had escaped detection. "Do you want to tell me how you managed to sneak into the show and onto *Liquidity*? I'm all ears."

CHAPTER 15

As they exited the boat show parking lot, Mattie turned towards Casey and declared solemnly, "I don't think we were ever officially introduced. I am Mattie Cartwright." She stuck out her hand to shake Casey's.

"I think my brother did introduce us back at the pavilion this morning," she wrinkled her brows. "God, that seems like forever ago."

"It does indeed," Mattie sighed. "And how, may I ask, were you expecting to get back to your dorm tonight?"

"My brother gave me money to take an Uber, but I used it to buy a new bikini at the mall. I was going to hitch a ride back to campus. My friends and I hitch around Coral Gables all the time." She stuck out her thumb to emphasis the point. "Oh my gosh." She looked at the car's dashboard clock. "I was supposed to call Sky hours ago when I got back to campus. I'm sure he's worried to death and mad as hell that he hasn't heard from me."

"Well then you'd better call him." Mattie said firmly. "And right now."

"But I don't want him to know what I did...sneaking back onto the boat show grounds and *Liquidity*." Casey looked panicked. "You won't tell him, will you? He'll kill me. I swear, he really will. Sometimes he runs out of patience with me and then there's hell to pay. Please don't say anything."

"Listen, it's your story to tell. I warn you though… telling the truth is always easier in the end. Secrets are no good and they always come out at the most inopportune time. Just imagine if he got scared that something had happened to you? He might have gone to your dorm, only to find out that you hadn't been there all afternoon or evening, and then been so worried that he called the campus police or maybe even the Miami police."

"Crap! Do you think he'd really do that?" She was panicked by the thought.

"I don't know, Casey. I only met him this morning. He seemed pretty level-headed, but I have no idea how he would react if he thought something had happened to you. He seemed pretty protective. But here, let's end the suspense. Call him now. And another thing," she turned the car around and headed in the direction of interstate I95. "I'm definitely not letting you hitch hike on my watch. It's not safe. There are lots of crazy people around. I am driving you back to UM myself."

Casey reluctantly dialed her brother. "Sorry I forgot to call," she said in a fake light-hearted voice. "Everything's fine and I'll be going to bed soon. Thanks for today, Sky. It was fun being with you." She was about to hang up and felt proud of herself. She had not lied to him, but she had not incriminated herself either. And she *would* be going to bed soon - as soon as Mattie dropped her off. The effects of the beer she had with Ned and the trauma of being discovered as a stow-away had exhausted her. She felt sleepy but was still pumped up from the exhilaration of her latest caper. No matter what Mattie said, or how she decreed that Casey and Ned had committed some unpardonable sin, it had been fun. She really liked Ned and was determined to see him again, no matter what… even if she had to miss Thanksgiving with Sky and their parents to be in Fort Lauderdale with him.

"Hold on, hold on." Mattie heard Sky shouting into the phone. "Damn it, Casey. Where are you? What the hell's going on?"

Casey tossed the phone into Mattie's lap.

"Casey," Sky bellowed angrily into the phone again. "Don't you dare hang up on me. I'm at your dorm with your roommate and she says she hasn't seen you all day. Where are you?"

"She's with me," Mattie picked up the phone from off her lap and interrupted Sky's tirade. "It's Mattie Cartwright. You met me at the Lux pavilion this morning, remember? You asked me to get you and your sister onto one of the mega yachts."

"Yes, I remember." He was stunned. "Casey's with you?" Sky clearly remembered the stunning woman at the Lux pavilion, but he had no idea how or why she would have hooked up with his little sister. "I thought she went to the mall to meet her friends, and then was going back to school. Help me out here. I don't understand any of this. Please tell me what's going on with my sister."

"It's really quite simple." Mattie began, trying to make her voice sound casual, but she was flustered. She did not want to lie to Sky, but she felt the urge to protect Casey too. Her passenger's face had turned suddenly pale, and Casey looked as though she was about to cry.

"As I understand it, your sister did go to the mall after the show and she bought some clothes, a bathing suit, I think," Mattie explained cautiously. She looked at the bundled-up red bikini top dripping water onto her car's floormat. "Anyway, I kind of stumbled upon her, and one thing led to another. I offered her a ride back to school. We're on I-95 now at Ives Dairy Road and should be in Coral Gables within the hour. I'm sorry, but I have to hang up now. I hate driving on this highway with all the huge trucks and motorcycles. It scares me and talking on the phone is too distracting." At least that part was true, she thought. "I'll have Casey back at UM soon so don't worry. Good night, Sky."

Casey looked at Mattie gratefully. She had not told her brother about sneaking onto the boat and she'd made everything sound normal. "Thank you, Mattie. Thanks for covering for me."

"I remember what it's like to be young and impulsive," Mattie answered and smiled wistfully. "But I will not lie to your bother. Let's hope he drops the matter now, so I don't have to ever tell him the truth."

"Okay. I get it, but thanks again." Casey was so relieved. Mattie was pretty cool after all. Most adults were not nearly as understanding or patient. Casey was used to talking her way out of problems of her own making, and she was impressed by the way Mattie had spoken to her brother. He was not an easy person to fool. She had handled the problem masterfully.

"As long as we've got at least an hour in the car together, tell me more about yourself…and your brother," Mattie added casually. "I bet there's an interesting story there."

That was all the encouragement Casey needed. She obliged Mattie and talked non-stop for the rest of the drive. She explained about her childhood in Tampa, her high school graduation last spring and mentioned that her father was retired, and her mother, Mary, taught piano. "Mom is one of those old-fashioned mothers who enjoyed taking care of her home and her family and finds that fulfilling enough. She never wanted or needed a separate career. Raising Sky and I was enough excitement for her, she claims. Personally, I think my parent's lives are a little boring, but each to his own. At least they are still together. So many of my friend's parents are divorced or remarried."

"You are lucky that you had both a mother and a father growing up.

My dad died when I was little, and I never had a male figure in the house. I used to dream about having another father, but my mother never remarried. It was just the two of us, but we managed to have a good life and we are super close, best friends, actually."

"I can't imagine being best friends with my mom," Casey looked at Mattie and was a little bewildered. "Mom's nice and all, and of course, I love her, but best friends, no. She's too strait-laced.

"Anyway," Casey continued. "Mom and Dad had Sky right away, the year after they married, but I was an accident, an "oops" baby twelve years later. At least that's what they tell me. Even with the huge age difference between us, I adore my brother and we are very close. I had my choice of several universities but I picked UM so I could be near him."

Casey took a breath and looked out the window as the spectacular Miami skyline came into view. "Sky has recently joined an internal medicine practice in North Miami and even though he works long hours, he always makes time to visit campus and take me out as often as possible. He's really a great brother," Casey said affectionately.

"He does sound wonderful," Mattie commented. "You're lucky. I envy you. I'm the only child of a single mother. I always wanted a big family with brothers and sisters, but it wasn't in the cards. I hope to have a large family of my own one day soon."

"Most of the time Sky's pretty cool," Casey admitted. "But sometimes he can be a real pain."

"I understand that is exactly why God made big brothers," Mattie laughed. She found Casey refreshing. And there was something so familiar about her. "The main entrance is straight ahead. Tell me how to get to your dorm and promise me that if you want to see Ned again, you'll do it the proper way…no more sneaking around and trespassing on mega yachts."

"I promise," Casey said earnestly and smiled. "And Mattie, I've had a really cool time with you. Do you think we could get together again... maybe go out on a boat someday for real?"

"Possibly." Mattie handed Casey her business card. "Give me a call and some advance notice, and I'll try to arrange something. It won't be on a mega yacht, but I have lots of friends with nice pleasure boats. We could take a ride down the intracoastal and look at all the mansions, maybe see a manatee or two. And you can bring your brother along. By the way, I think that new boyfriend of yours, Ned, is very cute. You make a nice-looking couple. But play it straight. Don't put his job in jeopardy again."

Casey was relieved when they stopped in front of her dorm. She had expected to find Sky angrily pacing around the courtyard waiting to confront her, but the place was empty. He must have decided that his sister was in good hands with Mattie and gone home. Casey slid out of Mattie's car, picked up her bathing suit, and with a casual wave, darted inside the building. "See you soon."

Mattie was disappointed. She had hoped Sky might be there waiting to be sure Casey was all right and thank her for giving his sister a ride. Now because of her impulsive trip to Coral Gables, she had another hour's drive back to Ft. Lauderdale and had to find a way to return Evan's cell phone. It was turning out to be an exhausting day, much more so than she had anticipated... and she still had Saturday and Sunday to work the show.

Secretly pleased that she had, in some small way, helped Casey and Ned foster their new romance, she turned her car around and headed back north. *Oh, to be that young again*, she thought wistfully and turned on the radio.

CHAPTER 16

Mattie was at the office bright and early the next morning. Fortified by a double dose of *Starbucks* strongest coffee, she was ready to complete her paperwork from yesterday and to check her client list for today's showings. She picked up a stack of brochures for the yachts she had scheduled to visit and placed them in her Lux Charters canvas bag. The Senator from Wisconsin, whom she'd worked with yesterday, was returning at 11:00 a.m. to make a final decision between two boats. And one of the senior partners from one of Miami's largest law firms was due at 2:00 p.m. Mattie was well prepared for both clients and was determined to have them both signed up by the end of the day.

Evan Stone had called and left her a message asking if she would leave his phone with her office receptionist and he'd send someone over to pick it up. He thanked her for going back to secure it and asked her out to dinner that evening in gratitude. She was disappointed that she would not have the chance to see him again, but it was her firm policy not to date her clients. She reluctantly wrote him a short note politely declining his invitation. She left it with his phone at the reception desk. She did not expect to see Evan again but hoped his charter in the Mediterranean would go well next summer and that he would refer his friends to her. He could be an extremely helpful contact for her and for Lux Charters.

After a quick cup of coffee and a short conversation with Charles in which she updated him about the charters she had arranged the day before, she drove to the boat show. There, she thanked Martin, the security guard, for his discretion and help last night with the "Casey situation" and prepared to get to work. She looked over at *Liquidity*, with its shiny decks glistening in the sunlight and thought she saw Ned standing on one of decks with a shimmy cloth in his hand supervising some of the crew. On a whim, she waved briefly, but he did not see her. She realized that she had not mentioned Casey's afterhours encounter with Ned to Charles that morning and wondered if subconsciously she was trying to protect her new young friend, the exuberant teenager.

The pavilion was crowded with boating enthusiasts, dressed in shorts and boat shoes, and lathered in sunscreen. Mattie made her way slowly through the crowd to the booth, stopping to chat with a few people she knew. When she arrived at her station, she saw a large crystal vase filled with two dozen gorgeous long-stemmed red roses. The vase was sitting prominently on the desktop for all to admire.

"Someone has a secret admirer," Linda chuckled. "Tell me about him."

"These are for me?" Mattie was surprised. Who would send her such expensive flowers and why? Maybe it was Evan's way of thanking her for finding his phone. She pulled the card off the little clip and read it with anticipation.

"Pretty flowers for a pretty lady. Thanks for taking care of Casey. Please let me take you to dinner a week from this Saturday. If you'll text me your home address, I'll pick you up at 7:00." It was signed, Sky Cooper,

MD, brother of the mischievous Casey, and it included his office and cell phone numbers with a smiley face emoji.

Mattie laughed out loud. She had not fooled him a bit and was secretly pleased by his attention and his sense of humor. She stared at the card and the flowers for a long time. Last night she had hoped to see Sky but never expected he would ask her out on a date. Or was it a date? Maybe he was simply trying to be polite and felt an obligation to her. She was not sure what to do. She knew little or nothing about him except that he was a doctor in a medical group practice somewhere in the Miami area and he had a playful younger sister. However, he was so darn cute! And, he wasn't a client, so why not? She could certainly have dinner with him without breaking any of her own rules. What could be the harm?

The Senator from Wisconsin approached the booth, so Mattie had to stop thinking about Sky and the flowers and concentrate on business. She spent the rest of the day showing him and several others, different yachts and did not get home until after eight that evening. The Senator had gone back and forth and finally declared that chartering a mega yacht was too expensive for him and would send the wrong message to his constituents. Mattie was sorry to have wasted so much time with him, but that was part of sales. Every client was not a success story. She understood his dilemma. However, several other prospects were about to make commitments, and Mattie planned to follow up with them in the next few days after the show ended. She kicked off her shoes, poured herself a glass of Pinot Noir and pulled the florist card out of her purse. *Should she accept Sky's invitation?* She was very tempted.

Last night on their drive to UM, Casey had told Mattie how all of her girlfriends had crushes on Sky, and Mattie could understand why. There was something so reassuring and kind about him, and he was unbelievably sexy. Maybe it was foolish, but what did she have to lose by going to one dinner with him? With Chad gone, she was not dating anyone at the moment and had no real prospects. Without giving herself time to change her mind, she sent Sky a text with her address and said that she would be looking forward to a week from Saturday evening. Then she worried all week about whether she had made the right decision and what she should wear.

CHAPTER 17

This year's boat show was very profitable for Mattie. She had negotiated several new charters for mega yachts, two for smaller boats for the upcoming summer, and another charter for the fall in the British Virgin Islands. She spent the two days after the show reaching out to all the contacts she'd made and compiling files for the upcoming charters.

Between Dr. Grant, Evan Stone, and the new charters she had signed up, she was on track for a banner year. It was not the money that motivated her, although she did enjoy seeing her bank balance rise. It was the sense of accomplishment she felt when she knew she had found the right synergy between customer, yacht, and crew.

Charles had been very proud of her, and of all his brokers, and was planning to take the whole office out for drinks on Saturday night to celebrate. He also wanted to introduce his newest hire, Candice Logan, to everyone. Mattie had met her previously and felt she would make a good addition to the team. She sheepishly explained that she had a date and would not be able to join in the festivities.

"My, my," Charles laughed and looked at her suspiciously. Normally Mattie was always free to socialize with her office buddies. "Since when is dating more important to you that an office outing?"

"Since now," she blushed. "On Saturday I have a first date with a man I'd like to get to know better. We met at our pavilion, but he's not a customer, just a drop-dead hunk of gorgeous manhood."

"And what do you really think about him?" Charles grinned at his protege. He had not seen Mattie so enthusiastic about a man like this before. "You're not usually smitten so quickly."

"It's hard to explain. I feel like I've known him all my life and yet we just met. This might be a 'one and done' date, but I want to give it my best shot. I really like his little sister too. I met them as a kind of a package deal. He's a doctor, and she's a college student at UM."

"That sounds intriguing. Keep me posted." He gave her a bear hug. "The party won't be the same without you but go have fun. If your date fizzles, we'll be at Johnny V's on Las Olas. Come by."

"Okay," Mattie answered, but she silently prayed that her date with Sky would work out. She was anxious to see him again. And to figure out if her attraction to him was real.

Even Brenda questioned her daughter's sudden interest in Sky. "What's so unusual about him?" she asked over dinner that night. "It is not like you to be so excited about a man."

"I don't know Mom. Really, I don't. It's chemistry, I suppose. I've only spoken ten sentences to Sky in total, but I feel like he's an old friend. And Casey, I feel a real connection with her too. She reminds me so much of myself as a young woman…totally boy crazy, all arms and legs, no boobs and very little common sense. But she's very sweet…truly likable."

Brenda chuckled. "I remember those times when you were a teenager, and, frankly, I'm glad those tumultuous years are over. You were quite a handful back then, and you're much more fun as an adult."

Mattie grinned and hugged her mother affectionately. They enjoyed dinner together and an extra glass of wine. Mattie stayed around long enough to help with the dishes, then drove home to her condo on the beach.

CHAPTER 18

Mattie was looking forward to her dinner with Sky. She worried that she had not heard from him since his original invitation. She hoped he did not regret asking her out.

Casey had called her and left a voice message. She had learned from Sky that he was taking Mattie out on Saturday, and she hoped the evening would go well. Casey reminded Mattie to keep her adventure on *Liquidity* a secret. Mattie tried returning the call. She wanted to assure Casey that her secret was safe, but she was unable to reach her.

Not knowing which restaurant Sky planned to take her to was a bit unnerving. Mattie had no idea how to dress. Ft. Lauderdale and Miami restaurants were notoriously casual. A diner's attire could range from shorts and flip flops to colorful dresses, or slacks in bold florescent pinks, oranges, and yellows with coordinating tops. Mattie's taste tended to be more conservative, so she selected a soft peach-colored V neck dress that nipped in at her waist and ended 3 inches above her knees. She planned to wear gold, high-heeled strappy sandals, and gold accessories. She did not want to tower over Sky, but she recalled that he was tall himself.

After she checked her lipstick and applied another coat of gloss, she sprayed herself with her favorite perfume, and sat in the condo lobby, waiting for Sky. He arrived in his red Honda exactly on time, which Mattie appreciated. In her mind, being on time showed consideration and respect.

"Hi," he said warmly. "I'm happy to see you again, Mattie."

"And I you," she grinned before he hopped out of the car and opened the door for her.

When they were both seated, he pushed a button and the car's top automatically went up and closed in place. "I don't want to mess up that beautiful hair of yours," he explained. "My mother always told me to be respectful of the effort that women make to style theirs. Mom still has gorgeous hair, although she complains constantly that it's getting too thin."

"Where does your mother live?" Mattie asked casually, although she already knew the answer from her conversation with Casey.

"She and my dad live in Tampa. Dad's retired. He was security guard for Home Depot. My mom has always been a stay-at-home mother, but she taught most of our friends and neighbors how to play the piano. She is musically talented, and our home life always revolved around all kinds of music and family sing-a-longs."

"That sounds wonderfully wholesome."

"It was…and is. Neither of my parent's drink. Actually, both are recovering alcoholics who met years ago at an AA meeting. To maintain their sobriety, they avoid the temptations of the bar scene and cocktail parties and prefer to entertain their friends and socialize in the safe environment of their own home. They have been happily married for many, many, years, so I guess they're doing something right. They drummed into Casey and me as kids that once a person is an alcoholic, they are always only a sip away from becoming a drunk again. So, they don't tolerate any drinking around them."

"I can understand that. I've heard that giving up alcohol is exceedingly difficult...harder than stopping smoking. I wouldn't know though. I've never smoked."

"Yes, giving it up is hard. The alcohol causes a physical craving. As kids, Casey and I went to some *ALON* meetings, which is where the children and other relatives of AA members learn to understand the insidious 'disease' and to cope with it. To be supportive of our parents, we always invited our friends over for musical evenings, and we used to play hilarious games of *Name That Tune*. I have to brag and say that I usually won. The refreshments were always *Dr. Pepper* or *Mountain Dew*." He rolled his eyes. "I, for one, enjoy a cold one from time to time, but don't ever tell my mother."

"No, I won't," Mattie chuckled. "Those times sound like fun. I cannot carry a tune, so I would definitely not fit in with your family." She laughed a little self-consciously. "Is there a big age difference between you and your sister?"

"Yes, twelve years. I am the first child from my father's second marriage, but my mother's first. Dad was divorced thirty-five ago. He never wanted children back then. He was too young and immature for the responsibility. However, when he met my mother, all of that changed. I guess he grew up pretty fast. My parents claim that I was eagerly planned, and they love to tease Casey that she was a surprise. I do not believe them though. I know that after me, Dad seriously wanted at least one little girl, and he adores my sister. They are very sweet together. I can't imagine him without Casey in his life."

Sky turned onto Federal Highway. "I made reservations at Casa D'Angelo. I hope that's okay?"

"Absolutely, I love Italian food, and that's one of my favorite restaurants."

"I've been told the food is excellent, so I'm eager to try it. Being new to the area, I have to trust recommendations and reviews."

A few minutes later they were seated at a table by the window, enjoying chunks of parmesan cheese and delicious green olives. "Tell me about yourself," Sky asked. "I want to know everything. Do you come from a big family...have sisters or brothers?"

"No. I wish. Unfortunately, I am an only child. My father died when I was very little. I don't remember him at all. I've only seen a picture. My mother raised me by herself and never remarried. She's really a terrific lady and I keep hoping some nice man will come along and sweep her off her feet, but she claims my father was so special, and that he spoiled her so badly that no other man could compare."

"That's kind of sad." He remarked as he glanced at the menu before the waiter came over to announce the long list of specials. He and Mattie were impressed with the lovely ambiance, the first-class service and the outstanding menu selections...but the two of them were there primarily to get to know each other. "It's wonderful that your mother had such a great love, but to be alone forever afterwards must be depressing for her at times. I can see how you would hope she'd find someone to be with."

He took a sip of his wine and nodded with conviction. "Casey and I were raised like only children because of the age difference between us, but it was always reassuring to know I had a sibling...and what a brat she turned out to be. She can be quite a challenge."

Mattie bit back a smile. She did not believe that he thought Casey was a challenge. His affection for his little sister was written all over his handsome face, and his eyes lit up when he mentioned her name. But he was right. She now knew from personal experience that Casey could be a handful.

"Now that we have the small talk out of the way, when are you going to fess up and tell me the real truth about how you came to be driving Casey thirty miles out of your way last weekend? I know there is more to the story than either of you has let on. I had hoped Casey would confess, but her mouth is as tightly closed as a clam shell."

"I can't betray a confidence," Mattie giggled. "But I assure you, Casey was always fine and in no real danger. She was involved in a silly prank. There's nothing for you to worry about. I was delighted to drive her back to campus and have the chance to get to know her. She's really delightful, and very funny. We had a good talk. She told me that she's thrilled that you're working in the Miami area. For all her show of independence, I think she is happy and comforted to have you nearby."

"Yes. We're a close family, but enough talk about us boring Coopers. Tell me more about yourself, and how the beautiful Mattie Cartwright got into chartering mega yachts. That must be a fascinating business, I would guess."

Almost two hours later, over cappuccinos and tiramisu, the two were still talking, laughing, and enjoying each other's company. Mattie was relaxed and content to listen to Sky describe his passion for medicine and his love of children. He was equally impressed with her work ethic and how successful she had become as a yacht broker. They discovered that they shared many common interests in novels, politics, and philosophy. They even followed the same sports teams and loved watching old movies. When the waiters started to yawn, Sky reluctantly stood up and announced that they had better leave the restaurant before they were physically thrown out. He gently took her hand and guided her out the door to the parking lot.

"I've had a wonderful evening," she said easily when he pulled his car into her condo driveway. "The evening's flown by. I don't think we ever stopped talking."

Staring into her deep green eyes, he asked hopefully, "Are you free tomorrow night? And every night thereafter. We still have so much more to learn about each other."

Mattie laughed. She knew she should play hard to get, but she was such an honest person and not into games. She liked Sky more than she thought possible after such a short time. "Yes," she stole a sideways glance at him. "I am definitely free. But why don't you come to my place, and I'll cook for you? I'm told that I make a decent Lasagna."

"You're on. What time? I'll bring the Chianti." He brushed his lips against her soft cheek. "Until tomorrow."

"Until tomorrow." She turned towards the front door, attempting to restrain herself and trying not to jump in the air with joy. Her heart was racing. He seemed like the perfect man for her. She couldn't wait to call Linda and tell her all about Sky. Only time would prove her intuition right or wrong, but for whatever reason, she felt deep within her that she had met her destiny…the man she wanted to spend the rest of her life with. Sadly, she had no idea what tragedy and heartache waited around the corner.

CHAPTER 19

Mattie cooked dinner for Sky the next night. The evening went very well and after that, they spent as much time together as possible, and often included Casey in their plans.

The last days of fall (hardly discernible in the warm Florida climate) sped by. Mattie was putting in ten-to-twelve-hour days at Lux Charters, and Sky's hours establishing a new practice were no better. He was gaining more and more patients as his reputation for giving excellent care spread throughout the community.

In early November, Mattie and Charles flew to Antigua for their large boat show designed to feature new boats for charter and to introduce their crews to brokers. Usually, she enjoyed the annual show and complained that it was too short. Not this year. She could not wait to return to Ft. Lauderdale and to Sky. They continued their romance via Facetime and text messages while she was away, but it was not the same. Any time apart was painful for them both, and they constantly wondered how they had existed before they had met each other. In the midst of a hot, whirlwind romance, they could not keep their hands off each other and were constantly talking and texting during their workdays, counting the hours until they could be together in the evenings.

In mid-November, Sky informed Mattie that he would be taking Casey home to Tampa for Thanksgiving and spending the weekend with his parents. He invited Mattie to come along, and Casey enthusiastically chimed in, begging her to join them. They both wanted their parents to meet Mattie.

Casey had already informed Sky and her parents that on the Friday morning after Thanksgiving she would be taking the *Greyhound* bus back to Miami to get in extra study time before her exams. Her parents were impressed by Casey's sudden studiousness, but Mattie strongly suspected her story was not the truth…that Casey was planning to spend the time in Ft. Lauderdale with Ned. It wasn't Mattie's place to cause problems, so she did not share her suspicions with Sky.

After considerable thought, Mattie turned down the Tampa invitation. She was disappointed about not going but felt it would be disloyal to leave her mother alone for the holiday on such short notice. Instead, she invited Brenda, Charles, Linda, and her fiancée, Ted, to her condo and served them a delicious traditional holiday feast. Charles carved the turkey, and Linda brought sweet potatoes with marshmallows. It was a wonderful occasion, but Mattie missed Sky terribly and could not wait for him to return home.

"I wish Sky could have been here with us," Mattie said sadly. "I want you all to meet him. He's really special. I think in time we could have a future together."

"He sure seems to have captured your heart." Charles smiled warmly at Mattie and winked at Brenda. "In all the years I've known you, Mattie, I've never seen you so taken with a man. And I notice that you are not spending all your time at the office hanging out with me anymore. That's a good sign."

Mattie blushed and took a sip of her wine. "I'll be the first to admit that I've never been this in love before! It's a wonderful feeling."

"What is it about this particular man that takes your breath away?" Brenda was curious. She too had noticed how enamored her daughter seemed to be with this young physician. She wondered if what Mattie felt was real love, like what she'd felt for Mattie's father years ago. She remembered the breathless stolen kisses and hanging on her husband's every word. She wished that kind of happiness for her daughter. Mattie, although she was popular and always had a man around, had not had a serious romance before. Brenda feared she was naive and didn't want her to be hurt. She prayed that Dr. Sky was the real thing.

Brenda remembered all too well that when she first met Mattie's father, she had fallen madly in love. He had been unbelievably handsome and witty, with the most gorgeous eyes and dimples and could tell a story that made the whole room laugh. He had been her entire world until she announced that she was pregnant. That's when he changed…when his drinking got out of control.

His boss fired him for imbibing on the job. He was too ashamed to tell Brenda, so instead he started spending all his time at local bars. He reeked of alcohol, slurred his words, walked precariously into walls, and tripped going up and down the stairs. She was frightened that he would kill himself in a car accident and often hid his keys in order to keep him off the roads. He would rant and scream at her until she had to give them back. Then he'd angrily weave his way out of the house and end up at the nearest dive to drink the night away.

He awoke every morning with a massive hangover and nothing Brenda said or did could persuade him to give up the bottle. Their marriage deteriorated beyond repair. The memories of that horrible time were still painful to Brenda. She needed to meet Sky to assure herself that he was not a problem drinker, and that Mattie would never face the same situation.

Mattie, lost in her own thoughts about Sky, had not noticed Brenda's worried expression. "There are so many wonderful things about Sky," she persisted. "It's hard to know where to begin. He adores his family and loves children. He almost went into pediatrics instead of internal medicine because of it. I find that so appealing, and he is so humble. He doesn't brag about himself, and he really listens to me when I speak. And," she continued doggedly, "he doesn't spend all night looking at his phone. He has it set so a special ringer lets him know when a patient or the hospital is calling, and then he will answer it. Otherwise, it stays in his pocket, and he talks to me. I appreciate that so much. We go out to places and watch other couples not even looking at each other, spending their whole time together texting or talking on their cells. It's ridiculous."

"Well, from your description, Sky sounds like a wonderful young man," Brenda admitted, but she still needed to see for herself. He sounded almost too good to be true. "When will I have the pleasure of meeting him?"

"Remember, we only met at Halloween," Mattie answered… "at the boat show. I wanted to wait until I knew him better before I introduced you. But now I think the timing is right. I feel like I've known him my whole life, but it's only been four wonderful weeks."

"You'd better let us meet him soon, young lady," Charles said sternly but his eyes twinkled. "I have to make sure he's good enough for my girl. I'm not sure I believe in all this love at first sight garbage. I want to see for myself that he's a solid citizen, and that he will take good care of you."

"Good grief, you two," Mattie winced. "We're just dating. We are not running off to be married. Relax."

"You'd better not," Brenda sighed and looked at Linda for moral support. "You understand, don't you? Charles and I just want the best for Mattie."

Yes, Mattie thought ironically. *And I want the best for you too. You and Charles are meant for each other, and you are both too stubborn to see it, when everyone else can.*

Mattie stood up and stretched. She expected Sky to Facetime her later. If her mother and Charles were still there, she would introduce them over the iPad, although she would have preferred that they meet in person. She knew Sky would win them over instantly with his first 'hello'.

"Anyone for pumpkin pie?" Brenda asked cheerfully as she began to clear the table. "Or pecan? I made both."

CHAPTER 20

Mattie was worried when she had not heard from Sky by midnight. He always called to say good night, even if he had just left her a few minutes before. She got undressed and into bed imagining all sorts of worrisome scenarios.

Maybe his parents had been alarmed by the suddenness and intensity of his romance and convinced Sky to slow down or break it off. Or maybe when he returned to his childhood home, he had realized that he and Mattie were from very different backgrounds and not nearly as compatible as his parents. Whatever the reason, Mattie tossed and turned most of the night, finally falling into a troubled sleep at five a.m. When she awoke, feeling anxious and exhausted, she dialed Sky's phone, but it went straight to voicemail. She tried several more times during the day as she worked at the office making last minutes checks on upcoming Christmas charters.

Holiday charters were always tricky because the crews had to decorate the yachts and provide festive atmospheres while being sensitive to the client's religious beliefs and specific tastes. Some guests wanted Christmas trees and brought their own decorations from home. A few came with their own family menorahs and candles. Some customers, over the years, had requested that a Santa Claus arrive in a variety of ways, the most unusual being on water skis. Others chose to have a sophisticated, formal meal with white glove service and wine pairings on Christmas Eve. Still others, for their own private reasons, hated the holidays and chartered at that time of year specifically to get away from their homes and avoid the celebrations entirely. Many captains loved to do holiday charters and had their own Santa suits which they wore annually at this time of year. Others hated all the hoopla around the holidays but did them anyway as part of the job.

Mattie checked her notes and recalled that one of her younger clients with small children had requested four red Christmas stockings to be filled with candy, oranges, and small trinkets and to be placed at the foot of their children's beds on Christmas Eve. She had already purchased the stockings, little gifts, and a dozen candy canes from *Michaels and CVS*. The yacht crew had everything needed and were in charge of stuffing the stockings and secretly placing them in the children's bedroom.

Mattie could not concentrate. She was really concerned about Sky now. What if he and Casey had been in an accident and never made it to his house in Tampa safely? His parents would not have known to call her. In a panic she tried to reach Casey again, but Casey's phone went unanswered also. Something was definitely wrong. Mattie could feel it in her bones. Sky was dependable, and this silence was not like him at all.

She locked up the office and drove home, planning to take a long solitary walk on the beach. That always relaxed her. Usually, watching the waves gently breaking onto the shore and seeing the seagulls and pelicans skimming over the water gave her a sense of peace and tranquility. But not today. She noticed ominous storm clouds in the distance, dark and foreboding, although the weather forecast had been for a sunny weekend.

She was suddenly afraid and began running quickly back to her condo. Just as she arrived at the steps off the beach, rain began to sputter, then fell in torrents. She was completely soaked by the time she reached the pool deck. Lightning flickered above like dozens of flash bulbs popping all over the sky, and thunder roared in the distance. She sprinted as fast as she could, careful to avoid slipping on the wet pool deck. Out of breath, she fell against the wall when she was safely inside the building. Thunder rumbled loudly as she stepped into the elevator and pushed the button to her floor, dripping pools of water on the floor.

Mattie changed out of her wet clothes and put on her favorite pair of sweatpants. Pouring herself a cup of hot chocolate, she sat on her sofa and watched the storm rage outside. She watched through the sliding glass doors as palm trees leaned horizontally from the heavy rain and high winds. A canvas lounge chair blew into the pool, sinking to the bottom. Normally she loved watching storms from the safety of her apartment but not now. She reached for the cashmere throw Brenda had bought her last Christmas and huddled under it, suddenly shivering.

Grabbing her phone, she searched for a message from Sky but there was only one text from her mother, thanking her for a wonderful Thanksgiving dinner, and another from Charles stating about the same thing. Frustrated, she tossed her phone angrily on the sofa and turned on the Netflix series she had been watching. Although the story was compelling, she could not pay attention to it. She switched off the television and paced restlessly around the room.

Frustrated, she marched into the kitchen and made herself a turkey sandwich from the day's leftovers, but she had no appetite. Angrily scraping the sandwich into the trash, she tossed the dish in the sink and returned to the living room window to stare out at the ocean once again.

The storm was over, and, magically, a colorful rainbow appeared in the sky. That was one of the amazing things about Florida's unique weather. It could look and feel like a hurricane outside and only a few minutes later, it could be a picture-perfect day. She wished she felt as calm inside as the weather appeared outside now. Her stomach was in knots, and she could feel a tension headache beginning to throb behind her eyeballs.

Mattie thought about taking a warm bath to relax and made her way towards the bathroom when her doorbell rang. She ran to answer it.

"Sky?" She called out hopefully. Flinging open the door, she looked at him in alarm.

He stood in her doorway, leaning heavily against the frame as if he couldn't stand up on his own. His complexion was ashen, and it was obvious that he was upset.

"What on earth? Sky, I was so worried when I didn't hear from you. What's wrong? Come in and tell me what's happened. Are you alright?"

"It's my mother," his voice began to crack. "She may be dying."

CHAPTER 21

Mattie led Sky to the sofa and poured him a stiff drink. "Now start at the beginning and tell me everything." She sat next to him and took his hand in hers, gently urging him to speak. His eyes were hooded in sadness, and she felt a slight tremor in his hand.

"Thanksgiving was wonderful," he began. "Mom cooked a delicious dinner and Dad handled the carving duties better than any surgeon. We had a few neighbors in so it was a lively scene. After stuffing ourselves, we watched the football game between the Dallas Cowboys and The Washington Football Team. The game was close, and it went into overtime. When it was over, and Washington had won by a last second field goal, we gathered around the piano and Mom led us in our favorite Christmas carols. As a family we have always started singing them on Thanksgiving night for as long as I can remember. It's a real Cooper family tradition." He was talking so fast that she barely understood him, and he was breathing so rapidly that the words literally tumbled out of his mouth.

"That all sounds nice," Mattie said softly and patted his hand again. She wanted him to get to the point. "So, what's the problem. What did you mean by saying your mom may be dying?"

"Sorry," he mumbled. "I'm not being very coherent. After the neighbors left, we settled down as a family in the kitchen for coffee and another piece of pie. That's when Mom broke the news that she'd been having a dry cough for a while and hadn't thought much about it until she began coughing up blood last week. Then she got worried, and so did Dad.

"I would imagine so," Mattie soothed.

Sky relayed the rest of the conversation as best as he could remember and said that he's been hurt that his mother had not consulted him right away. What was the point of having a doctor in the family, if they didn't call on him?"

"Mom came up with some lame answer about not wanting to worry me. Thankfully Dad stepped in and insisted that she call our family physician. The doctor ordered a chest X-ray and some blood work. Mom had all those tests done last week. When the radiologist viewed the X-ray, he thought he saw something suspicious, an abnormality. He called it a small lesion on her lung. He suggested Mom get a biopsy, which is scheduled for the first of December at Tampa General. I'm sorry I didn't tell you sooner, but I didn't want to ruin your Thanksgiving. Mom's doctor feels pretty confident that if there's anything there, it will be small and hopefully benign. But we won't know for sure until the pathology report comes back a few days after the procedure."

"When Mom finished talking, Casey started to cry. Dad hugged her.

"Your mom's a tough old bird," he told her, trying to lighten the mood. "She kicked a two pack a day cigarette habit and alcoholism. So...she can damn well kick this stupid thing on her lung." I thought he sounded more confident than he felt, but Dad was being brave for us all.

"OMG," Mattie groaned and looked at Sky compassionately. "How awful! You're the one in the family with real medical knowledge. What do you think?"

"It could be nothing, or it could be lung cancer," he answered solemnly. "In my medical practice I often have to reassure patients all the time that they or their loved ones will be all right…will survive some awful disease. And sometimes, unfortunately, I have to give them horrible news. I try to do it compassionately and calmly. But when it's your own mother who's sick, it's different. It is impossible for me to remain unemotional and detached. I suppose that's why doctors don't treat their own families. I'm sorry, Mattie. I should have called you right away. I wasn't thinking straight. Mom's been the glue that's held our family together. Her strength and attendance at the AA meetings have kept my father and her sober. I'm frightened what he might do if Mom is diagnosed with lung cancer. In the past, he's admitted that he didn't handle stress well, and he hit the bottle pretty hard back then. His drinking ruined his first marriage. I don't want that to happen again. And if God forbid, Mom dies. I don't know if Dad's strong enough to go on without her."

"I'm just a lay person," Mattie said calmly, her arm tightened around him in an affectionate hug. "But I think you are jumping way ahead of yourself and stressing unnecessarily. I know that's easy for me to say, but honestly you do not know anything specific yet. Maybe everything will be fine, or whatever your mother has will be easily cured. You cannot immediately start writing her obituary. For God's sake, Sky, remember your years and years of medical training. You need to muster all your strength and step up to support and take care of her…not bury her. And saying a few prayers wouldn't hurt either."

"I know you're right," he said, ashamed. "It's just that I was so stunned. This came out of nowhere. Mom's always been so healthy, and she was the one we ran to if anything was wrong. Dad is super worried too, and I can see the fear in his eyes."

"Are you going back to Tampa for the biopsy?"

"I wanted to, but Mom asked me to stay in Miami to be near Casey, who's a wreck over this. When Mom has the pathology results, we'll all get together and figure out the next steps. Until then, it's just a waiting game."

"Your mother sounds like a wise woman. I can't wait to meet her." Mattie was impressed with Mary's stoicism. "She certainly is setting a good example."

"She is…and so are you, Mattie. Thanks for listening and being so understanding. You and Mom are very much alike in that way. Before all this happened, I had planned to tell my parents about you…that we were falling in love. I brought pictures to show them and wanted to tell them everything about you. But when Mom told me about her lung issue, I just couldn't find the right words or be happy in front of her when she and Dad were suffering."

"I understand. There will be plenty of time to share news about us. You were right to keep quiet about us under the circumstances. She has too much on her plate to face the possibility that her only son might eventually be spirited away by a brazen woman from Ft. Lauderdale." She tried to lighten the mood with humor. "Let's put telling her about us on hold until we know your mother's going to be okay."

Sky took her in his arms and lifted her face to his, smothering her with kisses. "God, you smell so good," he whispered hoarsely. "I missed you so much and I'm so grateful I met you, my pretty lady. What would you think about having a houseguest tonight?" he teased. "I don't want to be alone. I need to hold and make love to you all night."

"I wouldn't have it any other way," she beamed with pleasure. "I was beginning to think we were the only couple in this day and age who didn't sleep together."

"We certainly can't have that." He said with a wink.

She led him to the bedroom as he began peeling off her clothes and removing his own.

CHAPTER 22

The next six days dragged by endlessly as Sky waited for his mother's biopsy procedure, and he tried to pretend it was business as usual at work. Casey remained on the campus of UM, half-heartedly studying for her exams and spending hours on the phone with Ned. She and Ned had not been able to meet over Thanksgiving weekend because of Mary's announcement about her lung condition, but they had become constant phone buddies and talked or texted each other several times a day.

Ned and *Liquidity* were back in town for another ten days, provisioning and preparing the ship for their twelve-night Christmas/New Year's Eve charter. The guests would fly to St. Barts to board the mega yacht there for the holiday cruise. Ned told Casey how beautiful the boat was, covered with red, green, and silver balls hanging from the ceilings everywhere and four professionally decorated Christmas trees in the public rooms. He took pictures and texted them to her. He and Casey made plans to meet over the weekend. Ned had borrowed a friend's car and had asked permission of Captain Llanos to pick up Casey and bring her to the boat to show her around before he took her out for dinner and back to campus.

The captain had become exceptionally fond of his new first mate in a short time. He saw a lot of himself in the young man. Ned was knowledgeable, entertaining, and dependable. He got along well with the other crew members and was an asset to the yacht. As long as Ned did his job, he was free to pursue his girlfriend in his free time. Captain Llanos had been a young sailor in love once too. He remembered the rush.

Casey had called Mattie to tell her how excited she was about seeing the yacht and Ned again. She wanted Mattie's reassurance that it was okay to have a little fun while she waited for her mother's pathology reports. Casey felt guilty being happy while everyone else was waiting on pins and needles for a diagnosis. Mattie promised her that although she did not know Mary, she felt sure she would want her daughter to enjoy herself and not be maudlin. There was still every reason to be hopeful. She warned Casey to pretend, in front of Captain Llanos, that this was her first-time onboard *Liquidity*. "Your earlier visit is still our secret," she chuckled conspiratorially. "I never mentioned anything about it to anyone, not even your brother."

The weeks between Thanksgiving and New Year' Eve were the slowest of the year for Mattie. Anyone wanting to charter had already down so, and Charles normally closed the office so the staff could enjoy a little time off before "the season" began in earnest in January.

Charles and Brenda had, in the past, gone to *The Capital Grille* for a fancy dinner on December 5th, to celebrate Brenda's birthday. Mattie was always included, but this year she begged off, explaining that December 5th was most likely the day Sky's mother would get her report, and she wanted to be with him, and Casey if they needed her, when they heard the results.

She had not told her mother or Charles how serious she and Sky were about each other. The two were falling more deeply in love everyday but wanted to take their time making future plans. They had only been dating a few months but were looking forward to a future together. For all practical purposes, they were already living together. Sky had stayed over with her the night he returned from Thanksgiving and never spent another night at his own place. Each time he came over, he brought more clothes and personal items. His electric shaver and toothbrush were happily ensconced in the master bathroom and his favorite waffle iron and Keurig machine had found a home on her kitchen counter. If it was not for the worry about his mother's health, it would have been the happiest time in both their lives. However, worry hung over them constantly.

If everything turned out all right, Sky was planning to drive Mattie to Tampa the weekend before Christmas to introduce her to his parents. He knew his mother and father would take to Mattie right away, as Casey had. And they would be thrilled that Sky had found such a wonderful woman.

Brenda was used to dropping by Mattie's apartment all the time to visit, but now if she did so, she would see the evidence of Sky living there. It would upset her to realize that her daughter was in an intimate relationship with a man she had never met. Mother and daughter had always been so close, and Mattie hated keeping the secret from her…and from Charles. She hoped it was not selfish, but she couldn't wait for the pathology results to come in, so she and Sky could get on with their lives and express their happiness together. She felt like they were sneaking around, and she hated the dishonesty of it.

Brenda was conservative by nature so Mattie knew her mother would feel that she and Sky were rushing into their relationship rather than taking their time getting to know everything possible about each other. Brenda had admitted often to her daughter that she fell madly in love with Mattie's father at first sight and throwing caution aside, married him shortly thereafter. Brenda claimed she never regretted the decision and only death had separated them. Hopefully, remembering how she had felt back then would sway Brenda in Mattie's impulsive favor.

As soon as everything was okay with Sky's mother, Mattie was going to have a long talk with her mother and tell her everything. Then she'd introduce Sky and hope for the best. She was positive that Brenda would adore him once she got to know him. Charles would probably put up a fuss about their living arrangements and be gruff at first, but when he saw how in love the two were, she knew he would give his support…or so she hoped.

The morning of December 5th was bright and sunny with hardly a cloud on the horizon. "This beautiful weather bodes well for good news," Mattie looked lovingly at Sky as they drank their morning coffee. "The waiting is almost over."

Sky had taken the day off and was going to *Zoom* his parents, his mother's doctors, and Casey so they would all hear the news at the same time. That way, nothing could be misinterpreted or misunderstood. Mattie kept glancing at the clock on the stove. Time was moving so slowly, and with every passing minute, she could see Sky becoming more agitated. Finally, his I-Pad binged and lit up with an invitation to join a Zoom meeting. Mattie blew Sky an air kiss and backed out of the kitchen so she would not be seen on camera. She stayed just outside the door so she could hear the conversations.

Sky's father spoke first, and from his tone of voice, Sky could not decide if the news he was about to share was good or bad. "Everyone, this has been a terrible time for the Cooper family and made us realize how very much we all love your mother. She is the heart and soul of this family, and I am thrilled to announce that unless she gets hit by a train or a bus, she will probably outlive us all. Her pathology report was completely negative, and her lungs are cancer free." His voice broke as he grabbed his wife's hand. "The good Lord has answered our prayers."

Casey did not hear anything ese. She let out a big 'whoopie'. "Way to go Mom!"

Mattie smiled and tears came to her eyes.

Sky took a few deep breaths and steadied his voice. He asked the doctors a few specific medical questions and was soon convinced that all the right things had been done and that his mother was going to be fine."

Mary's eyes glistened with happy tears. "I love you all," she spoke in a choked voice. "God saved me and your father from the temptation of alcohol many years ago. Today, He has saved us all from the agonies of cancer. This is going to be the best Christmas the Cooper family has ever had, and I can't wait to start decorating the house and baking. Thank you all for your love and support. I'm going to disconnect now and decompress, but I'll speak to each of you soon. And Casey, you cannot use me and my health as an excuse any longer. Study for those exams, honey. See you soon."

The I-Pad went blank. Mattie ran back into the kitchen and hugged Sky, tears of happiness running down her face. "See, I told you so. Everything's going to be fine."

"You were right," he said, the relief apparent in his voice and posture. "And now we have to let your mom and Charles and my parents know that we're a couple. Are you ready for the big reveal?"

"As ready as I'll ever be," she grinned happily, the worries of the last few days fading away. "But do we have to tell them right this minute? I think we need to privately celebrate the good news ourselves first and I can think of a way I'd like to spend the rest of the day."

"Oh, really." He came up behind her and rubbed her ass suggestively. "Last one to the bed is a rotten egg."

They both laughed and raced each other to the bedroom where they stayed for most of the afternoon. Mattie called her mother later that evening to wish her a happy birthday and to ask her how her celebration dinner with Charles went. She shared the good news about Sky's mother. "Mom," Mattie said mysteriously. "Can I come over tomorrow for breakfast? We need to talk."

CHAPTER 23

Mattie arrived at Brenda's townhouse at eight a.m. She brought fresh pastries from *Croissant Times*, as if eating the sugary delicacies would make the conversation and news about Sky living with her easier for Brenda to tolerate

"What's the big mystery," Brenda asked getting right to the point in her usual manner.

"It's all good," Mattie answered. "But I haven't been completely honest with you about my relationship with Sky and how far it's gone. I was afraid you would think we were moving too quickly, and I did not want to hear your criticism and have to defend myself. Mom, I am so in love and have never been happier. Sky and I are so compatible. We agree on almost everything, and the chemistry between us is mind blowing. He's the absolute perfect man for me."

"Wow!" Brenda was relieved. "I was afraid you were going to give me some awful news. I assume Sky feels the same way about you?"

Mattie blushed. "Yes, he does. He's five years younger than me – thirty - but that doesn't make any difference to either of us. I guess technically that makes me a cougar." She chuckled. "He has a growing internal medicine practice in North Miami and it's doing really well. He's from a close family on the west coast, Tampa, and has one sister, Casey, who I've mentioned. Sky's twelve years older than his sister, but they are super connected, and, in many ways, he acts like her dad. It's really sweet. He adores her and so do I."

"Whoa. Slow down darling. I need time to take this all in. You're going so fast."

"Sorry," Mattie laughed and continued. "I have not met his parents yet, but he wants to take me to his home next weekend. His father is a retired security guard for *Home Depot* and his mother is a stay-at-home housewife and a piano teacher. From the way he describes them, they are a really wholesome bunch...kind of like The Brady Bunch. Maybe too wholesome for me," she laughed nervously. "They don't drink a drop of liquor and I doubt they ever swear. Sky says many years ago they both had drinking problems and met at an AA meeting. They've been sober and together for thirty years and as far as I can see, they've done a great job raising their two kids. I hope if Sky and I ever marry, that we do as well with our own kids one day."

"This all sounds very nice, honey, but what aren't you telling me? I know you pretty well and you're holding something back." She could tell Mattie was leaving out something pretty important from the way her daughter was squirming in the chair and twisting her hair nervously between her fingers.

Mattie tried to think of a diplomatic way to tell Brenda she was sleeping and living with Sky, but there were no subtle words to state the facts. Frustrated, she couldn't help herself and blurted out the news that she knew would upset her mother. "The day after Thanksgiving, the day after Sky learned about his mother's possible lung cancer, he came back from Tampa to tell me. He stayed over at my condo. We've been living together ever since."

The room was silent except for the persistent sound of the grandfather clock ticking in the background. Mattie waited for her mother to say something, but Brenda remained stone faced and silent. Mattie could see that her religious, Catholic, mother was shocked and none too pleased by the news. It didn't matter that Mattie was a grown woman in her thirties. She was still Brenda's little girl and in Brenda's eyes, obligated to live by the moral code by which she'd been raised. Sleeping around before marriage was a definite 'no, no'. Brenda was old-fashioned and made no apologies about it. Sometimes Brenda's rigidity had been hard on Mattie, but she had never openly defied her mother...until now.

"Mom, say something," Mattie begged. "I have found a wonderful man, who loves and cares for me. This is great news. Please be happy for me."

"I honestly don't know what to say." Brenda could not hide her hurt and disappointment. "I don't know what upsets me more...the fact that you kept the seriousness of this relationship a secret from me, or that you would invite a complete stranger to move in with you before your own mother has a chance to meet him."

"Mom, it wasn't like that. It wasn't planned. It just kind of happened. And he's not a stranger to me. You will love him if you just give him a chance. Remember, you told me that you and my father fell madly in love on your first date and married only a few months later. This is exactly the same."

And see how well that turned out, Brenda thought caustically remembering her miserable marriage and consequent divorce, but she could not share those thoughts with Mattie. She had never been truthful about that part of her past.

"What's the rush to get so serious so soon? Is it babies you want? There's plenty of time for that if Sky's the right man. Women have babies into their forties nowadays. Can't you give me and his parents a little time to adjust to this new relationship? I still don't understand why you kept this from me until now?" She was trying to absorb the news and not overreact.

"I didn't mean to keep you in the dark, Mom." Mattie rolled her eyes in frustration. "We just wanted to keep things private between the two of us in the beginning…to see how things played out. But now we are certain that we are meant to be together. We want to shout our love to the whole world. I see now that we were being thoughtless and self-ish. I am sorry, Mom. Please, forgive me!" Mattie's eyes were wide with unshed tears. She loved her mother deeply and never wanted to hurt or disappoint her.

"I really don't have a choice, now do I?" Her dashed feelings were visible on her face. "But I love you more than life itself and have always wanted and prayed for only the best for you. Everything I've ever done has been to give you a decent, God fearing, happy life. I guess I will have to get used to this new reality and sharing you with this man. I'll try really hard to be loving and accepting if he genuinely loves and treats you well." She tried to smile for her daughter's sake, but it was difficult. "Please invite him to dinner soon so I can finally put a face to the recipient of all your glowing remarks."

"Thank you, Mom. I'll do better than that. You don't have to wait for dinner. Sky's sitting in his car in the driveway and is as anxious to meet you as you are to meet him. Let me go and invite him in."

Mattie went to the front door and happily waved at Sky, giving him the thumbs up sign.

"Good morning, Mrs. Cartwright," Sky smiled broadly when he entered the house. "It's wonderful to finally make your acquaintance. You are as beautiful as your daughter. I suppose this meeting is long overdue, and I truly apologize for that."

"Come in Sky," Brenda said as warmly as she could. "Apparently, we have a lot to talk about."

Even though she was skeptical, Brenda instantly liked Sky's wholesome good looks and manners. She saw nothing off hand that she could criticize. Unlike so many of the young men today, he was clean shaven, nicely dressed, and his eyes, a penetrating, unusual shade of green, reminded her of someone she'd known before. He was tall, thin, and very handsome, with no discernable tattoos (a big plus in her opinion). The two made a lovely couple. She watched as he took Mattie's hand, and she could see that they were very much in love.

Brenda normally took her time sizing up people and did not form instant opinions; but there was something about Sky that pleased and reassured her. She could understand why Mattie was so drawn to him. She was herself.

The three sat around Brenda's table chatting and sharing stories. Sky answered all of Brenda's questions and promised her that he loved Mattie and would take care of her always. By the end of this first visit, Brenda felt comfortable that Mattie had indeed made a great decision and that she was about to embark on a wonderful new chapter of her life. They made plans to meet Charles for dinner that night at *Rainbow Palace* and to share the news with him over gourmet Chinese food.

"That went as well as we could have expected," Sky said with relief after they left Brenda's. "I really like your mother, and I think she likes me. Now all we have to do is convince Charles about us, and we will have the Cartwright side of the family onboard. Then it's my parents' turn."

"Charles is a softie when it comes to me. I'm not worried, but I really want your mother and father to like me." She was worried. Not everyone was as accepting and understanding as Brenda.

"They will, Pretty Lady. Dad will fall all over you, and Mom too. She's a little more reserved but the kindest woman in the world. As long as you like pasta, there will always be a place for you at her table."

"I hope so," Mattie sighed. "At least we'll know one way or the other about how they feel about us as a couple by the end of the weekend. Tampa, here we come."

CHAPTER 24

At their introductory dinner, Charles and Sky had instantly liked each other, so that potential obstacle was averted.

On the drive to Tampa, Casey, Sky, and Mattie kept up a running dialogue. The three were never at a loss for something to say. The conversation was about everything and nothing. Sky had confessed to Casey that he had moved into Mattie's condo, and she was happy for them. He explained that the real point of this pre-Christmas visit was not only to bring Casey home for her Christmas vacation, but more importantly, to introduce Mattie to the parents and bring them up to date on their romance.

It was then that Casey realized that her parents knew next to nothing about Mattie. They knew that Sky was infatuated with someone from Ft. Lauderdale, but not that Mattie and he were living together. That would be a lot for them to take in at their first meeting. They had just endured the agony of Mary's cancer scare and were still pretty emotional.

"I'm counting on you to help win your parents over," Mattie spoke seriously to Casey. "I'm sure it's going to be hard for them to accept me so quickly. They must have preconceived ideas of the type of woman Sky should be with."

"No worries," Casey laughed. "You'll make them happy, and I'll scare the shit out of them if they're not nice to you."

"Ladies, please," Sky gasped. "No joking about this visit. We are not preparing for a war, more like a happy homecoming. And Casey, I think I should talk to the folks alone first with Mattie. Can you find some marbles or dolls to play with and stay out of our hair for a while?" He joked, but was half serious. "Please Ducky. Behave for once. I want to talk to Mom and Dad alone."

"Not on your life, big brother. I am not making myself scarce. I want to be in on all the action."

"Casey, please," Mattie implored her. "I think I'll come as enough of a shock, so we don't need you stirring up the pot. I really need to be able to count on you to help us."

"Okay, okay," Casey giggled. "But if things go south, just shout. I have Dad wrapped around my little finger."

"Enough, enough," Sky interrupted their banter. "Mattie, that's our house at the end of the street…the white one with the pink shutters."

"It's beautiful." She admired the lovely two-story stucco home with its perfectly groomed landscaping and colorful flowers planted in enormous clay pots on the front porch. There was even an old-fashioned white wooden swing hanging from the ceiling. "This is right out of *House and Garden* magazine," Mattie remarked. "It's breathtaking. Who's the gardener?"

"Mom, she loves her plants and flowers. She sings to them and credits that with their stunning brilliance, although I believe it's all in the *Miracle Grow*." He laughed. "She has a green thumb in the garden and magic fingers on the piano keyboard." Sky stepped out of the car and gently began pushing a more than a little hesitant Mattie up the front steps.

"Wait," Mattie stopped short. "What if they don't like me? What will we do then?"

"That won't happen," Sky assured her. "Everything will be fine. Like your mother, my parents only want me to be happy and once they see that I am with you, that will be the end of it."

Casey joked and slashed her head off in a mock gesture. "Let's go inside and face the guillotine...one for all and all for one." She thought Sky and Mattie were being ridiculous. What was the big deal? Who wouldn't like Mattie?

Casey opened the front door, which was never locked, and called out, "Mom, Dad, we're home and we've brought company."

CHAPTER 25

Sky held Mattie's hand and squeezed it tightly as they walked through the neatly organized front room of the house and into the kitchen where he knew his mother would be cooking something. Mary was standing over the sink, washing glasses and pushing strands of long gray hair off her face. The kitchen was warm and smelled of recent baking.

"Mom, this is Mattie Cartwright. The woman I told you about," Sky said proudly, nudging Mattie forward.

"Hello Mattie," Mary said warmly. "Welcome to Tampa. I have some nice cold lemonade in the fridge and freshly baked chocolate chip cookies. Please take a seat and help yourself." Mary walked over to Sky and hugged him. "You look thin. Are you eating enough?" She was all mother when it came to her children.

"Hello, you must be Mattie?" Sky's father said pleasantly as he came inside from mulching the flowerbeds in the backyard. "You're as pretty as Sky said. Welcome to our home."

"Thank you, Mr. Cooper," Mattie answered. She had not expected such a nice, warm reception and was pleased. Her fears began to subside. After all, she and Sky hadn't committed a crime. They had just fallen in love and moved in together.

"Call me Camden. Mr. Cooper was my father's name." He sat down next to Mattie and began nibbling on a warm cookie. "These are delicious, Mary."

Sky's mother smiled at her husband. "And please call me Mary.," she said to Mattie. "We are a very informal family. Tell us about yourself, and how you met Sky. We want to know all about you. Sky tells us you're quite a businesswoman, a yacht broker, I believe?"

"Mom, please don't start with the twenty questions," Sky chuckled. "I told you we met at the Ft Lauderdale boat show in October and have been dating ever since. I might as well tell you, she's one very special lady, and we're pretty serious about each other. She is the one for me, Mom... the one you always told me to wait for." His eyes were full of love as he smiled at Mattie.

Camden Cooper started to stare at Mattie and dropped his cookie on the tabletop, frozen in place. He felt his heart begin to race. Sweat leaked from his scalp down to his forehead. He gazed directly into Mattie's gorgeous green eyes and then quickly back to those of his son. They were the same shape and the identical color. He began to tremble and had difficulty swallowing the lump in his throat as he watched a nightmare unfold before his eyes. No one in the room realized anything was wrong, that disaster was about to erupt. Only Camden...He was at first unnerved, and then scared to death.

Camden pinched himself and forced himself to look deeply into Mattie's eyes again and then back to his son's eyes. They were identical, down to the same small flecks of gold. Chills ran down his spine and he felt suddenly nauseous. "Mattie, tell me about your parents and your life in Ft. Lauderdale." He spoke in a hoarse, halting voice and hardly dared to breathe.

"There's not much to tell really," Mattie smiled innocently, still holding Sky's hand. "I grew up with my mother, Brenda Cartwright. She was widowed when I was very little. My father died in the military service. My mother raised me in the Catholic church and supported me on her salary at the bank, where she was a branch department head. I went to the University of Florida and then after a few years working at Macy's, I started working at Lux Charters for its owner, Charles Cord. I own a condo on the beach between Commercial Boulevard and Atlantic Avenue if you are familiar with the Ft. Lauderdale area. My mother lives only a few blocks away in a townhouse in Lauderdale by the Sea. It's kind of a dull story, actually. The most exciting thing that has ever happened to me is meeting your son…and Casey, of course." She smiled and winked at Sky's sister. Camden detected an unmistakable trace of a dimple on her face and jerked his head involuntarily.

"Where was your mother born?" He abruptly cut Mattie off. "Was it in Massachusetts?"

"Yes, Boston." Mattie answered looking astonished. "How on earth did you guess that?"

"Because when I was a young man, I lived in Ft. Lauderdale for a short time and dated a beautiful girl named Brenda Cartwright. She was tall and looked a great deal like yourself. I'm sure it's just a coincidence." Although, he did not sound convinced. "Do you happen to have a picture of her?"

"Sure." Mattie pulled out her cell phone. "I have dozens…some from when she and I were much younger, and some taken just last week." She handed her phone to Sky's father. "Here, take a look. Could it possibly be that you once dated my mom? If true, what a small world. That would be an amazing coincidence." She looked at Sky and he nodded his agreement.

"How old would your mother be now?" Camden stubbornly persisted. He was becoming increasingly agitated. Mary was watching him closely. He was not behaving in his usual affable way. She had never known her husband to be so rude. Something was wrong, but she could not imagine what.

"Her birthday was December 5th, and she turned fifty-six then." Mattie answered. "Do you think my mother is the same girl you knew when you lived in Ft. Lauderdale?" She was more than a little curious and puzzled by Camden's brusqueness.

"I believe so," Camden struggled to keep the panic out of his voice. He rung his hands together nervously. "Yes, I think it's very possible."

"Wow," Mattie digested it. "And now so many years later, here I am, a guest in your home. Wait until I tell her. I'm sure she'll remember dating a handsome man like yourself."

Camden did not respond but studied the pictures of Brenda carefully a second time. With shaking hands, he returned the camera to Mattie. "Did your mother ever tell you your dad's last name?"

"Of course," Mattie watched him carefully. *What a weird question.* Camden Cooper was acting very strangely indeed. "My father's name was Frank Cartwright, but as I've said, he passed away when I was too young to remember him. I was born in September of 1984 and my father, a marine, died while on active duty sometime that same year."

Camden stood up abruptly, almost upending the table, and bolted from the room. "Mary," he shouted at his wife. "Come outside. Sky, Mattie, Casey, stay put. We'll be right back."

Mattie shot Sky a puzzled look. What on earth was happening? It was baffling.

Sky had no idea what was going on in his father's head. He had never seen him behave so erratically. Normally Camden was a gracious host and always pleasant and congenial with his guests.

"Sometimes I don't get my parents at all," Casey offered, munching on a cookie, and shaking her head. "They can be so bizarre. What's up with all the questions about Mattie's mom and dad? You'd think he'd want to know more about Mattie herself."

"I agree." Sky was perplexed. Mattie had not said or done anything to agitate his father and yet Camden looked shell-shocked, bordering on furious.

CHAPTER 26

Camden waited for Mary to meet him outside in the yard where he could speak freely and not be overheard. "I need a drink," he groaned. "And I mean a really strong one."

"Don't even joke about that Cam. For heaven's sake. What's the matter with you? That poor girl inside must think you're a real nutcase. What's going on?"

He sat down on one of the patio chairs with a thud and wrung his hands together. "Mary, remember I told you that I had a baby girl with my first wife, but that I was a no-good bastard and never took responsibility for the child. I baled on them the day my wife brought the baby home from the hospital. That baby's name was Mattie. Don't you see what I'm getting at? Where I'm going with this?"

"No, Cam, I'm sorry but I don't. What are you trying to say?" Mary was more confused than ever by Camden's strange behavior and his frightened expression worried her.

Camden was exasperated. "Mary, for God's sake! Don't you see how much Sky and Mattie look alike…the same eyes, the sample dimples, and both so tall. There is such a strong family resemblance between the two. Surely you see it?" He was almost pleading with her.

"After I walked out on my family," he continued in a monotone. "I felt so guilty that, as you know, I wandered around the country, boozing, and doing odd jobs for almost two years until I ended up in Tampa and found work in the shipyards. A buddy there recognized the signs of alcoholism. He dragged me to my first AA meeting and that's where I met you and the rest is history?"

"Yes," Mary answered warily as her eyes narrowed. "I know all that sordid history but why bring it up now? This is not the time nor the place. What are you trying to say and for heaven's sake, why dredge that all up now when Sky is here with his lovely girlfriend? So, what if they look a bit alike. Nothing wrong with that. They're both gorgeous. They'll probably make beautiful babies one day."

"Mary, please don't be so bloody dense! Concentrate, and listen to me. Look very closely at Mattie. You have to see what I do. Mattie Cartwright is really Mattie Cooper, my first-born daughter...she is the baby I deserted 35 years ago, and Brenda Cartwright is her mother, my ex-wife. I have no idea what atrocious lies her mother has told her, but obviously she never told Mattie my real name or that I had abandoned them. And I certainly was never a marine and clearly I did not die in action."

Mary looked at her husband in horror. She was speechless.

"I don't want to alarm Mattie or Sky, but we all have to get to the bottom of this...to know the truth, and tonight. This can't wait! You must understand the awful ramifications for them, for all of us. If my suspicions are true, Mattie and Sky can never marry or ever have children together. It would be an incestuous relationship and probably illegal. They are genetically related, *half brother and sister*. Oh my God. I never expected anything like this." He wrung his hands together and rocked back and forth in agony. "I have to reach Mattie's mother right away and determine if she is my first wife. I remember she took back her maiden name as part of our divorce settlement, so I'm pretty sure I'm right about all of this. Oh God, this cannot be happening! It's a catastrophe!"

"Oh, my Lord. No, it cannot be!" Mary fell to her knees praying silently, rocking back and forth on the ground, grasping the horrible significance of her husband's words. If he was correct, the truth would ruin so many lives. Poor Sky and Mattie. *Please God don't let this be true!* She prayed fervently rubbing the gold cross hanging around her neck. "Please, oh please dear heavenly Father, don't let it be true!"

Camden tried to comfort his wife, but there were no words. He could not wait another minute to find out the truth. He pulled out his phone and Googled "Brenda Cartwright" in Ft. Lauderdale. In less than thirty seconds he had her phone number and address. "Brenda, Brenda Cartwright, this is Camden Cooper," he choaked over the phoneline. "And I believe our daughter Mattie is sitting in my kitchen at the moment with my son, Sky."

All he heard from the other end was a woman's hysterical voice shrieking uncontrollably. "No, no, no. It can't be!" Brenda instantly knew that the voice on the phone was her ex-husband, Cam. Even after all these years, she still recognized it.

"Brenda, I know this is a terrible shock, but you have to get a hold of yourself for our daughter's sake. We have to figure out what to do. This is a God-awful mess. Our kid's lives will be ruined if they stay together. We have to put a stop to their relationship."

Brenda shouted into the phone. "We don't have to do anything. You're as dead to me now Camden Cooper, as you were the day you walked out on me and Mattie. Don't you dare reappear in our lives now and go all parental on me, you sick drunken bastard."

"This is not about me or you, Brenda. Control yourself, please. This is about Mattie and the terrible mistake she would be making by remaining involved with Sky. For God's sake…they are related. We can't let that happen." He fought to control his temper. "I know you're shocked, but so am I, and believe me, so is my wife, Mary. None of us ever expected anything like this to happen."

"Does Mattie know?" Brenda tried to control her emotions and her shrill voice was barely audible.

"No, she does not know any of this yet. I wanted to confirm it with you first. But she will soon. We cannot keep it from her. She is in love with her half-brother, for God's sake. It's INCEST! Damn you Brenda… It's all your fault because of your lies. What were you thinking…telling her I was dead?

CHAPTER 27

It took Camden and Mary a few minutes to control their emotions before they were able to return to the kitchen. They needed to deal with the calamity Brenda and Camden had set in motion so many years ago. But how?

As soon as his parents came back inside, Sky looked from one to the other and picking up on their body language, intuitively knew something awful had happened. "Dad, Mom you're scaring us. What the hell's going on? Why are you both acting so weird?"

Mary looked lovingly at her son. "Your father and I have just confirmed something that unfortunately is going to affect us all, but Mattie and Sky the most," she said sadly, her voice barely audible. "I think we should all sit down and let your father explain…and I do mean *your* father," she said cryptically to Mattie. "There's something we have to tell you."

Mattie had no idea what was going on, but she was rapidly changing her mind about the Cooper family's stability and their mental health. It seemed everyone but Sky was an odd ball. She had made a mistake coming here and wanted to go home.

Camden led them all into the living room and sat down on the sofa.

He faced Sky and Mattie. Mary perched on the sofa's arm and held her husband's hand. They both looked deadly serious. Casey, having no idea what was about to be revealed, made herself comfortable sitting on the floor between her parents and Sky. They were all silent, waiting for Camden to explain.

"There's no way to make this any easier," he began nervously. "So, forgive me, but I have to just plow right in." He looked at his son and the innocent face of his newly discovered daughter. He knew he was going to crush them with his next words and break their hearts. It was inevitable.

"It seems that Mattie's mother," he began, "Brenda Cartwright, has not been truthful for many, many years. She is not a war widow. Thirty-five years ago, she married a good-for-nothing creep who was incapable of assuming responsibility for his own child. When she announced to her husband that she was pregnant, he reacted by drowning his insecurities in vodka, and, as soon as their baby was born, he packed his bags, left town, and never looked back. His abandoned wife had never heard a word from him again until today… except from his divorce lawyer.

"A few minutes ago…when I reached out to Brenda by phone, she confirmed my worst nightmare. Unfortunately," he continued, "that low-life creep who deserted his family back then was me, Camden Cooper. Mattie, in the plainest terms…I am your biological father. I was never in the marines, never died in the service of my country. I certainly was never a hero. I was a slimeball, SOB, and have spent a lot of years trying to become a better person. I'm sure your mother thought she was being kind in hiding these facts from you but look what her terrible deception has caused."

Mattie and Sky looked at each other in utter disbelief. It was too soon for them to grasp the significance of what Camden had told them. Mary looked at the two young people, so in love and could see that they were totally confused. "What my husband is trying to say," she said in a hushed whisper, "is that Mattie and Sky have different mothers, Brenda, and myself, but you both have the same father, Camden Cooper. That genetically makes you half brother and sister."

CHAPTER 28

Mattie could not stay in the Cooper's house another minute. The walls were closing in on her, and she felt like screaming. Her head throbbed. She could not begin to cope with the realities of what Camden and Mary had tried to explain. Incest? With Sky? It could not be true. It simply was not possible.

They were so in love...so perfect for each other. How could their attraction to one another be labeled something so dirty and revolting? Why was this happening? She had no idea what to do next, but she needed to find answers and to demand the truth from her mother. How could Brenda have lied for all these years and kept Mattie's father's identity, and the fact that he was alive, a secret? It was unconscionable.

"Please take me home," Mattie ran into Sky's arms and begged him to take her home. "I have to get out of here." She felt like she would collapse to the floor if he let go.

Sky said a quick goodbye to Casey and Mary but ignored Camden completely. Casey was crying hysterically and clung fiercely to her brother. "Please don't go Sky. Stay with me or take me with you. I don't want to be here with them." She angrily pointed to her parents. "They're such hypocrites."

"I can't, Ducky." Sky's scathing contempt for his father was evident. "I have to get Mattie away from here and home now. We need time alone to figure out what to do with this mess and then confront Mattie's mother. Hang in there, Ducky. I'll come back for you soon"

Casey nodded reluctantly but continued to sob. "At least promise me you'll come home for Christmas."

He promised but was not sure how he would get through the holiday there. He was so livid with his father for walking out on Brenda and Mattie and for the horrendous consequences of that selfish behavior. Only his love for his sister and mother would make him return to Tampa ever again.

Camden had never mentioned having a child from his previous marriage and now the reality of that baby had kicked Sky in his gut. He had to leave his family home now, or he feared he might take a punch at his father.

As they drove back to Ft. Lauderdale, both in a state of shock, Mattie and Sky spoke candidly and tried to understand the full meaning of what Camden had just told them. But the information was mind-boggling, and, no matter how they looked at the facts, there was no way they could see for them to legally continue to be together as lovers. They were siblings by blood.

Their union was against the law. If people knew that they had the same father, they would be shocked and disgusted. Mattie did not know much about incest, but she did understand that if she and Sky were to have children, they could be genetically compromised. Under no circumstances would she subject any children of hers to that risk. It was unfathomable. And Sky would not either.

"I'm not ready to give up on us so soon," Sky pounded his fist on the steering wheel. "None of this is our fault. I'll check with an attorney to see if we have any options. We cannot be blamed for the sins of our father and your mother's secrets. Saying the words "our father" made bile rise in his throat.

"I suppose we could stay together and agree to never have children," Mattie said, searching desperately for a sliver of hope. "But we'd be lying to the world, and eventually one or both of us would miss having kids and resent the situation and each other. We can't let that happen."

"So then, we'll adopt." Sky suggested hopefully. "Plenty of people make their families that way. No reason we can't also." He smiled tentatively. "Would you consider that?"

"It wouldn't work," Mattie moaned. "We'd have to lie to everyone for the rest of our lives and pretend that we couldn't have children of our own? And how would we deal with explaining that you and I have the same father? …the children's grandfather. Oh God, Sky. This is such a mess. I don't know what to do."

Mattie stared out the window, lost in thought. Ironically, she should be happy that she had found the father she had been told was dead, but that didn't make up for the hurt and the anger she felt towards her mother. She could not understand how any man could simply walk out on his family and make no attempt to communicate or check on them ever again. She wondered, had he ever searched the internet or contacted a private detective to find her? Apparently not! His behavior had been so callous, so unlike everything Sky had told her about his father. It was like Camden was two different people.

Mattie was not sure she could ever forgive Camden. And she was positive she would *never* forgive her mother. What a horrible secret Brenda kept all these years…and why? The first thing Mattie would do when she went to her mother's house would be to take that damn picture of her supposed father off the mantle and smash it into a million pieces. What a hypocritical travesty! A marine hero, indeed! Camden had been a selfish coward, not a hero.

Sky was also lost in private thought as he drove along the highway. He was so distracted that he almost missed the exit, and he was incensed that his supposedly pious, self-righteous father had wantonly deserted Brenda and Mattie thirty-five years ago without a care as to what might have happened to them. Camden had apparently forgotten one of AA's important 12 steps to sobriety…the one about seeking forgiveness from those you have harmed and making amends to them. Instead, he had simply tossed them aside and started a second family with no regard for his first. Sky shook his head in disbelief. It was all too much to absorb. He had always loved and respected his father, but no more. His world was falling apart, and he was helpless to stop it.

Mattie and Sky did not speak for the rest of the trip home. Both were too devastated to make small talk and too emotional to discuss their precarious situation. It was the longest car ride either of them could ever remember. Sky was sitting only a few inches from her, but Mattie had never felt so alone in her life.

CHAPTER 29

Camden and Mary watched in agony as Sky and Mattie drove away. Camden tried to justify his former behavior by blaming his addiction to alcohol and railing at Brenda for telling the horrendous lie that he was dead. Still, all of his excuses did nothing to mitigate the pain he and Brenda had caused their children and the intense, almost indescribable pain he had seen in his two children's eyes when he told them the truth. He was completely despondent, and, for the first time in three decades, was seriously desperate enough to search out the nearest bar. Thankfully, there was no liquor in his home.

"I'm going to talk to Brenda again and try to figure this all out," he swore angrily. "I am so sorry for my part in this, Mary. I've ruined my kid's lives."

"Don't be so hard on yourself. It seems there's enough blame to go around," she said sadly, dabbing at the tears that continuously dripped from her eyes. She saw the pitiful look on her husband's face and feared he was close to falling apart. "Cam, we need to find an AA meeting right away. Call your sponsor. You can't afford to slip now…not when your family and I need you so much."

"I don't want any damn meeting." He stormed out of the house.

He had never spoken harshly to her before. "No platitudes or believing in a higher power are going to make this abomination go away." He was unable to conceal his anger. It was directed at himself and Brenda, not at Mary.

"Cam, please come back," she called desperately and ran after him. It was too late. He jumped into his car and peeled out of the driveway in a fury. Mary fell to her knees. "Holy Mother of God," she prayed. "Don't let Cam take a drink."

CHAPTER 30

After the drive from Tampa, Mattie and Sky went back to her condo where she sat alone on her balcony sadly looking out at the ocean. Eventually Sky wandered out and took a seat in the chair next to her. "I don't know what to say, Mattie. This is so unbelievable. I love you more than ever. I'm so angry at my father, and your mother, and at the world in general. I don't know what to do."

"I know," Mattie murmured. As much as she longed to hold him, kiss him, she could not. He was the man she adored, and who she had thought would one day be the father of her children. Now he was like the poison apple in the Bible story about the Garden of Eden. He was suddenly forbidden fruit. "There's so much to say, and yet I can't think of a thing. It's as if I'm emotionally paralyzed."

She stared forlornly at a random seagull on the beach and watched it casually skimming the water. It was so carefree, and she was in such emotional turmoil. How was this possible? How had life changed and turned upside down in a few short hours? Her mind was reeling out of control.

"I suppose, now that I know Cam is my father, I will be expected to try get to know him, and Mary, because I guess she's my step-mother? But Sky, I don't think I have the energy for it, or even want to. The idea is appalling. All I really know is that I can *never* forgive him for deserting me. And yet, I know he's your father too…and you love him. I am so mixed up. It doesn't seem right or fair that now, because of my mother's lies, I should insinuate myself into *your* family as Cam's daughter. I had wanted to be a part of it, so badly, but as your girlfriend and maybe someday in the future as your wife…but never *ever* as your half-sister."

"I don't know how I'm…we're … supposed to act going forward," Sky groaned, pacing around the room in anger. "Do you honestly think that one day we will be able to sit around a dinner table and act like we're one big happy, extended family? How can we ignore our love and passion and face the terrible truth that is tearing us apart? I don't think I can do it, Mattie…at least not yet. I cannot even stand being in the same room with you and not touching or holding you. Right now, more than anything in the world, I want to take you in my arms and run away to someplace where we will never be found. I am so tempted to do that."

"I understand. I really do. Just seeing you here and knowing we will no longer be living together, no longer making love, rips my soul apart. I feel so lost and desperate. Intellectually I know we can't be together ever again in an intimate way, but emotionally I can't accept it. The only good that has come from this mess is that I truly have a little sister now, and a great one at that. She's not responsible for any of this mess."

"And you have a brother - instead of a lover," he said bitterly, automatically reaching for her hand, but then he withdrew it immediately as if his fingers were on fire. Old habits would be hard to break. He wanted desperately to touch her…to feel her warmth, to taste her lips, to smell her hair… Instead, he could only watch her from a distance, hating the cruel trick genetics had played on them and the dirty secret that was responsible.

Mattie looked at Sky with intense passion. She could feel her heart literally breaking one tiny piece at a time. "I want you to make love to me," she agonized, "at least one last time, but I know we can't, or at least we shouldn't." She started to sob uncontrollably. "Life is so unfair!"

"No, we shouldn't," he said miserably, wanting desperately to take her in his arms and comfort her. He stood up, looking forlornly at the ocean. "Are you going to confront your mother? I think you should."

"At some point I'll have to, but not now. I know it sounds childish, but I hate her for what she did to us, and I want her to suffer...to pay for it. I don't think I can tolerate the sight of her now."

"I know you feel that way now, and I'm just as furious at my dad. However, for our own sanity we're going to have to learn to deal with this, or we'll both lose our families forever. I don't want that for either of us."

"I can't think about that now," Mattie snapped. "I want someone to pay for this atrocity!" She exhaled sharply in exasperation. "It's so damn unfair!"

"I bet my father will want to make a grandiose gesture and welcome you into the Cooper family. I'm sure he feels awful about what he did and causing you such pain. While I can't forgive him, I don't want you to feel guilty about establishing some kind of connection with him. You deserve a chance to decide if you want him, or any of us, in your life going forward; but I know I can't be around to watch." He stood up slowly, carrying the burdens of the world and his family genetics on his shoulders. "I'll always love you, Pretty Lady...always and forever."

He started walking slowly back into the living room. "I'm taking some of my clothes now and this week when you're at work, I'll come by for the rest."

Mattie could not bear to watch him leave. She clamped her eyes shut as tightly as possible and sat silently rocking back and forth in misery until she heard her front door close behind him. Then she broke into uncontrollable sobs that shook her whole body from a place deep within her.

"Goodbye, my love," she whispered. "Goodbye, my life."

PART TWO

CONSEQUENCES

CHAPTER 31

Mattie could not face Charles or anyone at Lux. Her emotions were out of control. She suffered from bouts of hysterical crying, when she raged at her mother and the whole world. At other times she crawled into bed, pulled the covers up to her neck and lay motionless for hours. Nothing she did relieved the unbearable pain of her separation from Sky and the disgusting implications of incest.

One morning, she felt driven to do something drastic, so she methodically went through her apartment, room by room, emptying drawers and closets of anything that belonged to, or reminded her, of Sky. She packed up the rest of his clothes and personal belongings, even the coffee machine and waffle maker. After shoving them into various pillowcases and plastic bags, she lugged them to the condo's reception desk and left instructions that Sky Cooper would be coming by to pick them up. She also left specific orders that he was not to be admitted to her apartment under and circumstances, ever again

She hoped that the physical act of purging her place of his things would make her feel better. She had been cautiously optimistic about it, but now seeing the empty shelves and bare closets only made her feel sadder and more alone.

Her phone rang constantly at all times of the day and night. From the caller ID, she knew it was her mother. Mattie never answered. There was no one she wanted to talk to, least of all Brenda. No one could take her pain away. No one could do anything that would fill the huge hole in her aching heart.

After more than two weeks of living in her pajamas and eating only enough peanut butter to sustain her, she forced herself to take a hot shower, washed and fixed her hair, and, afterwards, she felt a little more human. She was restless at home, wandering around the rooms with nothing to do and no one to talk to. On the spur of the moment, she decided to brave the office because work had always made her happy, even though she would have to make some plausible explanation for Sky's absence and for her foul mood. She'd say as little as possible, and certainly not reveal that she had discovered the awful truth that she and Sky were related. She prayed that the office staff would quickly lose interest in her personal love life and leave her alone to do her job.

Since she didn't have any potential clients lined up, she would go through the local yacht and sailing club directories in the area and make cold calls. She hated to do that, but she had to keep herself busy and her mind off of Sky. In her misery, Mattie had forgotten all about Christmas and the holidays, and that Charles normally closed Lux Charters for the week before Christmas until New Year's Day. When she walked into her office, expecting it to be full of people, the place was deserted, and it took her a moment to realize why. She was pleased that she would not have to discuss Sky with her co-workers, at least for a few more days. With relief, she headed toward her desk.

When she sat down, she noticed Charles, who as usual, was busy working at his desk. Candice, the attractive woman that she'd met previously, was sitting in there with him. They were huddled close together and appeared to be engrossed in some kind of project. Mattie had no interest in conversing with them and hoped her presence would go unnoticed. She was not that lucky. Charles looked up, surprised to see her, and immediately came out to speak with her.

"Mattie," he began cautiously, taking her in his arms and hugging her fiercely. "I've been so worried about you. Brenda told me what happened between you and Sky. I am so sorry, honey. You don't deserve this. Is there anything I can do to help? This is a terrible situation."

"No," she answered sharply. "There's nothing anyone can do. Forgive me, Charles. None of this is your fault, but I just can't talk about it… about any of it."

"I understand, but Brenda is so worried and wants…"

Her expression turned ominous, and she cut him off before he could finish his sentence. "I don't care what my mother wants! She is the reason for this whole disaster, and she has totally ruined my life. Why aren't you furious at her too? She's lied to you year after year about being a war widow, probably milking your sympathies and God knows what else. I will never trust her *again*, and I don't see how you can either."

"Honey, I am furious with her, believe me. When she told me about Camden's phone call and about everything that has happened since, I was so shaken and disappointed, and I told her as much in no uncertain terms. I believed she and I had an honest, open relationship, but in truth, it was built on her secrets and lies. I was floored by her dishonesty." He stepped closer to Mattie and reached for her hand. "However, I've had time to reflect on Brenda's behavior and I think I understand why she lied about Camden. Remember, she was very young and alone with a tiny baby to raise. At the time, she thought she was protecting you, and she never in a million years expected Camden Cooper to waltz back into her life, and certainly not in this convoluted way."

Mattie was not sympathetic. "I mean it," she hissed, withdrawing her hand from his. "I have nothing but scathing contempt for her and can't take it that you are siding with her. Don't utter another word about my sainted, lying, secretive mother, or I'll leave this office and never come back." Her face was deadly pale, and her voice was frigid. Charles had never seen her so angry. He was frightened by the intensity of the rage and raw emotions he saw on her beautiful face. He decided to back off. They could have this conversation sometime in the future when her emotions were under better control.

"Okay, Mattie. Whatever you want," he said with a tired smile. "You need time to heal. Just know that I'll always be here for you. And I am NOT on your mother's side. I simply understand the situation from her perspective. I love you and that will never change. But now, you'll have to excuse me. Candice and I are working on a deal, and I have to get back to her. Will you be all right?"

"Yes," Mattie mumbled softly, regretting taking her temper out on him. He was just trying to be kind and helpful. She waved half-heartedly to Candice and began leafing through the papers and the stack of mail on her desk. She was too upset to concentrate properly and suddenly felt stifled in the office. She did not have the stomach to make cold calls today, and only wanted to run somewhere and hide from the world.

It was obvious to Charles that his conversation with Mattie was going nowhere. She had no wish to speak with him further about her mother. He returned to his office, shaking his head in dismay and closed the door. It was a heartbreaking situation...and one for which there was no apparent solution.

"Let me just make this one call," he said to Candice, who was waiting patiently for him. "I'll just be a minute."

He picked up his cell and whispered, "Brenda, Mattie's come into the office, but she's in no shape to talk to you. I'll keep an eye on her for you, but you need to give her plenty of space, or she just might flee this town altogether. She's completely devastated and not thinking rationally. She blames you for everything. I believe, knowing her so well, that she'll come around in time, but for now you need to stop reaching out to her and to respect her privacy."

"Oh, Charles, I'm so sorry, and I feel so guilty. When Cam walked out, I was desperate to protect Mattie from the hurt and shame. I wanted to avoid hurting her any further. I honestly thought I was doing the best thing for everyone. Letting her believe he had died kept her from having to face what an irresponsible louse her father really was, and she was free to think of him with love instead of with bitterness. She had no abandonment issues as a child. I don't know how I can ever make things right between us again. Would you come over and keep me company for dinner tonight. I really need to see your friendly face and talk this through some more. I'll make your favorite meatloaf, please."

"No, Brenda. I'm sorry, but I am not ready to forgive your lies so easily yet either. I need time to digest all of this. And besides," he looked at Candice and smiled. "I have other plans for this evening."

"All right, "Brenda responded hesitantly. She had not expected Charles to be all warm and fuzzy after her betrayal, but she was alarmed by his sharp words. She knew she deserved his wrath, but it was hard for her to hear it. She wondered what kind of plans he'd referred to and with whom?

"What you did to Mattie was deplorable," he continued, "but no one could have predicted that things would turn out this way." He was trying to remain neutral because he cared so much about both mother and daughter, but his sympathies lay with Mattie.

"Have you heard from Camden?" He was curious about how the Cooper household was handling the situation. "Camden must be feeling pretty guilty about all of this. If he had stayed married to you and raised Mattie as his own, none of this would have happened. Has he said anything about how Sky is coping?"

"Yes, he's called me several times. He's apologetic and has asked me over and over again to forgive him for leaving. But he has not forgiven me for lying to our daughter. I am trying hard to let go of my anger towards him, but it's very difficult. So, I completely understand what Mattie is feeling towards me. To make matters worse for Cam, Sky is not speaking to him or returning his calls either. This is such a mess. Everyone involved is miserable and it's all my fault."

"I know it seems that way now. However," Charles declared somberly, "the one good thing about nasty messes is that once they are dealt with and cleaned up, things usually return to normal in time. Remember, if Jesus could forgive Peter for betraying him three times, then I think eventually Mattie and Sky will forgive you and Camden too."

"I don't think that will happen. There's no way to clean this up," Brenda lamented, her voice choking as tears started streaming down her face. "There's simply no way I can ever make this right for Mattie and Sky, or make you trust me again. Never in a million years." She willed herself to get control of her emotions, but her tears showed no sign of abating. She had brought all of this misery on herself and saw no way out.

"You are a religious person, Brenda. Trust that God has a plan for you, and that he will fix this situation one way or another, but in His own time and not necessarily as you expect."

Charles put the phone down. His once warm and trusting relationship with Brenda was being severely tested, and he was not sure how he felt about her under the circumstances. He sighed heavily, glancing back at Mattie's desk. She had taken all her papers and mail and fled.

"Ready to get back to work?" He asked Candice. "Sorry for the interruption."

CHAPTER 32

Mattie had to get out of the office. It was depressing her with its festive red and green Christmas decorations and the silver, six-foot Menorah. She did not want any reminders of the holidays this year and could not stand Charles trying to be sympathetic. Scooping up her papers and the mail, she ran out of the building, determined to work from home and leave Charles and Candice to do whatever they were doing. Maybe in the new year she could find answers and a way to resolve her issues with her mother, but not yet. She was still feeling utterly sorry for herself and missing Sky every single minute of every day. Thoughts and memories of him were always present.

The nights were the worst for her. She hugged the pillow that had been his and cried until there were no more tears. Then she dreamt about him, and, when she awoke, she was crying again in an endless loop of depression.

After escaping from the office, she returned home and stopped by the condo's front desk to ask if Mr. Cooper had picked up his things.

"Yes, Ms. Cartwright," the attendant answered. "He came by about an hour ago." Mattie was relieved. At least that part of the breakup was over. "And he left you a note."

She hastily grabbed the envelope with a trembling hand and walked into her apartment, placing all the papers and mail on the kitchen table. She began to sort through it. There were dozens of holiday cards from friends, business acquaintances, yacht captains, and other charter companies. She haphazardly tossed them in the trash. She was in no mood for holiday cheer.

Picking up the note from Sky, she caressed it gently, running her fingers over the paper where his fingers had touched. Slowly, he began to read it, recognizing Sky's familiar scrawl.

"Mattie, my love, I consulted an attorney as we discussed, and sadly he validated what you, my parents and I thought about our situation. This is his direct quote. *'Mr. Cooper, you and your half-sister, Mattie Cartwright, are involved in what we legally call "Accidental Incest". That is when sexual activity or marriage occurs between persons who were unaware of a family relationship between them. Our Florida courts have determined that half siblings are prohibited from marrying. To be more specific, a man may not marry any woman to whom he is related by lineal consanguinity, nor his sister, nor his aunt, nor his niece. Florida Statute #741.21.'*

"I'm afraid that pretty much says it all. Agreeing to stop seeing each other romantically was the right and only decision we could have made under the circumstances. I truly hope you find the happiness you deserve with someone else. I will always love you, Sky."

CHAPTER 33

Mattie paced around her apartment. She had been expecting this conclusion from Sky's attorney but seeing it in black and white and in Sky's handwriting made it undeniably real. There was no way to keep even a sliver of hope that she could be with Sky intimately...ever. Their hope for a future together was definitely over...smashed to death by Brenda's secret.

She sat down on her sofa and lost herself in memories of her times with Sky. Finally realizing that it was pointless to dwell in the past, she forced herself to get up and go through the rest of the mail she had brought home from the office. One oversized black envelope caught her attention. It was an unusual size with fancy gold lettering. Who used black envelopes? Curious, she ripped it open. An engraved invitation and several inserts fell out as well as a typed letter. Intrigued, she took the time to pour herself a glass of wine and began to read.

Dear Mattie,

My guests and the itinerary for my upcoming Mediterranean charter in June on Liquidity have been finalized. I will be entertaining several groups of business associates and friends

and thought you might enjoy coming along for one of the
weeks to see the chartering business from a guest's perspec-
tive. I bet you've never done that. I'd like to suggest that you
fly to Nice and join me onboard there for the third week of
June. My guests that week will all be actors, singers, and the
writers of my new show. I know you would enjoy yourself,
and, as a temptation, Kevin Costner will be onboard. He'll
be nursing his marital wounds on my dime. Maybe you
could ease his pain. (Ha, ha) Please consider coming along.
I would very much like to be with you, so let me know. Best
wishes for happy holidays,
Evan Stone.

Mattie stared at the letter and then at the inserts which gave all the particulars about that week's ports and itinerary, the guests who would be onboard, all the pertinent yacht information, weather predictions, attire suggested, and details of flights into and out of Nice. It sounded like a dream- come-true trip by anyone's standards.

Evan's quite efficient, Mattie thought, smiling for the first time in days. She appreciated the invitation but, even if she broke her own rule about socializing with clients, there was no way she felt like flying to Europe and socializing with a bunch of rich celebrities. She barely felt able to string coherent sentences together, much less endure days and days of small talk and feign interest in a trip.

She quickly pulled out the RSVP card that accompanied the invitation and jotted down a polite refusal, citing too much work and some personal problems. She wished Evan a smooth trip and reminded him to call her if he wanted to make plans for another charter in the future.

Depressed and feeling like there was nothing that could ever make her happy again, she tossed the invitation in the trash and left the RSVP card on the table to mail the next day. Paying no attention to the fact that it was still only the afternoon, she crawled into bed and pulled the covers up to her neck.

CHAPTER 34

Mattie forced herself to stop her isolation and returned to work at the end of January. As soon as she walked through the office door, she abruptly announced that she and Sky had broken up over the holidays and that she preferred not to talk about him in the future. Her colleagues expressed their sympathies and returned to their own tasks. The upcoming charter season was more important to them than Mattie's love life.

Linda gave her a quizzical look but asked no questions in the public venue with so many people around. "I need to speak to you later," she whispered to her friend, but Mattie ignored her. Linda could see Mattie was depressed and lethargic. They had not done their usual morning runs or even spoken since before Christmas. Linda had never seen Mattie so withdrawn and sad. Every time Linda called her, with a suggestion about doing something or going someplace, Mattie made an excuse and hung up or didn't bother to answer her phone or e mails at all.

She was still carefully monitoring her calls, always checking the phone I.D. She did not want to miss any communications from clients but had not spoken to her mother since learning the truth about Camden. Brenda continued to reach out to her constantly. Mattie never picked up the phone. She angrily erased all of her mother's voice messages without listening to them and continued to blame her for everything.

Camden had called Mattie several times to check on her. He told her that he and Mary wanted her to be a part of their life if she'd allow it and asked if they could all meet. Mattie thanked him half-heartedly and promised she'd think about it, but it was too soon. She was not ready to open up those festering wounds yet. The Coopers were shattered by their son's suffering and unable to conceal their agony at being partly responsible for it. They had not been in the holiday spirit that year. The atmosphere in their household was bleak and everyone was glad when January came.

Sky continued to see Casey and they took long walks around the UM campus.

"I'm really into Ned," Casey stated proudly on one of those occasions. "We're seeing each other exclusively." That announcement made Sky chuckle in spite of himself. "Exactly how many times have you been out with him, Ducky?" He asked gently, trying to hide a smile. "Exclusive, really? Isn't it a little too soon?"

"Four times," she answered indignantly. "And it would have been much more, but he's never here. He is always off on the yacht somewhere. Mom wants to meet him and says I can invite him here for a weekend sometime soon. If I do, will you come also?"

"I guess so," he said but without any enthusiasm. Thinking about Casey's escapade on *Liquidity* made him miss Mattie. He did not think it was possible to care about a person so deeply. The ache in his heart and the pain of their separation, rather than getting better with time, continued to get worse. His friends offered to fix him up, to introduce him to some new women, but he claimed it was much too soon. He had no interest now and doubted he ever would.

He spent all his time with his patients or Casey. Nothing and no one else interested him. He had become a virtual hermit, unable to eat or sleep properly. He wandered through his days and nights in a fog of grief and depression. The only escape was his work. He was first and foremost a physician and he cared deeply about all of his patients. He was able to compartmentalize his feelings, so they never jeopardized the care he gave. Sky was an outstanding doctor, diligent about the medical advice he dispensed.

Charles, tired of seeing Mattie moping around, had insisted on taking her out to dinner to cheer her up. He proclaimed that enough was enough, and that she had to pull herself together and get on with her life. He missed their good times together. She reluctantly agreed to go with him on the condition that Brenda's or Sky's names would not be mentioned.

At dinner, Mattie told him about Evan's nice invitation. Charles had been surprised and not realized Evan was interested in a personal relationship with her. Mattie's rejection of the cruise signaled that she was not ready to move onto another man. It was still too soon after the debacle with Sky. It was too bad, he thought. A relaxing week in the Med with a bunch of movie stars would be good for her. The week away might take her mind off her troubles. It certainly would not make matters any worse.

In the first few months of the new year, Mattie became more of a workaholic than ever before. She left her desk only to attend yoga classes and to work at the Palm Beach boat show where she connected with her clients, in person or by phone. She saw no friends except for an occasional drink with Linda, and she continued to avoid her mother.

In the long hours she put in at Lux, Mattie had come up with an interesting business idea and was busy developing it…a new computer software program. It would automatically match potential clients with certain ships, based on a detailed questionnaire and a few trick questions designed to weed out the financially insolvent. With one click of a button, a client could respond to all the questions on Mattie's new app, and Mattie could implement the client's requests immediately. She was excited about its potential and about presenting it to Charles. If she could sell the app to others in the chartering business and it became an industry standard, the program might save so much time, and so many unnecessary and unproductive meetings. It could also make her some money from the subscription fees. It was like a dating service, matching boats, and people. She decided to call it *Nautical Options*.

In early April she made an appointment to meet with Charles after hours when the office was empty, and she brought her computer and a few notes into his office. "This is what I've been working on so secretively these last few months," she explained proudly. "And I think, it, or some more sophisticated iteration of it, can revolutionize the way we do business in the future. You may be able to physically close down the office here and have your salespeople work from their homes. Think of the rent and utilities you'd be saving."

"That sounds interesting. Let me see what you're talking about." Charles pulled his chair to where he could see her screen, and she began to explain the concept. When her presentation was over, his eyes lit up. "I think you're on to something. It needs a little fine-tuning, but let's take this a step further and see what happens. I'll be glad to fund the initial costs for you, Mattie. However, we'll need to get patent protection and copyright the idea."

Nautical Options was just the thing to make her forget about Sky Cooper, and if people bought and used the app, it would definitely change the chartering business.

CHAPTER 35

Mattie and Charles worked together most evenings on *Nautical Options*. They had hired an excellent attorney and applied for a patent and a trademark and were beginning to speak to potential investors. Charles had suggested that possibly Dr. Tony or Evan Stone would be interested in putting up some initial money since both were entrepreneurial. Mattie did not want to impose on her new friendships with them by asking for money and squashed the idea. "Maybe I'll present the app to them later if we need a second round of capital," she told Charles. "But not now."

It was an exciting time, and surprisingly Mattie found herself dwelling less and less on Sky. She was excited about the future, and only when she was doing her yoga poses did her mind drift to thoughts about her former love. When that happened, she'd plunge into the downward dog pose and concentrate on the good things in her life. She took the fact that she could do that as a sign that she was healing emotionally. Designing *Nautical Options* and bringing it to market was her salvation. And another outlet for her sales abilities.

The phones were quiet after office hours, so Mattie and Charles could work uninterrupted on the new app. One night while they were working, the office phone rang and interrupted them. Instead of letting the answering service pick it up, she instinctively reached for it. "Mattie Cartwright, Lux Charters. How may I help you?" It was her automatic reply.

"Mattie, it's Tony Grant."

"Dr. Tony," she said, happy to hear from him. "Your captain on *My Lady Denise* said the cruise was a big success. He and his crew were very grateful for your generous gratuity."

"The whole experience was fabulous. The food was spectacular, and everyone had a wonderful time…so much so that I want to book another charter for this summer in Croatia, maybe in early July before it gets too hot. No children this time, however. Laura and I want to invite two couples to come with us. Is it too late to set it up?"

"No. I think I can find something appropriate. Do you want the same size yacht?"

"It can be a little smaller, but I want it to be an elegant experience for us and our guests."

"I think I have just the boat for you. *Atlantic Seas* is a 140-foot Frazier yacht with a master cabin and three guest suites. Look her up on the internet, and if you approve, I'll proceed. Captain Topovsky is fabulous, and I can request the same chef you had on *My Lady Denise*, if he's available."

"That sounds perfect. I don't need to look up the boat. I trust you. Can you get back to me quickly so I can schedule the time off from my show and invite our friends?"

"I'll try to have an answer and a price quote by tomorrow," she answered. "And I can't thank you enough for referring Evan Stone to me. He's delightful and we got along so well that he's invited me to join him for a week on his *Liquidity* charter in June. I am not able to go, but it was a lovely invitation."

Tony chuckled. "Evan told me that he was quite taken with you. When he is excited about something, or somebody, he can be very persistent. And believe me, he is definitely interested in spending more time with you." Mattie blushed, but thankfully Tony could not see her face turning red.

"I had no idea. We only saw each other for a day. Maybe we can get together some time in the future." She needed to change the subject. "Thanks again and I'll get back to you tomorrow."

CHAPTER 36

The next morning, Mattie reached out to chef Jeff Gunner and asked if he would be willing to work the charter for Dr. Tony and his wife in late June on *Atlantic Seas*. Chef Gunner responded that he had thoroughly enjoyed the Grants on their first charter, and he would be happy to cook for them again. Mattie secured the boat, checked with the captain to approve the chef, and locked in slips where needed. She prepared a tentative itinerary, doing the work first by hand using the old method, and then put the information into her app. She was amazed and pleased by how much easier and faster everything became using *Nautical Options*. She prepared a quote and the charter agreement. When she had everything in order, she e-mailed the information to Dr. Tony. Within two hours, she had the signed agreement back, and he had wired the deposit to Lux Charter's account. She was thrilled that he was pleased and that her app had worked so efficiently. She made a note to herself about ways to improve it even further, and to mention the changes to Charles at their next meeting.

Dr. Tony called Mattie to thank her for arranging everything so quickly and they promised to stay in touch. "Evan wanted me to try to persuade you to change your mind and join him on his cruise in June. Any chance of that?"

"I'm afraid not. I've been going through some pretty serious personal issues and now is not the time for me to take off on a pleasure cruise. Please thank Evan again - but the answer is still 'no'."

CHAPTER 37

Brenda was beyond frustrated by Mattie's indifference and her refusal to take her calls. The once inseparable mother and daughter were no closer to resolving their issues than when the incest issue came to light in December.

The holidays had long passed, and spring was here…a time that should be for renewal and new beginnings. Brenda talked to Charles endlessly about the Sky situation and she was exasperated and fed up with her unforgiving daughter. In retrospect, she understood that what she had done was awful. She admitted that openly, but it was not as if she had committed a murder. Even hardened criminals got occasional breaks from the legal system and were forgiven and granted parole. But not Brenda. Mattie was relentless in showing her distain. She remained heartless, keeping her mother at bay, and imprisoned in guilt and anguish. Even Charles, who still had not completely forgiven Brenda either, realized that the estrangement between mother and daughter should not continue.

Mattie was not only hurting her mother, but Charles, Camden and Mary, Casey and even Sky. By refusing any attempt by any of them to talk about and resolve the issues, she continued inflicting pain on them all. Charles, as close as he was to Mattie, felt awkward at the office with so many forbidden topics of discussion lying between them. Their light and happy banter had all but disappeared and been replaced by tension. Charles felt like he had lost a daughter too. The situation also strained his own relationship with Brenda, which he was trying to repair.

He had been having dinners with Candice from time to time for companionship. She was attractive, funny, and pleasant, but she was not Brenda. Charles had no romantic feelings for Candice and yearned to restore his friendship with Brenda.

Camden was feeling immense guilt and wanted badly to make amends with Brenda and especially with Mattie…but he was not given the opportunity. Mary wanted to ease her husband's guilt and open up her heart and her home to Camden's first-born child, to make her feel loved and a part of the Cooper family, but Mattie was unresponsive. Casey yearned for the friend and the sister she knew Mattie to be, and she desperately wanted to see her brother happy and carefree again. Everyone was miserable waiting for Mattie to do or say something…to open the door to some honest dialogue. It did not seem to be happening. At least not without a firm push from someone.

Brenda decided that the time of waiting for Mattie to make the first move had long since passed and she was more determined than ever to face her daughter and hash out all the misunderstandings. She knew Mattie would never come to her on her own. Her daughter was too hurt and stubborn. The only solution was for her to ambush Mattie at the Lux office when no one else was around.

"You have to do this for me," Brenda begged Charles. "I can't live like this a day longer…none of us should have to. Please, think up a reason to get Mattie to stay late, and let me be waiting in your office to confront her. There's no other way. If she was going to come around on her own, she would have done so by now."

"I don't know. I'm afraid if I trick Mattie into seeing you, she may cut me off completely too. We're involved in a new, exciting project together and as long as I don't mention you or Sky, it's almost like old times. I do not want to jeopardize that. She's not rational when it comes to you, and she blames you for everything that's wrong in her life. Mattie's as effi-cient as ever at work, lining up one lucrative charter after another. She's making so much money. She'll probably never be able to spend it, and because of the volume of her sales, I had to hire an assistant to help her. But when it comes to anything personal, she completely shuts down. I wonder if she might need some kind of professional help."

"I've thought of that, and frankly, Camden and Mary suggested it also, Brenda said. "They told me Sky has been seeing a psychiatrist regularly and it seems to be helping. According to them, he is happier and becom-ing reconciled to his new situation now. He is dating again, although no one seriously. He's even talking about planning a trip to Europe next spring or summer with some friends. That's a really positive sign. I can only wish the same for our Mattie."

"For everyone's sake, I'll make you a promise. I'll bring up the idea of therapy to her and if she refuses, I will make it a condition of her remaining at Lux. Of course, I would be bluffing. I can't afford to lose her to my competition, but that threat should be enough to scare her to go to a therapist."

"That would help a lot, Brenda said gratefully. "And if, after we talk, Mattie still wants no part of me, I will surely need therapy myself, but I will accept her choices. I cannot spend the rest of my life defending the indefensible or punishing myself further. I need her love and forgiveness, or I need to permanently separate myself from her and the pain she's causing. I can't take much more of this."

Charles took Brenda's hand gently in his. "You know I had hoped that the three of us would be a happy family one day. That's never going to happen now until and unless we tear down her walls of anger. I *will* help you Brenda, and I pray to God that Mattie listens, *really listens* to you. When would you like me to set this up?"

"No time like the present," Brenda answered softly. "Why wait?"

Charles picked up his phone and crossed his fingers. "Mattie dear, I have an idea about how we might get *Nautical Options* up and running in time to introduce it at this year's Ft. Lauderdale boat show. Can you come back to the office tonight, after your dinner, of course, to discuss it? Say around eight o'clock?"

Mattie agreed immediately. She had worked hard on *Nautical Options* and was anxious to test it out among her business colleagues. The boat show was the perfect time. "I'll be there, Charles. Thanks."

CHAPTER 38

Mattie walked into the Lux Charters office at five minutes to eight, eagerly anticipating her meeting with Charles. Promoting *Nautical Options* was the only thought on her mind. She had worked hard on its concept and was anxious to launch it. The main floor of the office, with its rows and rows of brokers' desks was silent and empty. Everyone had gone home. Only Charles' office was brightly lit. Mattie walked in, expecting to see him sitting behind his desk.

"I'm afraid it's just the two of us," Brenda stated firmly, stepping out from behind the door to face her daughter. Mattie paled and started to back up towards the door.

"This conversation between us is long overdue and tricking you into coming here was the only way I knew to accomplish that," Brenda said in a grim voice. "You have left me no choice."

"Well, I'm not staying around to have *any* conversation with you," Mattie declared angrily. She did not like being ambushed. Who the hell did her mother think she was?

"I think you'd better listen to every word your mother has to say," Charles said sternly, appearing in the doorway and blocking Mattie's exit.

He had hoped to listen to the conversation undetected, but it seemed that he was needed to referee the encounter between mother and daughter.

"I agreed to this deception to get you in here, but only because you refused to speak to your mother. And Mattie, if you try to leave, you'll have to physically run me over to do it. It's time you started acting like an adult and threw off that self-righteous attitude you've been nursing all these months. Your mother has some things she wants to say, and you are going to damn well listen. I know I am not your father, and can't order you around, but as your boss, I insist you hear her out. I'll be right on the other side of this door, and I won't let you leave until she's done. Are we clear?" Charles said fervently, standing his ground.

Mattie was stunned by the severe tone of his voice. He had never spoken to her that sharply before. She was clearly trapped in the room. There was no other way out of Charles' office, so she sat down in his desk chair with a thud and glared indignantly at Brenda.

"I guess I have no choice," she fumed. "Go on and get this conversation over with." She planned to sit as still as a statue and let her mother's chatter wash over her. She was still so furious at Brenda for her despicable lies and secrets and the heartbreaking consequences that resulted. She had no sympathy for her mother at all and now she was also angry at Charles.

Brenda was nervous. This was the moment she had prayed for, and yet, dreaded. Her hands were shaking, and she suddenly felt cold and clammy. Now was her one chance to reach Mattie, and she had to make every word count.

"Mattie, I have loved you from the moment you were conceived, and nothing has ever changed that. Everything I said and did, I did for you.

However, I cannot go on being punished by you for trying to be a good mother. I honestly thought I was making the right decision when your father abandoned us. Now upon reflection, I realize that what I did by pretending he was dead was cruel. My excuse is that by claiming to be a widow of a war hero, it made the situation easier on me. I did not have to face the scrutiny and questions from people asking why my husband deserted us. Had I done something unforgivable to drive him away? Was I such a bad person that he had to leave me?" Brenda's pain and frustration showed on her normally composed face.

"I understand now that Camden was insecure and immature and terrified of raising a child when he was still one himself. The responsibility was too much for him and he bolted, turning his back on both of us. But now – you are doing the same thing to me. Can you imagine how it feels to have your only child refuse to talk to you for months?

"I have had many serious talks with Camden since our worlds exploded, and I have found the strength to forgive him for leaving us all those years ago. And truthfully, I actually like the man he has become. He is a different person today, because of his marriage to Mary and his long affiliation with AA. I implore you to find it in your heart to forgive him too. He could be a wonderful addition to your life, as well as Mary and Casey…the big family you always wanted. And, of course, Sky if and when you are both ready."

Mattie stirred restlessly in the chair, but what her mother was saying made some sense. She was uncomfortable when faced with this new truth.

"I cannot allow the hurts and mistakes of my past to ruin my future any longer." Brenda spoke from her heart. "That's exactly what's happening. You are wallowing in self-pity instead of trying to see anything positive in this situation. If you're not careful you'll turn into a bitter, selfish woman. I don't say that to hurt you, darling, but simply because—regrettably, it's true."

Mattie started to protest but Brenda held her ground, not giving Mattie time to say anything in reply. She moved closer to her daughter and prayed that her words were making an impact.

"It hurts me to see you like this, but it's time you took some responsibility for your actions. No one, and especially not me, set out to hurt you or to tear your world apart," Brenda persisted. "However, bad things happen to good people. That is life and no, it's not fair. Nice, kind people get sick and die, or they are unjustly fired or served with surprise divorce papers. Many are maimed in horrible traffic accidents or paralyzed by neurological diseases. None of those things happened to you. Thank the good Lord."

Brenda had Mattie's attention, so she continued matter-of-factly. "You lost a great love. It's terribly sad. I understand that, but *it's not* the end of your life or Sky's. People recover from much worse. I probably can never convince you that what I did so many years ago by telling you that your father died was the right thing to do. But my lies freed you up to be a normal, happy child. You were not always looking around the corner hoping he'd be there. Thankfully, you faced no abandonment issues and had a pretty happy childhood…the best I could provide."

Mattie looked carefully into her mother's eyes and could tell Brenda was being sincere. She felt a pang of guilt but was not yet ready to let her mother off the hook.

"Now, unexpectantly your father is back, and he wants to be a part of your life! You now have him, a caring stepmother intent on welcoming you into her family, an adorable sister, and a brother. All they want is a chance to get to know and love you. And whether you want it or not, you'll always have me and my love too."

Mattie could feel her eyes tearing up as she began to realize how much her behavior had hurt her mother. She started to say something, but Brenda continued. "By most standards, you are a lucky woman. It's only your unwillingness to look at the whole picture and forgive us that's making you so miserable and unhappy. Your anger at me and your father has colored how you interface with everyone else. For instance, you have been very rude to poor Charles who had nothing to do with any of this.

"I forced this meeting on you," Brenda said simply, "because I believe you need professional help, some kind of therapy to help you cope. What happened was horrific, but it's not insurmountable. Your love for Sky and his love for you, was sweet, innocent, and pure. You did nothing wrong or dirty by falling in love. Unfortunately, because of family genetics, any marriage between you would be prohibited. Children of yours with him might have serious genetic problems, the consequences of which are incalculable. You were fortunate that you learned of your situation before any babies came along. Can you try to look at it that way, please?"

Mattie abruptly stood up. She was indignant. "You can't seriously mean that I should be grateful to you that I did not have deformed or mentally challenged children? Are you saying you did me a big favor by finally telling the truth?" Mattie was furious again and hurling unfounded accusations at her mother.

"No, of course not," Brenda snapped back. "Having to break up with Sky was and is heart-wrenching, but you don't have to cut him or me out of your life forever. We can make peace with the past. It can happen.

Please Mattie, I brought you up as a good Christian. Can you try to put some of the principles you learned from church and the Bible into practice; and seek God's help in finding forgiveness?"

Brenda was worn out from her emotional outburst. She had nothing more to say. Standing silently by Mattie she waited for her to respond. But Charles could not keep quiet any longer. He marched back into the room and took Brenda's hand.

"Mattie, your mother has been your best friend from the moment you were born. I understand that you were hurt and shocked by the lies she told you, but they were for your own good, I might add. There is no excuse for the way you've behaved and treated her. It's time to grow up. I, no *we*, want our old Mattie back, *not* the angry, self-righteous woman standing in this room with us." Charles paused for a moment to gauge Mattie's reaction. "If you are willing, I'll arrange for you to see a therapist. I'm certain that talking this all out with a neutral trained professional will help put things in perspective for you. Do you think you can do that? … for me and for your mother…and mostly for yourself?"

Mattie looked down at her hands as tears leaked from the corners of her eyes. She felt suddenly ashamed. Sky's parentage was not his fault any more than it was hers. Why had she taken her anger out on Sky when he was hurting just as much? Her mom was right. She was being selfish and stubborn. She wanted to make things right, to stop the awful anger and pain that she carried around with her. She knew now that she was wrong…her mother did deserve to be forgiven.

"All right." She sighed deeply. "You win. I'll get some therapy." She looked up at Brenda and Charles with a tired smile. "And I'll try to forgive. That's all I can promise for now. I know your words are genuine and I want to be the 'old me' again."

"That's a good start," Charles replied in a choked voice and bent over to hug Mattie.

"That's all I can hope for." Brenda hardly dared to breathe. She backed away as if to leave, then turned back around. "Mattie, may I hug you, darling?"

Mattie looked into her mother's tortured eyes. She could not hold onto her anger any longer. She walked over to Brenda and hugged her. "Mom, I've really missed you. I'm sorry for the way I've behaved."

Charles, with tears in his eyes, left the room to allow mother and daughter their privacy and time to reconnect.

CHAPTER 39

The next eight months were emotionally painful and yet exhilarating for Mattie. She worked as hard as ever at Lux Charters and signed up a record number of charters. She also followed through on her promise to start therapy. She began counselling with Dr. Reese Bristow, a well-known post-trauma stress specialist in Miami. After an initial bumpy start, they got along nicely and communicated well. Mattie came to trust him and to rely on his advice.

At her first appointment, Dr. Bristow introduced himself and began by saying, "The simplest way I can explain what's happened is that in dealing with the fallout from your intimate relationship with your half-brother, you experienced severe stress induced by emotional trauma. In much the same way, war veterans suffer from PTS after witnessing wartime atrocities, your brain has been traumatized by the incest revelation. You innocently fell in love and then stepped on a virtual land mind, blowing your emotions to smithereens. Now like an injured vet who must endure the surgeries and rehabilitation in order to heal, you must do the same thing with your emotions. You will not recover in a day. There is no easy fix, but I will be your partner in this journey, and I'll help you explore your options and work through them. In the process you may discover some very interesting things you never knew about yourself, and hopefully realize that you are a worthwhile and decent person, and open to finding a new love when the time is right."

"That all sounds rather simplistic," Mattie said curtly. The doctor was a little too cavalier for her liking. "Can you be more specific about how you think you can help me?"

"Yes. Certainly. Please understand that I am not dismissing the severity of the trauma you've been through. I'm only trying to point out that recovery is possible with my support and guidance coupled with a lot of hard work on your part. You will be able to unlock the healing process and move towards a happier and more emotionally stable future." He looked at his new patient with empathy. It was hard to imagine that such a beautiful, composed young woman could be living with such pain. "Are you willing to give it and me a try, Mattie?"

Remembering her promise to her mother and Charles, she nodded in the affirmative and then began months of therapy. In the beginning, Dr. Bristow let Mattie pour her heart out, over and over, with the requisite tears and tissues. Finally, after a few very emotional sessions, she was able to speak calmly about her feelings without sobbing, and she began to make real strides towards understanding what was going on in her brain and in her heart.

"This is not going to be quick or easy," the doctor warned. "We have to go through the recovery process in an orderly manner, like living through the various stages of grief. They are well defined, and each phase must be completed before proceeding to the next. You will have to take baby steps at first. Don't feel you have to heal 100% to see improvement in the quality of your life. It will come in time. You will feel better day by day as you begin the process and accept what has happened."

"Do you think Sky and I can ever be friends, just friends?" The question was always on her mind.

"Yes, I do if he's gone to therapy also. Neither of you are to blame for what's happened, but you both have to accept it and have the courage and strength to redirect the romantic love you felt for each other, to a more platonic one."

At first Mattie was skeptical and hesitant because she did not always understand where Dr. Bristow was leading the conversations. However, after each session she began to feel a little more hopeful that she would soon be like her old self again, only wiser. Dr. Bristow taught her to be patient and persistent, insisting that Mattie set realistic goals for her recovery and not demand perfection from herself.

The three steps in the trauma recovery process that the doctor advocated were, *first step:* establishing a safety zone, a place where Mattie could feel completely safe with a protective hedge around her emotions. That step was achieved fairly quickly as Mattie trusted the doctor implicitly and was not shy about sharing her feelings. As a matter of fact, it felt good to shout and scream and get them out in the open. She did not have to pretend to be brave.

The *second step* was retelling the story of the traumatic event so many times that there was literally nothing more to say about the subject. This second step was more difficult. It took many sessions. With each telling, Mattie had to face the hard reality of her true feelings about her mother's deception, her father's desertion, and the catastrophic loss of Sky. With each review of the story, another fact or perception emerged, giving her pause to think with more clarity about the situation. Finally, Mattie arrived at the point of understanding and forgiveness…forgiving her mother, her father and even Sky, although none of it had been his fault. She, as a woman, had unreasonably hoped that Sky, as a man, could make everything better and was devastated when she realized that he too was only human, and he could not alter the facts to suit their romance and give them a happy ending.

The *third step* in Mattie's emotional recovery was for her to reintegrate herself back into the world of sociability and allow herself to feel laughter, hope and love again. She did this in baby steps as Dr. Bristow had suggested. She began by resuming her daily runs and happy hours with Linda. Then she began dating again. She hosted a bridal shower for Linda at the end of the summer and proudly acted as her maid of honor at Linda's September wedding to Ted. Mattie took an active interest in her friends again, spent time with her mother and Charles. She called Casey and began going out with her too. They soon resumed their sisterly bond. Mattie still was not ready to deal face to face with her father and Mary, but she would in time. She no longer harbored any ill will towards her father but getting to know him just wasn't a huge priority for her. There were too many other things she wanted to do first. The only thing missing from her life was the intimacy of having a special man in her life, but she was willing to wait for the right one to come along.

Mattie continued to work at Lux and handled all her clients easily and efficiently, and now that Charles had hired Ellie as her personal assistant, she had more free time. She flew to New York on two separate occasions with some friends and took in a few shows on Broadway. On the most recent trip there, Dr. Tony invited her to watch a taping of his television show and then he and his wife Laura took her out to dinner. They had a lovely evening and spoke about arranging for a third charter the following year. Dr. Tony mentioned that his friend, Evan Stone had enjoyed his cruise on *Liquidity* so much the previous summer that he was contemplating repeating it again.

Mattie smiled. "Please tell him to call me if I can be of assistance." It had been many months since she had thought about the handsome producer. It might be fun to see him again.

"I'll be sure to tell him," Dr. Tony replied with a sly smile. "I think all he needs is a little encouragement. He was quite taken with you, as I recall." He winked at his wife and unaccountably, Mattie blushed.

ROMANCE, AGAIN

CHAPTER 40

It was the end of September and Mattie was in the office bright and early. She had recently returned from a successful week in Monaco where she had been working the boat show there. Representing Lux Charters, she negotiated a half dozen international charters for the following summer in Spain and Portugal. Mattie reacquainted herself with several European yacht owners she had known from previous shows and attended several cocktail parties onboard their ships. It had been a quick trip, a strictly business one, but highly successful. She had been anxious to return home to prepare for the upcoming Ft. Lauderdale boat show which would begin in a month. It had been two years since she first met Sky at that show and so much had happened. She was anxious to begin there with a clean slate, as Dr. Bristow had urged.

The bell on the front door jingled, catching Mattie's attention. She glanced up expecting to see Charles or one of her co-workers. Instead, Evan Stone came strutting through the door wearing a huge grin and approached her desk.

"Good morning, Mattie".

"Well, hello stranger," she smiled warmly. "What in the world are you doing here?"

"I just happened to be in the neighborhood," he joked. "And I thought I'd take a chance that you were here and drop by."

Her smile widened. "I'm glad you did." She was slightly flustered and hoped her excitement did not show. She had hoped he might call her sometime to arrange another charter, but she never expected him to casually walk through the front door. She was glad that she had worn her gray slacks and matching silk blouse with red trim. It was one of her nicest outfits and she knew she looked sexy in it. She had debated dressing more casually, in white jeans and a tee, as she expected no clients that day and had planned to spend the time going through her paperwork and beginning to make her schedule for the VIP Day of the boat show.

"As long as I'm here, can I take you out for breakfast? I have two hours before I have to leave for a *Miami Intrigues* taping in Key Biscayne."

"I'd love that," she said enthusiastically. "Just let me grab my bag and lock up."

He put his arm around her affectionately. "It's so good to see you again. Where shall we go?"

"How about the Pelican Beach Hotel? It's one of my favorite bars at night, but in the day, they serve breakfast and lunch on their wide porch overlooking the sand and the ocean. It's very nice."

"Whatever you want," his arm tightened around her waist in a hug. He pointed to a black sedan parked out front. "Just direct the driver."

Ten minutes later they were drinking freshly squeezed orange juice and ordering French Toast with syrup and fresh strawberries.

"How have you been?" he asked casually. "You look as beautiful as ever."

"Just fine," she responded nonchalantly, pleased by his compliment. This was not the time or place to tell him about Sky and her subsequent months of therapy. "Business has been very good and thankfully we've escaped two hurricane seasons with no major storms hitting here."

"Yes, I know. I keep an eye on the weather during hurricane season."

"Seriously, why are you here, Evan?" Mattie was curious. There was no way he happened to be in the neighborhood.

"I told you. I'm in Miami for a week finishing up some shots for the season's finale of *Miami Intrigues*. I couldn't be this close to the gorgeous Mattie Cartwright and not come visit."

Mattie bit back a smile. "Where are you staying?"

"The Mandarin Oriental on Brickell Key in Miami."

She knew the luxury hotel well. It was at least an hour's drive from there to her office, maybe longer in rush hour traffic. She looked at her watch. It wasn't quite eight o'clock yet. "You must have left at the crack of dawn."

"I did but losing a little sleep to see you is well worth it."

She did not know what to say, so she signaled the waitress and avoided answering him by asking for a cup of coffee. She was not much of a flirt and couldn't tell if he was being sincere or simply playing with her.

They spent the next hour flirting and engaging in small talk. Evan told her about how successful the Miami television show was and that he was considering a few ideas for other shows. She asked about his cruise on *Liquidity,* and he raved about the experience. "As a matter of fact," he admitted. "I had such a nice time that I'd like to duplicate the entire trip again next summer, same ports, same activities but with different guests this time. I spoke to Captain Llanos recently and he thinks the ship is still available in June and July. Can you check, and if it is, book it for me please."

Mattie knew all her yacht schedules by heart. She assured him that *Liquidity* was available. It was booked for the last week of May in Greece with a European soccer player and his French girlfriend. However, the boat could easily change course afterwards to pick up Evan and his guests in Nice.

"That's wonderful news. Should we go back to your office now and make it official? or," he suddenly had a much better idea. "Can I send a car for you later today and bring you and the paperwork to Miami to have dinner with me?"

Mattie willed herself to sound casual. "I have a strict policy not to socialize with my clients. It can make for awkward situations. However, since I've already had breakfast with you, I don't suppose a dinner will hurt anything. Thank you, Evan. I would love to join you and I'll bring all the papers with me. But I must warn you, the price has gone up $10,000 a week since last year. Are you all right with that?"

He pretended to be shocked. "I guess I'll have to be. I think I can afford it."

They drove back to her office, chatting the whole way. "I'll have the car service at your place at 6:00. What's your home address?" He jotted it down and left with a wave. "See you tonight."

Mattie walked back into her office with a smile on her face. "Charles," she looked sheepish. "I'm taking the rest of the day off. I'll be back tomorrow." She picked up the paperwork for a new charter and left. Once in her car, she called her hairdresser and asked for an appointment for color and a blow dry. She wanted to look her best for Evan. She had not felt this happy and eager to see someone in a long, long time.

CHAPTER 41

Mattie had dinner twice more with Evan that week, once in Miami and once in Ft. Lauderdale. Then he had to return to California for business. They had both enjoyed their time together, but Mattie was cautious and wanted to proceed slowly. She was gun-shy after Sky and never wanted to experience the hurt she had felt from her breakup with him ever again. The best way to avoid that was to remain as aloof as possible to protect her heart.

The holidays came and went that year very uneventfully. Mattie went out on several dates but wasn't excited about any of them. She spent Christmas with Charles and Brenda. Casey came over to Mattie's condo to exchange gifts and told her that the Cooper family was celebrating in Tampa as usual. Sky was coming home for a few days and bringing his latest girlfriend, whom Casey was anxious to meet.

Mattie spent a quiet New Year's Eve at home and at midnight her time, just as the crystal ball began its descent in Times Square, Evan called. He had been at a party in L.A. and said he'd been thinking about her all evening. He missed her and had an idea. She listened as he explained that he would like her to join him and a few friends on his charter cruise in June. He wanted her to stay for a week or two, or for however long she felt she could be away. And he emphasized that he wanted to see her as often as he could before then. "Will you consider it, Mattie? It's time you officially broke your rule about dating clients. Will you meet me in Nice and sail with me on *Liquidity?*"

Her heart said yes but her brain said no. She wavered back and forth for two days and finally broke down. She called him back. "Evan, I've been wrestling with what to do about the cruise. There are things that have happened to me in my private life that I have not shared with you, and they have made me very leery about becoming involved in a new romance. I really enjoy being with you, as I'm sure you know, and obviously we have a mutual attraction. So," she paused to take a breath. "I've decided that I'll happily come on the cruise with you as long as you keep your expectations in check. We will have to take it slowly - a day at a time and see how it goes. And Evan, to be clear up front, I will need my own room."

Her heart sank when he took so long to respond, and she was overwhelmed with a terrible sense of foreboding. Had she scared him away? Been too demanding and ungrateful for the lovely invitation? Had she broken up a relationship before it had a chance to begin?

"You drive a hard bargain, Ms. Cartwright," he finally replied smoothly. "I will comply with all your requests as long as you grant me one of my own."

"Which is?"

"Wear that beautiful dress you wore when we went out to dinner in Miami…the long red one with the white thigh trim. I want all my friends to see you in that."

She exhaled. She had not realized she'd been holding her breath. "Okay," she answered. "You have a deal."

They talked some more and went over a lot of specific details about the cruise and the kinds of activities she'd like to do. He mentioned that he would like to invite Dr. Tony Grant and his wife Laura. Mattie was thrilled. She liked them both very much and was really looking forward to her first real vacation in years.

For the first time in her life, she indulged herself in what she had previously thought frivolous - the world of fashion. She spent a fortune on a new wardrobe. Her mission was to impress Evan and make him proud when he introduced her to his friends.

Mattie and Linda drove to Miami, Boca Raton and Palm Beach searching for treasures from the fancy boutiques there and searched department stores in nearby malls. Mattie was intent on developing a new, personal style for herself...using soft flowing fabrics in sensuous colors, showing off her figure in an understated but elegant way. She bought Louboutin stilettos in every color and exquisite, expensive costume jewelry to accompany her new outfits. By the time she and Linda were through shopping, she had spent tens of thousands of dollars and the results were breathtaking. She had purchased so many new hats, swimsuits, cover ups, shorts, linen slacks, cropped capris, and dresses that she decided to send them ahead to the ship in several large suitcases. That way she would not have to bother with dragging them through the airport in France. Her years of saving and watching her bank balance grow had stopped. Now whatever she saw that she wanted, within reason, she bought.

When Brenda raised an eyebrow and questioned how much she had spent on her new clothes, Mattie only laughed. "What good is my making all this money, if I can't enjoy some of it?"

"You have a point, but what have you done with my frugal daughter?"

"I'm still the same person, Mom," Mattie chuckled, "simply better dressed. One of the benefits of therapy is that it showed me that there is more than one way to look at things. Now I see new clothes as a way of giving myself pleasure…a form of gratification and a way of rewarding myself for my hard work. Some people congratulate themselves with food or by taking exotic vacations. I guess my gift to myself is clothes… and lots of them."

The night before she was to leave for Nice, France, Mattie had dinner with her mother, Charles, and Casey. They enjoyed French onion soup with delicious, melted Gruyere cheese, rare steaks with truffle fries, and Caesar salads at the *Capital Grille*. It was odd how they always ordered the same food when they went out. Their painful past tensions had long been forgotten. They truly were relaxed around each other and enjoyed the evening together.

"I'm so jealous," Casey announced holding a crispy fry in her fingers. "I can't believe you're going to be on *Liquidity* with *my* boyfriend, and I'm stuck here in Florida."

"I won't exactly be with Ned," Mattie chuckled. "But I will make sure he behaves and calls you whenever he can."

"Is that supposed to make me feel better?" Casey pouted and revealed a secret. "I'm seriously thinking of quitting college next semester and getting a job as a stewardess on whatever boat Ned is working on…We've talked about it. He wants me to finish college, but I think I'm winning him over, slowly."

"Well, I agree with Ned. You should finish college." Mattie said with alarm. "Your parents would be terribly upset. You cannot just take a year off to sail around the world with your boyfriend. That is very immature, Casey. Really, I'm disappointed in you."

"For what it's worth, I agree," Charles added, but kindly. "It's a romantic idea, Casey, I suppose, but you have to be realistic. One can't just decide to be a stew and then have your pick of any boat you want to work on. You would have to serve an apprenticeship and work your way up…and of course, the boat's captain would have to approve you as a member of his or her crew. Many of them frown on their crew or their staffs being involved in personal relationships with each other because if things don't work out, there can be a lot of tension and problems."

"Well, Ned and I won't be having any problems," Casey asserted defiantly. "We're in love."

"Oh my," Brenda sighed, not knowing what she should say. This had to be between Cam, Mary and Casey, and she knew enough to keep her opinions to herself. *Oh, to have the confidence and naivete of the young,* she thought.

Mattie did not want to dash Casey's dreams. She knew what that felt like. However, she was certain how Cam and Mary would feel about their daughter giving up college to follow a boy around the high seas. It was odd to care so much about this young girl, who she hardly knew, but now was very much her little sister. Life had certainly provided some surprises in the last year.

They finished their dinner, and everyone wished Mattie a safe and fun voyage. Charles hugged her warmly, then drove Brenda home. Casey came back to Mattie's apartment to spend the night. Mattie planned to drop her off at UM on the way to the Miami airport in the morning. Casey had agreed to stay on the UM campus to take two courses in summer school. She had no interest in spending the summer in Tampa with her parents, and Ned was away in the Med. She might as well do something useful and get through as many courses as she could. Then if she did quit school, she could resume again later with less credits needed to earn her degree.

CHAPTER 42

Mattie arrived in Nice, France and was met by a uniformed limo driver Evan had sent to bring her to the yacht. Even after the overnight flight, she looked refreshed and pretty. Dressed in a simple yellow silk shirtwaist dress, with a white straw hat and white heels, she looked like a celebrity. As she strolled through the airport, heads turned and people whispered, trying to figure out who she was. Mattie noticed the attention, so she put on her Tom Ford sunglasses and smiled. If people thought she was a movie star, then she would act the part. The financial investment in new clothes was already paying off. She hoped Evan would be impressed.

It was a short drive from the airport to the marina where *Liquidity* was docked. As soon as the limo pulled into the parking lot, Mattie saw the magnificent yacht in the background. Captain Llanos and Evan were standing by the entrance gate to the pier, waiting for her. She was so excited that she opened the car door and ran out to meet them, without waiting for the driver to help her.

"My God, you look gorgeous," Evan said appreciatively and gave her a big hug. "As fresh as a daisy."

"I did manage a few hours of sleep after watching a funny movie," she smiled innocently. "First class was wonderfully comfortable and had only a few passengers, so the flight attendants paid a lot of attention to me. It was delightful. Thank you for arranging it."

"It's good to see you, Mattie." Captain Llanos walked up to her and took her carry-on bag. "Welcome onboard...and as a guest this time."

Evan grabbed her hand and led her through the gate and down the docks to the yacht's gangplank. "Everyone is anxious to meet you, and as soon as you're settled in, we'll leave. We had planned to anchor off Monaco tonight, but a storm's coming there this afternoon, so we'll head to Cannes. As you know, that's the beauty of a charter. We don't have to follow a predetermined itinerary. I hope you won't be too disappointed, but Kevin Costner cancelled at the last minute, so I'm the only eligible bachelor on board at the moment." He smiled seductively.

"That's fine with me," Mattie grinned. "He's not really my type anyway."

Evan escorted her to her V.I.P. suite where all her suitcases had been unpacked and stored out of sight. "Make yourself comfortable. Everyone is in shorts or bathing suits up on the sundeck. You know where that is, so join us when you've changed. We'll have lunch in a while. I'm so pleased you're here." He hugged her warmly. "Welcome aboard."

"I'm thrilled to be here, Evan," Mattie said gratefully. "You have no idea how much I've been looking forward to this cruise."

"And to being with me, I hope." He squeezed her hand and kissed her lightly on her cheek. "Take your time. I'll be waiting for you with a frozen strawberry daiquiri in hand...that's what you said you liked, right?"

"You have a good memory," she laughed. "Thanks. I'll be along in a couple of minutes. I just have to go through the drawers and find where Alice put my bathing suits and sunscreen. She's still the head stew, isn't she?"

"I sure am," Alice grinned as she walked into the cabin. "Nice to see you Ms. Cartwright…and as a passenger, I mean. I unpacked all your things and I'll show you where everything is."

"I'll leave you ladies to do your thing," Evan smiled. "But Alice, don't keep Ms. Cartwright too long. I'm anxious to introduce her to the rest of my guests. I've waited a long time to see her again."

Mattie shooed him out the door with a grin. "I'll be as fast as I can." She turned to Alice. "Do you remember where you put my red bikini?"

"Yes, of course." The stewardess walked to the built-in dresser and pulled out the swimsuit. "Is this the one?"

"That's it," Mattie smiled. "And Alice, is Ned Sigler a member of the crew here?"

"Yes Ma'am, he certainly is…our first mate. We all like him a lot. He jokes around all the time and entertains us in the crew mess with funny stories, especially ones about his Florida girlfriend and their crazy antics. They are quite a pair, and it's a wonder they haven't been arrested for some of the silly things they do. He sneaks off the boat almost every night when we're docked in Ft. Lauderdale, and he meets her at different places. Then he has to sneak back onto the boat without being seen, and she has to get back inside her dorm. I think Ned must have paid off one of the security guards at the dock because he's never been caught. It all started when he snuck that girl onboard this yacht at the boat show two years ago and they had a romp in the hot tub." She giggled at the story. "He's a rascal that one."

"I'd heard something about that hot tub," Mattie snickered. Casey had told her some of the outrageous things she and Ned had done since the boat show caper, like sneaking into concerts and Heat basketball games. Supposedly Sky had met and approved of Ned and their budding romance. But Mattie was not convinced. Casey was prone to hyperbole and exaggeration.

I'll tell you more about Ned later, if you're interested, but Mr. Stone will be mad if I keep you here chatting. Let me help you change. Your sandals are on the floor of the closet and your coverups are in the bottom drawer."

Mattie put on her bikini and a soft red and white checked caftan with a slit up to the top of her thigh. "By the way," she said to Alice as she grabbed her hat and sunglasses. "I brought something for Ned from his girlfriend." She went to her purse and pulled out a stack of postcards and a small brown box. "Please give these to him."

"How do you know his mischievous girlfriend?" Alice stared at Mattie, curious.

"As it turns out, by a fortuitous twist of fate, his quirky girlfriend, Casey Cooper, is none other than my little sister."

CHAPTER 43

Mattie caused a commotion when she made a stunning entrance onto the pool deck. Evan immediately rose from his deck chair to introduce her to his guests. Some had arrived the night before and two couples had been onboard the previous week. He walked over to the bar and one of the crew handed him a frozen strawberry daiquiri in a tall, frosted glass, which he in turn gave to Mattie. He slowly led her around the sundeck, past the hot tub to the swimming pool. She could not help but glance at the infamous hot tub and smile…the scene of the crime, she thought to herself.

"Mattie Cartwright, these are my good friends from California, and they are all associated in one way or the other with my previous projects in Hollywood or with the *Dr. Tony Show,* or my new television series, *Miami Intrigues.* Matt and Suzie Peters, they're both writers for *Miami Intrigues,* as are Lance and Silvia Hurd. Silvia is my first cousin, but she hates to admit it because I embarrass her sometimes."

Mattie laughed and continued shaking everyone's hands. "And of course, you already know Tony and Laura Grant." Mattie smiled and gave them each a warm smile.

And here's Harry and Meg Stark. He's my co-producer on the *Dr.*

Tony Show and Megan is a well-known fashion and costume designer in the industry. I think you'll find her particularly interesting based on the fashion statement you've made here so far." He winked at Mattie and whispered in her ear. "You're the prettiest woman here by a long shot… the loveliest woman in the whole Mediterranean."

Mattie blushed but loved his compliment. Every penny she had invested in her new wardrobe had been worth it. She politely shook hands with Evan's other guests and was surprised by how comfortable she felt in the group…not at all intimidated by the elite company, and they seemed happy to have her join them.

"They are all in the V.I.P. suites across or down the hall from you." Evan explained. "The rest of this week's guests have been reduced to two couples who were supposed to board this evening when we were in Monaco. Now with the change in our itinerary, they'll have to hire cars and meet us in Cannes either later tonight, or they may prefer to stay the night in Monaco and drive down in the morning. I'm sure we'll hear from them soon once they've made their new plans."

Mattie removed her cover up and joined the others sitting by the pool's edge, sipping her drink, and chatting with Megan and Harry. Evan glanced over at her and immediately produced a tube of sunscreen. "I'm afraid I'm going to have to lather you down," he whispered provocatively. "Otherwise, you'll burn those pretty shoulders."

Without asking, he began to rub the cream on her shoulders, arms, and upper back in slow gentle strokes. She was about to protest, but his hands on her body felt so good, so sensual that she did not ask him to stop.

After an hour, Alice appeared by the pool to announce that lunch would be served on the deck below at the outdoor dining table, aft. The guests, one by one, dried themselves off and put on their shirts or cover ups. They used the outside staircase to reach the lower deck.

Taking their seats around the huge teak table, they were in awe of the lovely table settings and the centerpiece. Each day it would change. That was part of Alice's job, and she was highly creative. Today's theme was money. She had placed Monopoly dollar bills all over the tabletop. Miniature, silver piggy banks were placed at each place setting, filled with euro coins. Green placemats and plates completed the theme's look. A two-foot Lego copy of the famous bank in Monto Carlo sat in the middle of the table, commanding the diner's attention.

Mattie was sipping cold blueberry soup when she noticed Ned coming down the outside stairs. While the guests ate, he had apparently supervised the cleanup of the pool deck, the removal of the empty drink glasses, and replaced the beach towels by the lounge chairs. Mattie caught his eye, smiled, and waved. Then she noticed his wrist. He was wearing the thin leather bracelet Casey had bought him with his name branded onto it. She remembered when she and Casey had bought it at the Festival Flee Market last March. Alice had obviously given Ned the package from Casey.

Ned looked at her and mouthed the words "thank you". She smiled back. Casey would be pleased. He obviously liked his gift. Mattie would be sure to text her sister later that day.

"Ladies and Gentlemen," Evan said formally, raising his glass. "We are about to leave beautiful Nice and travel along the charming French Riviera to our new destination, Cannes. We'll try to double back to Monaco later in the week after the weather clears."

"Here, here," someone at the table called out. They all raised their glasses in a toast, as *Liquidity* seamlessly used her thrusters and backed out of the slip. In a few minutes, they were cruising in the Mediterranean Sea, past one beautiful scenic spot after another, enroute to their new anchorage spot.

Mattie took in the beautiful views, the gorgeous countryside scattered with amazing villas, and she had to pinch herself. This was beyond anything she could have imagined. She had described this to her clients many times over the years from pictures and videos she had seen, but never expected to be a part of it herself. She looked over at Evan and mouthed "Thank you". He responded by blowing her a kiss and mouthed back. "This is just the beginning."

As it turned out, it was just the beginning of the most wonderful time in her life.

CHAPTER 44

After a delicious lunch, Mattie began to feel the effects of jet lag, and although she hated to miss a second of the beautiful day at sea, she needed to nap. Excusing herself, she went below to lie down. When she opened her suite's door, she noticed an envelope that had been shoved under it and was lying on the carpet. Assuming it was an invitation to that night's dinner, she placed it on her nightstand and promptly fell asleep. When she awoke, she remembered the envelope and was surprised to find that it was from Ned Sigler.

"Thanks for bringing the letters and bracelet from Casey. We need your help with something. Can you meet me in the galley tomorrow after lunch? It's important. Ned"

I wonder what that's about. Mattie tossed on a pair of shorts and picked up the latest Peggy Chernow novel. She had gotten enough sun for one day, so decided to read her new favorite author in the air-conditioned comfort of the sky lounge and relax with a *Diet Coke*.

"Hi there," Suzie Peters greeted her as she entered the lounge. She noticed the novel in Mattie's hand. "I love a good book and I'm always looking for inspiration for new story lines for *Miami Intrigues*. Matt and I work closely with Lance and Silvia to come up with utterly unique plots.

When we think we have it right, that's when we tweak the story just a bit more. Our goal is that every last scene must leave the viewers hanging and waiting for the next episode. We want this new series to be Evan's television legacy and run for years and years like *Friends* or NCIS, but with an edgy, modern Miami feel. And the residuals will be fantastic."

"That sounds very ambitious. I wish you luck." Mattie smiled at Suzie. "What do you like to read for pleasure?"

"Mostly mysteries and some legal dramas, like Grisham. I really don't have much time to read for fun." She sighed wistfully and studied Mattie. "If it's not being too personal, may I ask if you and Evan are dating? Normally he brags to his friends about his women, but he's said nary a word about you except that you arranged this charter for him, and he considers you a good friend."

Mattie was a little hesitant to answer Suzie's question. She and Evan had formed a nice friendship after many long phone conversations, but they were not dating. However, the more she had seen of him, the more she wanted to get to know him better. She liked his sense of humor and that he was not flustered or angry when things went wrong, or when he was forced to change plans at the last minute. He was even keeled and just plain nice…so refreshing. That was a rarity for a famous celebrity, she imagined.

She was saved from having to answer Suzie's question when Evan strolled into the lounge with his own book. "There you are." He smiled at Mattie and took a seat beside her. "Did you have a good nap?"

"Yes, I feel much better, and I'm ready for a fun night."

"Well, my original plan called for our tender to take any guests wanting to spend the evening in Monaco ashore." He shrugged his shoulders. "Anyone preferring to stay on board can expect cocktails and a gourmet dinner here. Chef Gunner has prepared a delightful dinner. But now, with the change in destination, I'm not sure what's happening. Captain Llanos is calling ahead to Cannes to find us a reservation somewhere if needed, and then we can all decide what we want to do. Frankly, I love this boat and I'd be happy to stay onboard tonight and just relax. An added benefit is that an early evening would give you a chance to conquer your jet lag. So, let's wait and see what develops."

"I hate to miss one of Chef Gunner's gourmet meals, but I'd really like to go ashore to see a casino, if not tonight, maybe tomorrow. Would that be possible?" She hoped she was not being too forward in asking, but she'd heard so much about the European casinos and wanted to experience one for herself.

"Okay then. Your wish will be granted," Evan laughed. "Although, I confess, I'm not any good at craps or roulette. I'm a horrible gambler."

"So am I. But it could be fun. I'll set a limit on how much I'm willing to lose and not spend another dime. Notice I did not say *win*. I have no expectations in that regard. At home I've never won a single dollar from the scratch offs in my supermarket or at Lotto. And just so you know, I'm horrible at bingo too."

"Maybe your luck will change with me around." His eyes twinkled. "And, by the way, one of the couples that will be joining us here for the next week is the famous singing diva, Barbara Camp. I'm sure you've heard of her. She is performing a one woman show in a supper club in Monaco tonight, doing a small rendition of her hit Las Vegas extravaganza. We had tickets to her 8:00 p.m. performance and then she and her husband, Gio were going to join us for a midnight supper before coming onboard. Since that's not happening now, I guess she will not be arriving until tomorrow. She cannot back out of the performance at this late date.

So, that means we'll have at least another day and night in Cannes. Your trip to the casino is a certainty."

"Besides Barbara and Gio," Evan continued, "We were to meet one more couple in Monaco and bring them onboard with us. I guess with the change in our itinerary, they might stay there overnight to see Barbara's show and then catch up with us tomorrow. I don't want your jaw to drop when you recognize him from the movies."

"How about a hint? Initials maybe?" She prodded playfully. "Kevin Costner's been ruled out, I believe."

"Yes, but our mystery guest is just as famous. You'll have to wait and be surprised."

"Please, just a little hint." She begged playfully.

As hard as it was to resist her, he winked. "Sorry. My lips are sealed. You'll have to wait and be surprised."

CHAPTER 45

After several back-and-forth phone calls, details for the evening were confirmed. Mattie and Evan decided to go into Cannes, have an early dinner by themselves, and spend some time in the Casino. The other guests made separate plans to go ashore or decided to stay onboard.

After dinner, as Mattie walked into the casino on his arm, Evan was struck again by her exquisite beauty. She had piled her hair high on her head in a soft twist, showing off her long and smooth neck. Her black floor length dress was an elegant sheath with a thin gold belt tied at her waist. A thigh-high slit revealed her long and shapely legs and teased him to want to see more. She wore no jewelry except for a gold Cartier watch that Charles had given Mattie for her thirtieth birthday, and gold dangling earrings she had found in the vine covered Via Demario on her recent shopping trip to Worth Avenue in Palm Beach.

She looked like royalty, with her statuesque height and posture. Evan was proud to be by her side and knew the other men in the room were envious. Even in her stiletto heels, he still stood several inches above her. They made a handsome, distinguished couple and turned heads as they moved about. He noticed the paparazzi snapping pictures everywhere.

Mattie was causing quite a stir, but she was oblivious to it, concentrating on the sights and sounds in the room and proudly holding on to Evan's elbow.

He took Mattie's hand and led her to the nearest roulette table where he handed the croupier a couple of hundred Euro notes which he exchanged for casino chips which he piled in front of her. She knew the general principles of the game, but not the individual odds on where she should place the chips. Evan taught her to play single numbers for the largest payoffs but also about odd and even, red, and black, zero and double zeros, and how to place a chip on the lines to cover two or four numbers at a time. The game's strategy was more complicated than she had thought. She was having fun and loved the vibrancy around the wheel. All the players were intense, hoping for a big win and encouraging each other.

She loved watching the little silver metal ball speeding round and round after the dealer had spun the wheel and she waited anxiously to see where it landed. The first few spins were discouraging. She lost all the chips she put down. Then, on impulse, she decided to play her lucky numbers, which had never paid her anything before. But it was worth a try…7, 17, 24, and 27. She put a hundred-Euro chip on each number, eagerly leaned forward to watch the spin, and held her breath, squeezing Evan's hand in anticipation.

"I feel this is your lucky spin." He was being cautiously optimistic and draped his arm over her shoulder. Feeling her smooth skin sent a shiver through his body and he pulled her closer, enveloping her in an almost suffocating hug. "You smell wonderful," he whispered.

"Careful," she gasped. "You're going to squeeze the breath out of me."

"Sorry." He released her and grinned.

"Look, look at where the silver ball landed…smack dab on my number 17. I won!" She shouted with glee. "But how much?"

The dealer kept stacking more and more chips in front of her. "How much did I win?" She asked the dealer, barely able to contain her enthusiasm. It was not the money that excited her but the fact that for the first time ever, she was a winner.

"Oh my God," she was stunned when he replied. "Did you hear that, Evan? I won $3500 euros." The others around the table laughed and applauded.

"I told you I'd bring you luck." He gave her a high five. "Now let's cash out and head back to the boat. I don't want you to be tempted to play any more tonight. My heart can't take the suspense."

Between the two of them they carried the chips to the teller's cage and cashed out. They were still laughing and talking about her winnings as they returned to *Liquidity*.

Evan walked her to her door and kissed her lightly on her lips. "See you in the morning." She had hoped for more, but, although it took all his resolve, he turned like a perfect gentleman and walked away. She had no idea how much will-power it had taken for him to be so restrained.

She was too keyed up to sleep, so she picked up her book and read a few chapters. She finally dozed off, dreaming of the tiny, silver ball circling round and round.

CHAPTER 46

Mattie awoke refreshed. It had been a wonderful night, and it was only the first of many evenings still left to enjoy on this cruise. She was looking forward to meeting Barbara and Gio Camp and the mysterious movie star. But more than anything, she was eager to spend more time with Evan. He was fun to be with and they had had a wonderful time in Cannes.

After she showered, and dressed in capris and a tee shirt, she wandered to the upper deck where breakfast was served between 7:00 a.m. and 10:00 a.m. either at the "help yourself" bar containing coffees, fruit, croissants, and cold cereals or at the table where one could order eggs, omelets, French toast, or hot oatmeal.

Meg Stark was sitting alone at the table enjoying her eggs benedict and studying some costume designs on her I-Pad. She smiled at Mattie. "Good morning. Did you have any luck at the casino?"

"Oh yes! I won a couple thousand Euros at roulette. I think Evan must be my lucky charm. It was amazing! I've never won anything before in my life." She poured herself a cup of steaming hot American coffee and helped herself to a bowl of fruit.

"How about you?" she asked. "Was dinner on board good last might?"

"Yes. It was delicious. The chef made individual tournedos with fresh asparagus and crab stuffed baked potatoes…and for dessert, chocolate crème brulee."

She noticed Meg's I-Pad. "What have you got there?"

"These are my latest designs for *Miami Intrigues'* next episode. They need a little tweaking. I want them to be edgy and young, but I don't want our cast to look slutty. It's a fine line."

"May I take a look?"

"Sure. You have a good sense of fashion. Maybe you can see something I missed." Meg handed Mattie the I-Pad.

After scrolling through the sketches, Mattie remarked, "my first impression is that these are trendy and spot on for what you'd see people wearing in South Beach. I think adding some funky, chunky jewelry might finish the look."

Meg studied the pictures again carefully. "I think you're right, especially for the nighttime wear. Thanks so much. Sometimes an extra set of eyes is really helpful."

"De nada," Mattie laughed. "That's my first experience with fashion design. This cruise is turning out to be a lot of fun firsts for me."

The Peters and the Hurds came in for breakfast, and a while later Evan appeared on deck in designer shorts and a tight tee shirt that clung to his washboard abs. The Grants were with him, and he brought Barbara and Gio Camp to the table. "Everyone this is Barbara and Gio. They drove down from Monaco early this morning. Please introduce yourselves while I order breakfast for them and room service for their friends." He grinned mischievously at Mattie. "Tom Selleck and his wife, Jillie, will join us later. He's on a conference call back to the States at the moment and sends his apologies for missing breakfast with us."

Mattie's eyes opened wide. "Tom Selleck from "Magnum P.I" and "Blue Bloods?"

"The one and only," Evan grinned, thrilled to see Mattie's eyes light up with delight. "And look," he held up a sheet of computer paper. "This was on Facebook this morning." He handed Mattie a picture of herself with him at the casino in Cannes. The headline caption read, WHO IS THE RAVISHINGLY MYSTERIOUS WOMAN KEEPING EVAN STONE COMPANY THESE DAYS?

"Oh, my goodness," Mattie blushed. "I never saw anyone taking pictures of us."

"The paparazzi are everywhere, and they hang out in all the places where they expect celebrities to show up. Now that they have discovered you, they'll have a field day trying to figure out who you are, and if we are a couple. But don't worry. We are safe from their scrutiny on this boat, and they won't be able to get any more pictures of us as long as we're onboard. On land, though, that's a different story. And thankfully, they haven't figured out that we have the famous Dr. Tony and other celebrities with us."

Mattie was a little alarmed and looked at Evan with uncertainty.

"Don't worry," he reassured her. "I'll take care of them, if need be."

"If you say so. So, what's our schedule for today?"

"I thought we'd head to St. Tropez and have a look around. How's that sound?"

"Terrific," Lance Hurd interrupted and offered enthusiastically. "I want to see the famous beaches I've heard so much about."

"You don't fool anyone, dear. You just want to watch all the young girls in their string bikinis strutting around," his wife Silvia joked. "Lance calls those swim suits dental floss."

"I guarantee you that you won't find anyone looking better in a swim-suit than our own Mattie. You do remember her red bikini from yester-day?" Evan snickered, but was full of admiration, and Mattie blushed openly. It was a compliment, she knew, but she was still embarrassed. She was not used to so much public attention.

Evan tactfully changed the subject. He was aware of Mattie's dis-comfort and wanted to put her at ease. "There are so many private beach clubs in St. Tropez. That's what the town's really known for. I suggest those that want to check one out, come with Mattie and me to Le Club 55. It's the beach where Brigitte Bardot filmed *And God Created Woman.* It has become a top celebrity haunt and world-famous place ever since. I have guest passes at the club to swim, and we can enjoy a leisurely lunch there. With the sea as the background, and your feet in the sand, it's an idyllic experience. But if the sand and surf are not your thing, I've hired private cars for those that would rather shop or be on your own around the town. Let Granger, the ship's chief Engineer, know your preference. He'll make all the arrangements."

"How far is it?" Barbara asked, "to St. Tropez, I mean."

"We're already halfway there. It's about another hour cruising time. We'll dock, and you are free to come and go all day and night. We won't depart until late morning tomorrow. We'll begin to double back over the next few days from Cannes to Nice, Antibes, Cap Ferret, and finally to Monaco. Every destination is very close to the next, so you'll get to see everything from land or by sea. Granger can help each of you once you decide where you want to go. Think of *Liquidity* as your floating hotel, always available to welcome you. I know Jillie and Tom mentioned that they wanted to go to the beach club today, so that will be at least four of us there, but the more the merrier." He looked around the table. "Any other takers?"

The Grants enthusiastically nodded yes. "We'll come along," Laura added eagerly. "Although I can't compete with the dental floss set."

"You can hold your own," Tony grinned and patted his wife on her ass.

Mattie suddenly realized that she was supposed to meet Ned in the galley after lunch, but with the day's plan, she would be ashore by then. She excused herself from the group and went in search of the first mate.

Ned was in one of the V.I.P. suites talking to Alice as she changed the linens and refurbished the towels. Mattie found him there and asked if he had a minute to talk with her privately. She explained that she was going ashore for the day, so this was her only free time.

"Sure," he said looking to Alice for confirmation. "Do you need any help?"

"No, go ahead Ned," she smiled. "I'm almost done here."

As they walked away Mattie looked at him suspiciously. "What's going on and what does it have to do with Casey? Are you two in trouble again?"

"No," he answered defensively. "I guess you know that she and I have gotten pretty serious about each other, and we hate the time we have to be apart. I'm always at sea, and she's stuck on campus. Before I came away on this charter, she and I talked about our future, and we decided to go to a yacht employment agency to explore our options… just to see possibilities. The point was to see if Casey could be trained to be an assistant stew. If so, then we could request a joint placement for a year on the same yacht. Not *Liquidity*, of course, but a smaller one where she can train and perfect the housekeeping skills, she'll need to work on a mega yacht like this. The agency said it is a definite possibility.

They were impressed by my crew experience and by her enthusiasm and eagerness to learn about a career in boating. Captains are always looking for competent crews. Serving on a smaller yacht would be a demotion for me, but I'm not concerned about that at the moment. We want to be together and are willing to do whatever it takes to make that happen."

Mattie had suspected this from her recent discussions with Casey. "Do her mother and father know about this plan? Casey would have to drop out of college or at least postpone her studies for a year…not a smart thing to do in today's world. I'm sure the Coopers would be upset if Casey passes up the opportunity to get a college degree."

"No. Not yet. Her parents don't know anything about this yet. I've been to Tampa several times with her, and they seem to like me. Although at first, they questioned if I was too old for their daughter. Casey lied about her age when we first met, but I saw her driver's license and figured it out. I'm seven years older. That's not too bad, and she's pretty mature for her age except for her mischievous streak. I know this idea of working on a yacht will come as a surprise to the Coopers, and probably not a good one. That's where you come in." He looked at the floor and shuffled his feet nervously. "We need your help to convince them that it's okay. You're the perfect person. You know that being a member of a yacht crew provides a great opportunity for someone to be paid and see the world at the same time… before one marries, has mortgages and kids. You can point this out to the Coopers."

"I see you've thought a lot about this." Mattie reflected, but she still thought the idea was flawed. "I have to think about it some more before I can give you an answer. Ned, as Casey must have told you, I'm very new to the Cooper family, and not at all sure they will listen to anything I have to say or that it would carry much weight."

"Yes, I know all about you and Sky, and about your mother and Mr. Cooper. Casey tells me everything, but you know all about boats and what a great opportunity working on yachts can be. Please Mattie, we need your help...young love and all," he grinned awkwardly. "If we are going to make this move, Casey has to drop out of UM after this semester and sign a commitment agreement with the agency. And I have to give my notice to Captain Llanos. We don't have much time to waste."

Mattie was embarrassed that Ned knew so much about her private personal history, but it was unreasonable to expect Casey to keep such information from him. They were apparently a couple in every sense. "I'll think about it Ned. That's *all* I can promise, and I'll also talk to Casey."

"Thanks, for listening. Have a great day in St. Tropez. And, may I say, if I'm not being too personal, that I think I see romantic sparks between you and Mr. Stone. Maybe, if that's truly the case, you can empathize with how Casey and I feel about each other and reassure her parents."

Mattie walked away with a hint of a smile on her lips. Romantic sparks, indeed? But maybe Ned was right. Only time would tell. For right now, she was in a hurry to go ashore with Evan, and the Grants and to meet Tom and Jillie.

CHAPTER 47

The next week sped by quickly. Mattie had no idea how every day blended seamlessly into another without her giving a thought as to which day of the week it was, or what the hour. She moved blissfully from one activity to another, with Evan always by her side. She felt like she was living in a dream, but it was very real...as were her growing feelings for the very likable and attractive producer.

She and Evan went everywhere together. They were inseparable. Mattie loved being with him, but she also enjoyed talking and spending time with his other interesting and accomplished guests. The group was very compatible, and they liked being together: visiting local produce markets, walking through the quaint towns, enjoying the scenery, savoring the enticing smells, and the delicious tastes of the French Riviera. They ate sumptuous lunches and dinners in Cap Ferret, Eze, and Monaco and enjoyed croissants and pastries at local brasseries everywhere. They toured the castle and the church where Grace Kelly married Prince Rainier. They relaxed and swam off the boat in the Mediterranean Sea, water skiing and tubing behind wave runners and a speed boat.

On their last night in Monte Carlo, Mattie and Evan went off by themselves. They played craps and roulette at the casino made famous by James Bond and ate dinner at the Michelin three-star restaurant, Louis XV in the Hotel de Paris. Afterwards they danced the night away in one of the exclusive nightclubs and did not return to *Liquidity* until after three a.m. A member of the paparazzi spotted them at the restaurant and began snapping pictures until Evan went up to him and had a "talk" in which several hundred American dollars found their way into the photographer's pocket, and he and his camera disappeared for the rest of the evening.

The next morning, Evan and Mattie said their goodbyes to their friends. The guests were heading home separately, but Tony and Laura were taking a private guided tour and meeting back up with Mattie and Evan in Mykonos in a few days.

When the last of the guests had departed, Mattie and Evan collapsed wearily in deck chairs by the pool and napped. It had been a magnificent but exhausting week. They were ready for a few days of peace and quiet while the mega yacht made her way to Greece.

When they awoke from their nap, Evan stretched and gazed affectionately at Mattie. "I have something serious to discuss with you. I've fought hard to restrain myself from acting like a love-struck teenager and showing my feelings in public while we had a boat full of guests. However, now that they have gone, I want to be selfish and have you all to myself, in every way." His voice was husky. "I've fallen in love with you, Mattie. It's that simple and straight forward. I know it's been quick, but when you think about it, we've known each other for two years. I hope you share my feelings."

She had hoped he felt that way about her and surprised herself by spontaneously pulling him towards her and kissing him. The taste of his lips made her heart jump. Their tongues met. She backed away so she could speak coherently. "I don't know if what I feel is love Evan. For me, it's been too soon. But I do have deep feelings for you, and I want us to become intimate. Before that can happen, I have to be honest with you." She looked at him and took a breath. "In the past I had a heartbreaking experience with a man I loved and still do in a way. I'm still getting over the pain and shock of it. Before you and I get into a deeper relationship, I have to tell you about him and the circumstances of our breakup. You have to understand what happened to fully understand and know me. Honesty between us is imperative. There can be no secrets. I've had enough of them to last a lifetime."

She sat down and painfully described her romance with Sky and the horror of discovering that he was her half-brother. Evan listened patiently without ever taking his eyes off of her face. If he was shocked, he did not show it. His face was full of compassion and love. When Mattie started to cry and tears rolled down her cheeks, he pulled out his handkerchief and wiped them away. Taking her by the hand, he quietly led her to his suite without saying a word.

"Darling Mattie, I cannot begin to understand the pain you went through. It is unfathomable. Sky sounds like a nice man and I'm sorry for him. I can only imagine what he feels like, having to give you up. I'm not sure I could do it so gracefully. We don't have to talk about this ever again, but thank you for trusting me enough to tell me that story. I will never tell another living soul."

"I'm so relieved," she said gratefully with a huge sigh. "I was afraid you'd think I was dirty or perverted somehow." Her voice quivered. "Incest is such a horrible word. I almost gag when I say it out loud."

"Your love affair was not incest, technically. You had no idea that you and Sky were related. You cannot be blamed in any way for what happened. You have to let go of the guilt; otherwise, you will never move on…and you must! You have to learn to live happily, forget past hurts and love again. That's where I come in." He took her in his arms, cradling her softly. "I love you, my darling. You are safe with me. And if I might lighten the mood a bit…I promise, we are NOT related!"

"I'm so glad you understand," Mattie smiled, finally feeling grounded and at ease. Being with Evan made her feel safe and protected. "I've been too ashamed to bring Sky up. The word incest has such horrible connotations. It's been horrible having to hide what happened."

"Never be ashamed to tell me anything. I will never judge you. Trust in that." He hugged her even more tightly this time. "Let's forget about everything that's gone before and pretend this is the first day of our cruise…a new beginning for us. What would you think about asking Alice to move your things into my suite?" Evan wanted to be with Mattie more than he could verbalize, and his feelings showed on his face as he kissed her deeply and waited for her answer.

"I think that's the best idea you've had since you agreed with my impulse to put a hundred euros on number seventeen in Cannes," she grinned. "I don't want to forget that…my lucky evening. And I'd love a handsome roommate like yourself. Yes, call Alice please."

"The nice thing is," he winked at her. "Alice can wait a while. We'll have the boat completely to ourselves for the next five and a half days while we make our way to Mykonos. It's about 1300 nautical miles to the port there. We'll have relaxing days at sea and amorous evenings. Can you take that much togetherness?"

"Yes, oh yes. It sounds perfect to me," she sighed happily. "And I look forward to meeting up with Tony and Laura again. He is such a nice man. If it weren't for him, I would never have met you."

"Yes, we owe him for that. He and Laura are lots of fun, and he's been my best friend since our college days at Yale."

"I didn't know you went to Yale. I would have picked you for a Stanford guy, being from the west coast and all."

"No, I'm a Bulldog fan forever." He grinned.

She looked out the large windows on the port side. "Before we reach Mykonos, what bodies of land will we be passing? I never thought to look at a map of the area."

"I don't know. We'll learn together. But I know Captain Llanos will take us through several bodies of water - the Mediterranean Sea, the Tyrrhenion Sea, the Sea of Crete, and the Aegean Sea. But he'll have to tell us when we're in what. I'll have no idea. One body of water looks pretty much like the next to me."

"The weather," he said with a smile, "is predicted to be good, and the waters should stay calm. I want this time to be the beginning of a wonderful life together. I'm not necessarily talking about marriage, although I am amenable to it. And, if it's too soon after Sky, I understand. But I want us to belong to each other...as in an exclusive, committed couple. Is that too much pressure for the paparazzi's most mysterious ravishing beauty?"

"No," she smiled and hugged him tightly. "Not at all. Should we call Alice now and ask her to move my things in here?"

"Yes, in good time, but first, we should initiate the bed. I want to be sure you'll be comfortable in here with me and that the mattress is up to your standards."

She smiled provocatively. "Ready when you are." Her tee shirt and bra fell to the floor.

CHAPTER 48

The next five days were perfect in every way for Mattie and Evan. They spent all their time making love, leisurely relaxing on the sundeck, or reading in the sky lounge or tucked comfortably in bed. They soaked daily in the hot tub, swam, and snorkeled off the swim platform, and rode wave-runners in concentric circles around the yacht, laughing and racing each other. They took long naps in the afternoons and played competitive games of Gin Rummy after dinner. Evan usually won but when Mattie did, it was cause for celebration and champagne.

Mattie's beautiful new wardrobe lay dormant in the dresser drawers or languished on padded hangers in the closet. Evan could not keep his hands off her, or her clothes on her. The crew had become accustomed to seeing the amorous couple all around the yacht dressed only in their plush, white terry *Liquidity* bathrobes and slippers. On several occasions, they even ate dinner in their robes and retired to their suite immediately after the meal.

Evan, being the consummate businessman, made time each morning to check in with his California, and New York offices while Mattie used that hour to text or call her mother, Charles, Linda, her assistant, Ellie and to answer her work-related e-mails. Ned's request to speak to

Casey's parents weighed heavily on Mattie's mind, but she had come up with an idea about how to handle the situation. However, she wanted to talk to Casey about it first.

"Hi," she said when Casey answered her cell. "How are things in Coral Gables?"

"Fine, I guess. It's hot as hell here though, and because of the humidity, there is no such thing as a good hair day." Casey sounded irritated. "But I miss Ned so much…and you too of course," she added hastily. "How is Ned?"

"He's fine, although he misses you also. He asked me to talk to Camden and Mary about allowing you to quit college and work on a charter yacht with him. I'm pretty sure that your parents won't be happy about it."

"That's why we need you to intervene." Casey added.

"I've given the idea a lot of thought, Casey, and I *cannot* go along with your plan. Going to college is such a privilege and the gateway to all kinds of possibilities. I cannot justify you giving it up to make beds and fold napkins. You think you love Ned and want to spend the rest of your life with him, and maybe that's true, but you're still so young. If the relationship doesn't work out, you will kick yourself for the rest of your life for passing up getting a degree."

"Listen to me, please. I think I have a solution that will make everyone happy and not upset your parents."

Casey calmed down slightly. "Go on. What's your idea?"

"I will never mention this crazy idea of yours to Camden and Mary. But what I will do…is contact Charles and ask him to give Ned a position as a salesman at Lux Charters. Ned can get his sales license and then help me as my right-arm. He will gain valuable experience. I need the extra help. My present assistant is leaving in a few weeks on her maternity leave, and I need to fill that position quickly.

"Another option is for Ned to strike out on his own, working in some other aspect of the yachting business, but on land…in Lauderdale or Miami until you finish school. That way, you will be in the same area, and you can take your time and see where this relationship is heading. After you graduate, whatever you decide, your parents will have to accept, and I will support you completely."

Casey thought about Mattie's suggestion for a moment. "I suppose that could work, but Ned would have to give up going to sea. And that's what he really loves. He might be miserable stuck on land 24-7."

"Yes, he may be, but it would only be for a short while. If he was willing to ask you to give up college to be with him, then I think it's only fair that he gives up going to sea in order to be with you. We are only talking two, or maybe even just one and a half years, depending on how many courses you take each semester. The time will fly by and then you two can sail around the world together if that's still your wish."

"Do you think Ned would do that for me? Give up his job and work with you?"

"There's only one way to find out. Do you want to call him and ask, or should I go speak with him right now?"

Mattie was pleased that Casey seemed to like the idea. Quitting UM would be a terrible mistake. In today's economy, a college degree was pretty much essential for one to succeed professionally.

"As long as you're there with Ned, you might as well sound him out." Casey said soberly. "Please convince him to go along with your plan. I can't stand being away from him. But I don't want him to be miserable and resent me either. This decision has to feel right to him."

"My goodness. You are suddenly sounding so mature and wise." Mattie was impressed. "Where is this deep insight coming from?"

"Mom and Dad made me go to counselling after they saw how much it helped Sky. I resisted at first, but eventually found it very helpful, and think I learned a lot from it. I still see that doctor here on campus once in a while. It's kind of nice to have someone to listen to all my crazy thoughts. Sometimes I say stuff I don't mean, just to see his reaction."

"You shouldn't do that," Mattie scolded. "But I'm proud of you, little sis. I'll get back in touch with you after I've talked to Ned. If he agrees, I'll call Charles."

"By the way," Casey said as casually as she could. She wanted to give Mattie some important information about her brother but did not want to upset her. "Sky has been dating a very nice nurse who works at the Baptist Hospital in Miami. I think they are getting pretty serious, because they just left yesterday together on a ten-day cruise from Athens. That doesn't freak you out, does it? I thought you should know."

"No. It does not upset me in the least. I genuinely want Sky to be happy...to be with someone he cares about." She was surprised at her unemotional and nonchalant reaction to Casey's news, but she honestly did want Sky to be happy. She had worked through her issues with Dr. Bristow and felt she had resolved any problems that might arise when she saw Sky again.

"So, how's it going with you and the hunky movie star, Evan?" Casey changed the subject.

"Very well," Mattie answered softly. "Very well, indeed."

CHAPTER 49

Brenda and Charles were having dinner at *Sea Watch*, a popular beachside restaurant in Pompano. It was located on the beach just north of Lauderdale by the Sea, where Brenda lived. They had been seated at a corner table on the porch where open windows brought in the cooling ocean breezes and the calming sounds of the palm fronds rustling gently against each other. It was almost sunset, and the beach was deserted except for a wedding party standing together by the shoreline. The bride and groom, holding hands and dressed in casual clothing, stood barefoot in the sand under a homemade trellis, reciting their vows to each other. Twenty guests were there to witness the ceremony. All were barefoot too.

Weddings on the beach were a common phenomenon in Florida. The sand and surf provided beautiful backdrops and were far less expensive venues for ceremonies than the elaborate interiors of hotels, restaurants, or private clubs. A beach wedding was usually followed by a low-key reception at a local restaurant or nearby hotel. The private dining room at *Sea Watch* had been reserved for this particular wedding reception. Brenda and Charles watched as the joyful wedding party, the bride and groom and their guests made their way, laughing and smiling, from the sand to the dining room to begin the festivities.

"They all look so innocent and carefree," Brenda said wistfully. "I don't think I was ever that young or free-spirited."

"I'm sure at one time you were. However, raising Mattie by yourself with no husband to help, forced you to grow up fast and to be responsible and mature beyond your years. Brenda, you are still a beautiful woman, and Mattie, thankfully, inherited her gorgeous looks from you, with the exception of her eyes, which are definitely Cam's."

"I have a confession to make," he said earnestly. "Please hear me out. As much as I have tried to deny it over the years, whenever I see you or hear your voice, I wish we had met and become a couple when I was younger, and that I could have been a real husband to you and father to Mattie. I don't know what has held me back, but after everything that's happened this past year, I've had a real epiphany. I know the importance of telling people that you love them. I hope Mattie knows how much I love her."

"Of course, she does. You are as close to a real father as she'll ever have. Camden may be her father by blood, but you have loved and cared for her all these years. She's every bit as much *your* daughter as she is his. Believe me, I know she feels that way, and so do I."

"Aren't family relationships strange?" Charles thought out loud. "Mattie came into my life by accident at a cocktail party and look how important she's become to me. I can't imagine my life without her. Now because of what's happened in the past, she has found the brother and sister she always wanted. Camden has been reunited with Mattie and she's trying to feel like a part of, and fit in with, the Cooper family. You've formed a warm relationship with Casey, and I can't even begin to figure out if she and Sky are related to you…it's too complicated, but it doesn't matter. You have graciously forgiven Camden and accept him, while encouraging his relationship with your daughter. That's a selfless act on your part. Most women would not be so kind or understanding. It's all really odd, but quite wonderful when you think about it. *I admire you profoundly.* If I haven't said it before, I'm saying it now."

He looked at her lovingly. "Brenda, since the day we met, back when I hired Mattie, you have been an important force and source of inspiration in my life. You have always tactfully reined in my impulsive nature and kept me grounded in reality. Whenever I had a wild ass scheme, you talked me down off the cliff and did it with kindness and common sense. Without you I may have tried to buy up all the charter companies in the US and consolidate them…ending up ridiculed by my peers and in bankruptcy court. I credit a lot of my success to your sage advice. The publicists have always given me credit for being such an astute businessman, but in truth, the majority of the recognition should go to you."

Brenda blushed, embarrassed by extravagant praise. She had been his sounding board for years. She believed in him whole heartedly and had only offered what she considered occasional advice, when asked.

Brenda beamed. She was thrilled that he appreciated her. "Thank you. I don't know what to say. Except, that the day you walked into Mattie's life was also the best day of my life too."

He suddenly looked very serious. "In my mind, there are still a few loose ends to tie up."

"Such as?" Brenda sipped her wine and looked at him with curiosity.

"Well, for one thing, I think Mattie and Sky need to meet face to face. I know everyone's been through counselling and are supposedly cured and moving forward. That's just psychobabble to me. I believe closing the loop on their doomed romance is important for her final healing, and maybe for Sky's too."

"I don't disagree. But so far, the timing has not been right. According to Cam, Sky's on a cruise with his new girlfriend, Carolyn, and as you know, Mattie is off, God knows where, in the Mediterranean with Evan Stone. I'm sure when they all get back to Florida, one or the other will reach out. If not, Casey will make it happen." Brenda smiled. "What other loose ends were you referring to?"

Charles studied Brenda carefully. This conversation was long overdue, but he had not had the courage to broach the subject before. Something or someone always got in the way or maybe he had been too much of a confirmed bachelor to make his feelings known. Taking a deep breath, he plunged ahead, praying he didn't stumble over his words.

"Brenda, you have been my best friend for over a decade now. We have seen each other and Mattie through some pretty scary times and some wonderful ones. This last year, finding out about your past has tested us all, but one thing has never changed. Even though I was disappointed, I have always had your back and you have had mine. That's remarkable and deserves some significant recognition."

"Go on," she whispered softly, looking into his eyes.

"I was thinking that, as neither of us is getting any younger, it might be fun to grow old together. Seeing that young couple on the beach reminded me of the happiness two people can bring to each other and frankly, it made me a little jealous. I'd love the security of knowing you were waiting for me at home each night after work, and that you'd be looking forward to being with me. When I retire, which I think will be soon, we can travel the world. I want to take you to all the places you've dreamed of seeing. We don't have to get married, if that makes you uncomfortable, but I do love you, and I want you to move in with me. My house is large, and I promise I would not crowd you. What do you say? Will you consider it?" He looked hopefully into her eyes, praying she would say yes.

Brenda looked at him with wide-eyed surprise. "Charles Cord, that's the most unromantic, boring, prosaic marriage proposal I've ever heard. How can you tell me in one breath that you love me, and then in another say you don't want to get married? What am I supposed to be? Your roommate?"

"No. I didn't mean it that way." His words had not come out right. "And I did *not* say that I didn't want to get married. I thought, after all these years, you might not want to. I was simply giving you "an out" in case you preferred to stay single. I was trying, albeit stupidly, to let you know that I want to be with you, anyway you'll have me." The more he talked the more ridiculous his words sounded, even to himself. "Oh, I really messed this up, Brenda. Let me start again."

He reached into his pants pocket and pulled out a small jewelry box. "I've been carrying this around for over a year, but never had the nerve to show it to you." He placed it on the dinner table and implored her. "Please marry me, Brenda Cartwright. I have loved you for a long time and want us to be together…to be a real conventional family. What do you say? Will you take a chance on an old man like me and become my wife?"

"Well, that was much better," Brenda said with a chuckle. "It only missed the bended knee approach or violins in the background. Let's call Mattie and tell her our happy news."

"What news? You haven't answered me yet." He looked confused.

"Dear Charles, I answered you years ago. It just took you all this time to get around to asking."

He reached across the table and took her hand. Brenda opened the box from Jon Paul Jeweler's and slipped the five-carat solitaire diamond on her ring finger. Her eyes glistened. "I do love you," she whispered intimately. "I always have."

They finished their wine and Brenda asked, "Are there any other loose ends before we call Mattie? I can't wait to share our news with her. She has wanted us to be together since the night she met you. I think she's given up hope, so this engagement will really make her happy."

"Yes, one more." He grinned. "What's for dessert?"

CHAPTER 50

Hi honey," Brenda spoke to Mattie on her cell phone. "Charles and I are having dinner at *Sea Watch* and have some happy news to share with you."

"Is it what I've been wanting to happen for years?" Mattie asked cautiously. She did not dare hope that her mother and Charles had finally admitted their true feelings for each other.

"I think so," Brenda stated happily. "Charles and I have decided that we're not getting any younger, and we want to get married and spend our old age together."

"That's wonderful, Mom!" Mattie exclaimed. "But stop with the old age nonsense. You both have many more happy and healthy years ahead of you. You can outrun and outwork most people your age. Put me on speaker so I can talk to Charles too, please."

"Hello, Mattie." Charles voice boomed over the phone. "What do you think about me making your mother a blushing bride?"

"I think it's fantastic news and about time. Have you set a date?" Mattie asked.

"No, this just happened, but at our age, why wait? Maybe in the fall before we all get crazy with the boat show. It'll be nothing fancy. Just family, good friends and good wine."

"Cake. There has to be cake." Brenda tapped Charles on his arm and insisted.

"Always a stickler for tradition, aren't you?" Charles winked at Brenda. "If you want cake, then we'll have a big, delicious one."

"If I might interrupt the wedding plans," Mattie chuckled. "I have something serious I'd like to run by Charles."

"Sure, what is it, honey?" He waited for Mattie to continue.

Mattie reminded Charles that her assistant was about to give birth and that she would be on maternity leave for a few months. She told him that she would like her replacement to be a member of Captain Llanos' crew, whom she had come to know well and really liked… a young man named Ned Sigler. She explained about his romance with Casey and about Casey's crazy idea to drop out of college and work on a yacht with him.

"Charles, I've mentioned Ned before, but not in this capacity." Mattie spoke earnestly.

"I agree with you, Mattie. Casey should not drop out of college. She'll always regret it. But what has this got to do with me?"

"I convinced Ned to come work with me at Lux while Casey finishes college. I know I should have asked you first, but I'm hoping you'll trust me on this and approve. I promise that he will be an asset to Lux. He knows so much about yachts and charters, and as a first mate, he is used to dealing with personnel and other problems quickly and efficiently. Even if Casey were not in the picture, I would hire him in a second as my assistant."

"If you want this young man, I will make it happen," Charles said. "I think it sounds like a good plan. As soon as he finishes this charter, ask him to give Captain Llanos proper notice and then bring him to see me. We'll work out the details later, and you can tell him the job is waiting for him as soon as he's able to start. I can see that you've come up with a good solution to what might have been another upsetting problem for Sky and his family. Smart thinking, honey."

"Thanks," Mattie said with relief, "and congratulations. We'll celebrate your engagement when I get back home. In the meantime, Mom, don't you dare pick out your wedding dress without me. Lately I've become very knowledgeable about fashion," she laughed.

"I promise I'll wait for you. But remember, our wedding is going to be small and not formal."

"That's fine. But it can still be elegant, and you have to wear something. You'll make a beautiful bride."

"Thanks, honey. How are you and Evan getting along?" She hoped that Evan's jet setter friends had made Mattie feel welcome and a part of their group. She knew Mattie had been eager to go on the cruise, and Brenda hoped her daughter wasn't losing her heart to an international playboy who would hurt her in the end. Mattie had been through enough already. Brenda did not want any more love catastrophes for her daughter, not after she had finally recovered from Sky. "Is he as fabulous as you thought he'd be?"

"Better, Mom. He's really wonderful," Mattie answered happily. "He takes really good care of me." She was not ready to confess her true feelings for Evan to the world yet. However, anyone looking at her when she was with him would sense it immediately. She was clearly head over heels in love.

"Well, have fun for the rest of the trip, and we'll see you in two weeks." Brenda handed the phone back to Charles.

"Take care, honey. I'm so happy you approve of your mother and me."

"Always have, always will," Mattie hung up. Her dream for her mother was coming true. Now if only hers would too.

"Evan," she called out to him in the bedroom. "I'll be with you in a minute. I just have to call Casey back and tell her everything's been straightened out and that Ned will be returning to Ft. Lauderdale to work with me after this charter. She will be so happy."

"It seems you've solved a lot of problems today." He called out to her. "But I have one more serious one."

"What's that?" She knew he was teasing her from the sound of his voice.

"I am stuck on this big bed and need some company. Can you help a poor lonely man out?

"I guess my call to Casey can wait." She went into the bedroom and closed the door softly behind her.

CHAPTER 51

"Mykonos is the most cosmopolitan island in Greece" Evan told Mattie as they walked hand in hand along the seaside, past one restaurant after another, featuring outside seating and spectacular views of the Aegean Sea. "It's sophistication is evident in its high-end boutiques, trendy art galleries and jewelry stores on every corner. They feature exquisite and unique gold pieces. I want to take you to my favorite jeweler," he smiled. "And believe it or not, the owner, Marcos, and his brother have a shop in Boca Raton, Florida. What a small world. Look, it's straight ahead."

Evan led Mattie into the small shop with a blue and white striped awning and was instantly greeted by Marcos, the owner. "Welcome back to Mykonos," Marcos shook Evan's hand. "Good to see you again. And Mr. Stone, I see you have brought a lovely lady with you." He smiled warmly at Mattie.

Evan made the introductions, and Marcos offered them each a bottle of water or a glass of the local wine. "It's hot here this time of year," Marcos explained. "One has to keep hydrated."

"Just like in Florida," Mattie nodded and looked around the shop, admiring the exquisite but simple jewelry, mostly gold pieces with an occasional embedded gemstone.

"I'd like to buy Ms. Cartwright a gold necklace and matching earrings. Something to remind her of our time in Mykonos. What do you suggest, Marcos?"

The proprietor unlocked a glass display case mounted on the wall and pulled out a beautiful necklace with interwoven strands of gold. He held it up for Mattie to inspect. "What do you think?"

"It's absolutely gorgeous," she replied. "And so stylish. I could wear it with jeans or with a formal gown." Evan reached around and fastened the clasp around her neck. Mattie admired the necklace in the mirror. "I've never seen anything like it. It's really something special."

"It's beautiful on you, Mattie. I'd like you to have it and the matching earrings. That way you'll always have a way to remember me and Mykonos."

She smiled at him gratefully. "I don't need jewelry to remind me of you."

"We'll take them both," Evan said firmly as he pulled out his black Amex card. "Mattie, do you want to wear them or take them in a box?"

"Oh, no box, please. I'd like to wear them. Thank you." She looked at Evan tenderly. "Thank you so much."

Marcos took a selfie picture of the three of them before they left the shop and handed Mattie his Mykonos and Boca Raton business cards. "In case you want a bracelet to match," he smiled and waved goodbye.

Mattie and Evan wandered hand in hand around the town, Hora, with its trademark windmills, whitewashed houses, and narrow, winding alleyways. They stopped for a snack of baklava and vanilla ice cream at *Kastro*'s on the waterfront, and Evan recognized a famous political novelist and her jazz musician husband seated at the next table. He waved politely to them but did not bother to stop to chat. After finishing their snack, Evan and Mattie left the restaurant and strolled in and out of dozens of small shops featuring local goods, souvenirs, and some exclusive designer boutiques. By the end of the afternoon, they had filled several large shopping bags with their personal purchases and some gifts to take home to friends and family.

Evan checked his Rolex. "It's almost five o'clock. We're supposed to meet Tony and Laura at 5:30 for cocktails. I guess we'd better start walking in their direction."

"Where are we meeting them?" Mattie asked, struggling a bit with her shopping bag and over-sized purse. She hadn't realized that she'd bought so many things.

"Not far from here."

They continued walking and stopped next at Alefkandra, known as the little 'Venice of Mykonos', an area famous for its bars and colorful buildings with their balconies suspended out over the Aegean Sea. "It's a great place to have a relaxing cocktail before we board the boat." He pointed to the sea. "I can see *Liquidity* anchored a little off to the left."

They arrived at the bar and happily took seats on the balcony. A few minutes later, Tony and Laura arrived, and the four began discussing their day and showing each other their purchases. Mattie displayed the jewelry Evan had bought her, which Laura greatly admired. The four had become good friends and were looking forward to taking more trips together in the future.

After their cocktails, as they were approaching the tender, Tony looked at Evan and winked. He could see that his friend was completely captivated by Mattie, and her with him. He mentally patted himself on his back. He had evidently done a good job of matchmaking. "I can't wait to see Santorini," Tony announced. "It's reputed to be such a beautiful place. Seeing it has been on my bucket list for ages."

CHAPTER 52

Liquidity cruised slowly between Mykonos and Santorini Greece while her passengers slept in after a late evening. The night before, the four had arranged to go ashore independently in the morning and meet at noon for lunch at a highly touted local restaurant.

From the forward deck, Mattie absorbed her first impressions of Santorini with a coffee mug in her hand. Approaching the island from the water was a spectacular way to see it. The entire top of the island was bright white, as if it sat under several feet of fresh powdered snow. The whole town appeared to be glistening as the brilliant mid-day sun hit and bounced off the whitewashed, cube-shaped structures with their mostly blue doors and windows, patterned after the colors in the Greek flag. The buildings – homes, shops, and restaurants were an astonishing array of creative and inspired architecture and were nestled comfortably into the steep cliffs.

Evan came up behind Mattie. "You'd better bring a scarf," he warned. "Santorini is known for its strong winds. They can be quite fierce at times. And you should wear your sunglasses to keep the dust from burning your eyes."

"Okay," she smiled and pulled out her Chanel sunglasses and a red scarf from her purse. "I read the helpful information sheet Captain Llanos slipped under our door last night. Like a good girl scout, I'm always prepared."

They went ashore, and Evan grinned at Mattie as he explained that to reach the town of Thera at the top of Santorini Island, one could either ride a donkey up the mountainside or take the cable car. Mattie wisely opted for the cable car. Once on top, they began strolling arm in arm through the narrow, winding streets, wandering in and out of shops selling souvenirs, local wines, and the Greek specialty drink, ouzo. "This is spectacular," Mattie raved. "I had no idea that Santorini was known for its wines."

"Yes, it is, and we have plans to visit a local winery tomorrow afternoon. It's my favorite one here - Santos Winery. The hot, sunny climate is perfect for growing grapes. But in the morning, I want to show you the volcano. We'll have a nice last day in Santorini."

"That'll be fun," she remarked. "I loved wine tasting when I visited Napa and Sonoma." She continued strolling hand-in-hand with Evan but noticed that she felt a little claustrophobic and was conscious of gathering crowds of tourists pushing their way through the narrow alleyways. "From the sudden increase in pedestrians, I guess some of the cruise ships must have arrived in port."

"I'm sure you're right. Santorini is on almost every Greek Isle cruise itinerary. It's so picturesque, and for "foodies", it's known for its authentic Greek cuisine. Thankfully, we have reservations for lunch. Tony took care of that. Otherwise, we'd never get a table in the height of the tourist season."

They made their way to the restaurant. Tony and Laura were already seated and sipping wine. "You two don't look too hungover," Tony laughed. "I have to confess that Laura and I had a hard time getting up this morning. We had Bloody Mary's and *Alka Seltzer* for breakfast."

They settled in to enjoy a leisurely lunch time, sampling some authentic Greek dishes: *Fava me Koukia* (mashed up fava beans), *Tomoto Gefthedes* (tomato fritters), Saganaki (fried cheese in filo pastry covered with honey), a huge Greek salad, and roasted lamb.

After a while, Laura looked at Evan. "Anyone for dessert?" she asked. The meal was her husband's treat. Tony loved to play host and Laura was a polished hostess, and they were both appreciative of Evan's hospitality.

"I couldn't eat another bite," Mattie answered with a grin. "I need to walk off some of these calories or the launch might sink on its way back to the yacht."

"I'll go with you," Laura offered. "I need to stretch my legs too. You guys please order desserts. Mattie and I will be back in a few minutes."

As Mattie and Laura got up from their chairs, Evan looked at Mattie and smiled knowingly. "I think the girls want to go back to the little dress shop in the courtyard. I saw Mattie eyeing the window goods before we came in here to eat."

"Guilty as charged," Mattie admitted. "It looked pretty intriguing"

Evan and Tony were content to relax, enjoying the food and wine. Mattie and Laura made their way to the doorway and headed towards the shop. Once inside, they took their time sorting through folded and hanging merchandise. Laura found a cotton blouse and skirt that she liked, and Mattie picked out a white dress with blue trim for herself. They were about to leave the shop, when a boisterous group of American tourists, wearing Celebrity Cruise baseball caps and tee shirts burst through the door, laughing, and joking with each other. Suddenly the small shop was filled to capacity.

Mattie could not help but overhear their conversations and thought she recognized one of the voices. *Was it possible?* She froze in place. Sky was standing two feet from her face with his arm draped around a very attractive brunette.

"Sky?" She managed to make her tongue work properly and to control her wobbly knees.

"Mattie?" His voice shook with emotion, and he dropped his arm from around his girlfriend's slim shoulders. Taking a step backwards, he gazed into her familiar face and stammered, "Mattie is that really you?"

RESOLUTION

CHAPTER 53

Ever since they broke up, Mattie had fantasized about the day when she would see Sky again. She plotted all kinds of scenarios in her mind, trying to think of clever and witty things to say when it happened. She wanted to look her best and show him that she had completely recovered from him. She expected to run into him sometime ...maybe when he was with Casey at a Dolphins football game, or at Cam and Mary's home in Tampa, or possibly in a restaurant in Miami or Ft. Lauderdale. But...she never in a million years imagined he would be standing just inches away from her in a tiny shop in Santorini, Greece.

Sky stared at her and looked as stunned to see her as she was to see him. He had always known this day would come. As a matter of fact, he had talked to his parents about trying to make it happen sooner rather than later, to clear the air between him and Mattie once and for all. Through the passage of time and some intense counselling, he had grieved and then accepted what had happened to them. He would always love Mattie but was receptive to finding another woman to love and to share his life. He thought Carolyn, his girlfriend, might be that woman.

Mattie looked at Sky and could see that he was happy. The strained look she'd seen on his face and the deep frown on his forehead when they had to end their affair had disappeared. He looked like he did the first day they met at the boat show. She had no idea what to say to him. The situation was awkward, and yet, she was so happy to see him looking so well and obviously connected to someone else. She wanted only good for him.

Unexpectedly, he swept her into his arms and hugged her tightly Then with a broad smile, he released her. "As Humphrey Bogart said in his famous line from the movie *Casablanca*, 'Of all the gin joints, in all the towns, in all the world, she walks into mine.' His gorgeous green eyes twinkled with merriment. He was truly happy to see her. His joy melted her heart.

Mattie could do nothing but laugh. The ice had finally been broken by Sky's trademark sense of humor. She knew everything would be all right between them now. Hearing his voice after such a long time seemed odd but was so comforting and welcome.

"Carolyn," he said proudly, reaching for his girlfriend's hand. "Meet my beautiful sister, Mattie."

CHAPTER 54

We can't talk here." Mattie glanced around the crowded store. "Can we go next door to the restaurant where my friends are waiting and speak privately for few minutes? Please. I have so much to say and to ask you about."

Sky nodded. "Lead the way." He took Carolyn's hand and approached his friends. "We'll meet you back on the ship for dinner." He left them with their curiosity and walked out of the store behind Mattie and Laura.

Laura had no idea what was going on, but she felt undercurrents between Mattie and her brother. "I'll take Carolyn to our table," she offered helpfully. "Why don't the two of you talk for a while and then join us?" She looked curiously at Mattie and then at Sky. The resemblance between them was uncanny. They could have been twins - not just brother and sister.

Mattie and Sky took seats at a small table by themselves. She looked over at Evan and could see by his quizzical expression that he was concerned and was not sure what was happening. He recognized Sky from pictures Mattie had shown him. He was worried about their unexpected reunion but gave Mattie the privacy she needed.

Evan attempted to make Carolyn feel welcome and ordered her a glass of wine. Carolyn did not seem stressed at all. She immediately began making conversation and told Tony that she was a huge fan of his television show and had purchased all of his books. Evan assumed she did not know about Mattie and Sky's previous affair. She seemed unconcerned about their reunion and private conversation.

Mattie studied Sky's handsome face. "Casey told me that you and your girlfriend were taking a cruise around the Greek Isles, but I never put two and two together, and certainly never thought there was a chance that we might run into each other here." She signaled the waiter and asked for a glass of water. What she really wanted was wine, but she refrained. "It's good to see you Sky. You look wonderful."

Sky smiled broadly. "You look fantastic, Mattie. As always, the prettiest woman in the place. Casey has kept me in the loop and told me you were dating some famous movie producer and that you are happy. Are you here with him?"

"Yes. His name is Evan Stone. I'm sure you'll recognize him. He was the client I was waiting for the day you and I met. He charted *Liquidity*, the mega yacht Casey wanted to see at the Ft. Lauderdale boat show… and here we are." She did not know what else or how much to say about her new relationship. He had said nothing about Carolyn.

Sky recognized Evan's name immediately and was impressed. He mentioned that he was a fan of *Miami Intrigues*. "Carolyn and I are on the cruise ship, *Celebrity Edge*. We're traveling with another physician friend and his girlfriend and have been having a ball. We are loving everything Greek. What about you?"

It was clear to Mattie that Sky was nervous. She tried to reassure him. "Sky, I'm happy you're having fun and that you have a new girlfriend, but please, enough small talk. I want to know about you. Are you really alright? I'm full of questions, like have you forgiven our father and my mother? Do you think we can ever be friends again, or will we have to avoid each other for the rest of our lives? There are so many important things we need to talk about."

"Whoa, slow down." He grinned. "I'm just a little skittish, I guess. Seeing you has been a shock…but a nice one." He took a sip of water and continued. "What happened between us really shook me up, and I've been through some pretty intensive therapy to sort it all out. I have definitely resolved my negative feeling about *our* parents. And yes, I have forgiven my father. If I want to be part of the family, and I really do, I had no choice. I'm happy with my work, and Carolyn and I are getting along great. As for you and I being friends …the answer is definitely yes. I want you in my life, Mattie. Do you think we can make this work?" He looked at her anxiously.

"I think so," she whispered with relief. "I want to. I've tried to forgive Cam and think that I have. But I cannot think of him as my father. Charles will always have that role for me. I had a harder time with my feelings for my mother. She and I were so close. I felt terribly betrayed and could not believe that she had lied to me for all those years. We've talked a lot since the truth came out and I understand what happened and that she believed she was doing the right thing. The two of us are in a good place now. But it took Charles knocking some sense into me and in a not too subtle way. Oh, and by the way, on a happy note, he and my mother are finally getting married."

"That's good news. Those two belong together." He glanced at his watch and suddenly stood up. "Sorry but I have to get Carolyn and go back to the ship. I don't want it to sail without us. When we all get home, let's have dinner together. I want you to get to know Carolyn. I think you'll like her. She, by the way, does not know anything about our romance and I don't see any reason to ever tell her or anyone. From now on its just Mattie and Sky, brother and sister, same father, different mothers. That's my story and I'm sticking to it." He grinned and squeezed Mattie's hand. "I'm so happy we ran into each other."

"Agreed." Mattie stood up also and gave him a warm hug. "I don't want to go through life having to make explanations about us. I'll walk you over to the table and introduce you to Evan and our friends the Grants, and then you and Carolyn can be off to the ship and the rest of your vacation. We will definitely plan to get together back in Ft. Lauderdale."

"Which one of us is going to tell Casey about this chance meeting?" Sky rolled his eyes in mock horror. "I can hear her now." He chuckled at the thought as he followed Mattie to the other table.

"I will," she said and shrugged her shoulders. "She's going to be so pissed off that she wasn't here to see us."

CHAPTER 55

Mattie and Evan hugged and said goodbye to Dr. Tony and Laura who were taking a ferry to Athens and then flying home from there. Mattie and Evan still had a few days left and had not decided where they would go next beyond the volcano and wine tasting excursion. They left that decision to Captain Llanos - as long as they were in Athens in three days to catch their flight to the States. They had all had a wonderful time being together and planned to meet again, maybe the following summer. Tony took Mattie aside and whispered that he wanted to charter another yacht over the Christmas holidays for his family as a surprise for his wife. He asked Mattie to arrange it.

"You are turning out to be one of my best clients," Mattie laughed. "I'll investigate the options and get in touch with you after I get back to Ft. Lauderdale." She kissed him goodbye. "Thanks for everything and especially for introducing me to Evan." Then she remembered. She could use her *Nautical Options* app from anywhere and look into cruises from the comfort of her bed onboard *Liquidity*.

Evan was quiet on the tender ride back to *Liquidity*. He gripped Mattie's hand tightly the whole way. It was as if he did not want to let go. He seemed pensive, maybe even sad. They hardly talked, and there was none of the usual casual banter back and forth between them. Evan was obviously troubled. She suspected it was about Sky. She sat patiently next to him, and watched the waves bounce off the boat and ripple back into the sea. She put her head on his shoulder, but he didn't speak until they were back on *Liquidity*.

When they were onboard, in the privacy of their bedroom, Evan took her in his arms and kissed Mattie passionately. He squeezed her so tightly that she had to push him away to catch her breath. The intensity and the look in his eyes alarmed her. She had never seen him like that.

"What's wrong?" she asked, taking his face tenderly in her hands and kissing him. "Tell me!"

Evan looked embarrassed but blurted out his fears. "Since the moment I saw you with Sky, I've been beside myself with worry. I have to know, Mattie. Did running into him stir up old feelings? Did being with Sky upset you? Did it make you fall out of love with me?"

"It was unsettling at first, I admit, and such a surprise," she answered honestly. "But I'm so glad that it happened. We had a little time to talk and assure each other that we are both okay now and looking forward to the future. We agreed that we would never mention to anyone that we had once been in love. There is no reason to dredge that up again. You know the truth, and that's important to me." She looked at Evan and saw the fear begin to fade from his eyes. "No one else has a need to know. I don't think Sky plans on telling Carolyn, but that could change sometime in the future, if they decide to marry. But that is up to him, and none of my concern."

"What else did you talk about?" He needed to know everything. He still felt threatened by her relationship with Sky. He could see that Mattie still had feelings for the man.

"We talked about forgiving our father and my mother, and how it had taken us both time and therapy to accomplish that. We also said we did not blame each other for what happened. How could we? Evan, I assure you, we have both accepted that what we had between us is over. We hope we can continue to see each other as siblings and rebuild a friendship again with no romantic feelings. It will not be difficult. When I saw him with Carolyn, I was actually relieved. It meant he had put our trauma in the past and moved on with someone new…Just as I have with you." She kissed him again, deeply. "Please, believe me, you have nothing to worry about. I'm all yours, completely.

"Come lie down with me then," he said hoarsely. "I need to hold you."

He was a strong man and pulled her to him, blowing his warm breath into her ears. She shivered with excitement, as she felt her knees begin to buckle. They tossed their clothes in a tangled mess on the floor, jumped into bed, and made love as never before. He sensuously ran his fingers all over her, stroking, kissing, and caressing her body. They teased each other until the tension was unbearable. Together they reached simultaneous climaxes in an explosion of passion she had not thought possible.

Mattie was exhausted and satiated. She lay blissfully in his arms. He squeezed her nipples until they stood out, firm and hard.

"I'll do it again," he smiled seductively. "But first I need to catch my breath. You have exhausted me, you little vamp." He was definitely out of breath. Rolling over to one side, he studied her body. "You are so breathtakingly beautiful. I think I'm going to find a part for you in one of my movies or television shows. I can't be selfish and keep you to myself. The whole world needs to see you."

"I'm not the actress type, but I'll happily perform for you," she said seductively and slid down his body caressing and kissing him everywhere.

As she lay with their bodies touching, she felt safe and at peace. Her life was full and all about the people in it now—Evan, Brenda, Charles, Casey, and even Cam, Mary, and Sky. It was no longer about what or who she'd lost, but about what she'd gained. She had loved Sky, but never with the ardor and passion she felt for Evan now. He had helped bring her out of her misery and shown her that she could enjoy life and love again. She began kissing him all over his body again until she saw signs of his arousal. "Our rest time is over." She mounted him.

After they climaxed a second time, Evan rolled over and propped himself up on one arm. He gazed at her with overwhelming love. "Let's take a shower, and then I think it's time we talked about our future."

CHAPTER 56

Mattie and Evan flew from Athens to New York together. They held hands for almost the entire trip and refused to sleep. They wanted to be awake together for as long as possible and dreaded their parting in only a few hours. After they landed and deplaned, they clung together in a long embrace in the terminal at JFK International Airport. Bystanders recognized Evan but thankfully left the couple alone to say their goodbyes. Mattie hated the idea of spending even one night apart, and Evan agreed. He reluctantly pulled apart from her when his flight to L.A. was announced. With a wink and a wave, he walked to his gate to catch his plane. Mattie watched him and waited until he was out of sight. Then she made her way to her own gate for the flight to Ft. Lauderdale.

Evan was a wise businessman as well as a producer. He understood that he could not return to Florida for at least two weeks. He had pressing issues to attend to in California that had arisen in the time he'd been away, and Mattie also expected to be inundated with a backlog of her own work. Charles had warned her that her entire desk was filled with paperwork and messages. Her trusted assistant , Ellie, delivered several weeks early. Baby and mother were fine, but the situation left Mattie frantic and in need of help. She had no assistant and Ned was not free to come work with her yet.

Ned had given his notice to Captain Llanos on the last day of Evan's charter, but he had a contractual agreement to stay on board *Liquidity* for one more ten-day charter to Ibiza, Spain. Then his replacement would take over, and he could fly back to Florida. Captain Llanos was sorry to see him leave but understood about his wanting to be near Casey. He left the door wide open for Ned to return anytime in the future, and possibly bring Casey if she was willing to be trained as a junior stew.

Mattie allowed herself two days to unpack, do laundry, grocery shop, pay bills, and recover from jet lag before she plunged into her job. When she arrived Monday morning at the office, bright and early to start her day, Charles and Brenda were already there waiting to welcome her with hot coffee and donuts. She was happy to see them both but took one look at her desk and panicked.

"I can hardly see the desktop through all the papers." She wailed. "I'd love to visit and fill you in on the trip, but I have to tackle this mess right away. Please forgive me. You'll have to leave me alone to get through it all. Frankly, I don't even see a place on my desk where I can put down the coffee cup."

"We understand," Charles said, "but it's great to have you back home. We both missed you terribly. This place isn't the same without you."

Mattie nodded politely and began to sort papers and messages into piles. One of the first things she needed to do was send Dr. Tony the paperwork for his surprise Christmas cruise. She had booked it through her app while at sea and had also spoken to Captain Llanos and asked if he would be available to captain the holiday charter. When he agreed, Mattie suggested a Caribbean cruise beginning in Saint Martin a few days before Christmas and ending in St Barts for a New Year's Eve celebration.

With everything in order, Mattie wrote a proposal and sent it to Tony's New York e-mail address for approval. She was sure he would be pleased with *Liquidity* and her crew. He already knew the boat well, as he had been on board the yacht and met Captain Llanos during their recent cruise to Mykonos and Santorini.

Most people in the boating community knew that St Barts was a special place to celebrate New Year's Eve. Mega yachts and dozens of smaller boats gathered in the harbor there to watch the festivities. The night sky above Fort Oscar lights up with magical fireworks. Superyachts moored in the harbor blast their fog horns in unison at midnight. Mattie knew that Tony and Laura would love it.

She worked twelve-hour days her first week back trying to catch up, but no matter how busy she kept herself, she missed Evan all the time. No matter what she was doing, he was constantly on her mind. They talked when they could, but the three-hour time difference was a problem. The two were miserable without each other, but both were responsible individuals and were busy doing the jobs they loved. It was obvious to each of them that their bi-coastal relationship had many challenges, and Mattie and Evan were not sure they could handle it. They promised each other that they would find a solution to the problem, even if one or the other had to change jobs and move.

CHAPTER 57

Casey spent the night with Mattie the following weekend. Evan was in Los Angeles, bogged down by problems on the set and an unexpected actors' strike. The two sisters caught up and ordered take out for dinner. Casey missed Ned and was counting the days until he returned, and so was Mattie but for different reasons. She needed Ned as her assistant in the worst way.

"Have you heard from Sky recently?" Mattie asked. "When we ran into each other in Santorini I didn't ask him when he was coming home."

"Yes. He got back earlier this week, but said he was too busy to get together until sometime next week. He plans to visit our parents next weekend, and he asked if I wanted to go with him."

"And?"

"And I said not this time. Ned will be back on Tuesday, and I want to spend time with him alone. He's really excited about working with you at Lux. I'm so glad Charles agreed to hire him."

"I am too, but you understand that he will need to put in a lot of hours in the beginning. The charter business is not a nine to five job, and his weekends will often have to be spent with clients or meeting with captains and crews and checking out other yachts. I'm going to expect him to be knowledgeable about our yacht inventory and to be available when I need him. The training Charles demands takes time and effort. He won't always be available when you want to see him."

"I know all that," she conceded and grinned impishly. "But his nights will be free."

"At least some of them," Mattie smiled at her sister's naivety and hoped things worked out with Ned. They were a cute couple, but Casey was still so young, and she had a lot of growing up to do.

"By the way, are you free tomorrow afternoon?"

"I suppose I could be. Why?" What was Casey up to this time, Mattie wondered.

"Dad finally is getting me a car. I won't have to depend on Sky to get around anymore. Isn't that super? Because I'm a sophomore, I'm allowed to keep a car on campus now. Dad and Mom are coming here tomorrow morning. Mom's driving their car and Dad will follow her in my new one. They say it's really nice…a blue Nissan. I'm so excited. They want to have lunch and then they'll head back to Tampa. I think it would be great if you'd come too. I know it would make them happy. What do you say?"

Mattie was caught off guard. She'd just told Casey that she was free, so coming up with an excuse now would look bad. And she did want to spend time with Cam and Mary and maybe having Casey along as a buffer was a good idea. "I guess I could, if you think your parents would be okay about my crashing their party," she said hesitantly. "Will Sky be there? It's not that I don't want to see him, but I'd rather see Cam and Mary first, before we have a whole freaking family reunion."

"I get it but remember, they are *your* parents now too, so of course they'll want to see you. I'll text them that you'd like to come along if that makes you feel better. And you did say that you and Sky got along great in Santorini. And that you both agreed to have dinner with each other and maybe with me too sometime soon."

"Yes, that's the plan. Don't worry. He's happy for me and Evan, and I'm pleased for him and Carolyn. We're good, Casey really. Our past is just that…the past."

CHAPTER 58

Mattie and Casey left for the restaurant to meet Cam and Mary. Casey was eager to see and drive her new car. She waited anxiously in the parking lot with Mattie, checking her watch repeatedly until she saw her family's SUV pull into the lot's entranceway with Mary behind the wheel. A few seconds later, a brand-new midnight blue Nissan sedan followed. Cam parked it and hopped out of the driver's seat. Casey ran to meet him and jumped into the car. "Dad, it's gorgeous," she raved, happily, running her fingers over the beige leather steering wheel and checking out the dashboard displays.

Cam handed her the keys and went around to the passenger side. "How about you drive us around the block a few times to get a feel for the car. You should set the side mirrors for safety." He handed her the manual. "You'll need to read up on everything, but for now, as long as you're comfortable, you can take her back to campus. If there is something you can't understand, call Sky. He knows everything about cars."

Cam showed Casey where the ignition button was, and Casey slowly backed out of the parking space heading to the highway.

Mary walked up to Mattie and gave her a quick hug. "Hi there. I guess it's just you and me for a while until Cam feels certain Casey understands how to control the car. He is very protective of her. How about you and I go get a table and order something cold to drink?"

"Sound good." Mattie said. "It's so nice of you to give Casey a car. She's beyond thrilled."

"We did it for selfish reasons," Mary admitted after she ordered two iced teas from the waitress and explained that they were waiting for two more guests. "We thought if Casey didn't have to ask Sky for his car all the time, she might drive over to Tampa and visit us more often. As it is now, she's dependent on his schedule, and he's so busy at work and dating Carolyn. Oh," she suddenly blushed." I hope I didn't say anything wrong. You know about Carolyn, don't you?"

"Yes, and you can mention Sky anytime to me. He's your son. I understand completely and when we ran into each other in Santorini, I met Carolyn. She's lovely. Sky and I had a good talk, and everything is fine between us. With the help of therapy, we have both put the past behind us and are happily in new relationships. It's a wonderful thing. You and Cam can stop worrying about us."

Mattie did not have time to say anything more because Casey and Cam arrived at the table. Casey was exuberant. She loved her car and could not wait to drive to Coral Gables and show it off to her friends. And when Ned came to town Tuesday, she planned to pick him up at the airport in it. She was thrilled!

"Sorry Mattie," Cam said apologetically. "This lunch was also to hear about your trip, but I had to be certain Casey could handle the car. Now, it's time to concentrate on you. Let's order and then you can tell us all about your cruise and about running into Sky." He took a long gulp of iced tea and looked at Mattie fondly. "Casey told us you're dating a famous movie producer. Mary and I want to hear *all* about him. My inquisitive wife was so curious that she went out and bought a copy of the *National Enquirer* and *Star Magazine* to see if she could find any articles about him. She found a picture of you with Evan Stone walking through a casino in Cannes. You two make quite an attractive couple."

Mattie smiled. "Yes, the paparazzi found me interesting," she laughed. "But Evan was pretty good at dodging them." She was surprisingly relaxed around Cam and Mary and loved seeing Casey so happy. What a change from her original, negative feelings about the Cooper family when they first met. All four of them ordered gazpacho soup, sandwiches, or salads. They chatted comfortably and finished the meal with generous slices of Key Lime Pie for dessert. Finally, Cam looked at his watch. "I hate to break up this wonderful afternoon, but Mary and I have a long drive home and I'd like to get there before dark. I guess we should leave soon, and Casey you need to get to campus and find your parking spot and register your car. I'd prefer you did that in the day light."

The lunch had been an easy ice breaker, and Mattie was glad she had agreed to come. Every Cooper family get together in the future would be easier, and easier and she was looking forward to the next one. She promised Cam that she would bring Evan to meet them when she could arrange it, explaining the problems of their busy lives and that they were trying to decide how to manage their bi-coastal relationship.

"Evan will be in Miami for a few weeks soon to continue filming new episodes of *Miami Intrigues* and we'll make some decisions then. Maybe we could squeeze in time for a visit then, but if not, soon. Thanks for a wonderful afternoon." Mattie stood up and hugged Cam, Mary, and Casey. "You all drive carefully and stay in touch."

After Mattie and Casey left, Cam turned to his wife. "I think that went well. Mattie could not have been warmer, and I love how well she and Casey get along. I hope she will be as relaxed around Sky when we all get together."

"So do I honey. But I believe she will. Everything is going to work out for all of us. I thank God for bringing Mattie into our lives, and now you have another daughter. We have a lot to be thankful for."

"I agree, but He could have done it in a less complicated way." Cam joked as he signed the check and tipped the waitress. "Let's go home, Mary."

CHAPTER 59

Sky and Carolyn had such a good time on their cruise and were so compatible that they decided to find an apartment and move in together. They enjoyed each other's company immensely and had so many common hobbies - tennis, boating, and the love of traveling. They both were voracious readers and loved watching the same Netflix and Hulu television series. They could spend a whole weekend bingeing on the programs, interrupted only if Sky got an emergency call from a patient. If that happened, Carolyn pushed the pause button on the remote, and they went into his office together or to the hospital together. She read in the waiting room while he tended to his patent. They loved being together and shared a keen interest in medicine, experimental and holistic treatments, and new protocols. They were as happy reading and discussing articles from *The New England Journal of Medicine* as they were the latest John Grisham thriller.

Casey enjoyed being with Sky and Carolyn too. They always suggested doing something different and fun together. Over the late summer weeks, they took Casey with them to the Everglades for an airboat ride. They went to the Miccosukee Indian reservation to watch alligator wrestling, and view exhibits showcasing the tribe's early life adapting to conditions in the Everglades. They watched demonstrations of doll making, beadwork, and basket weaving. Sky and Carolyn were active and spontaneous people and Casey loved being with them. Ned joined them when he could, which due to his busy schedule working with Mattie, was not often.

Casey, behind the wheel of her new car, drove them to the Keys where they bone fished, water skied, kayaked, and paddle boarded. They drove to the tip of Key West, the most southern spot in the United States, and strolled around Duval Street to watch the sunset over Mallory Square. Ned went with them several times to the Keys, and he and Casey continued to fall more and more in love. Sky got a kick out of watching them, but he gave Casey stern brotherly advice about safe sex and the use of condoms. Casey listened and took his advice to heart. No unwanted babies for her. She was growing up.

Mattie joined them once in a while when their adventures were closer to home. She was still super busy at work and all her free time was spent training Ned and preparing and organizing for the next Ft. Lauderdale boat show at the end of October. Remembering the show two years ago, she had already arranged for Ned to take Sky, Carolyn, and Casey on several mega yachts before the show officially opened as a special surprise. It was to be Casey's birthday gift this year from herself, not Sky. There was to be a celebratory cake onboard *Liquidity*, the last stop on the tour.

Ned and Mattie worked well together, and Mattie gave him two of her recent clients to handle at the boat show. He was also going to man the Lux booth for several shifts and hoped to make his own connections there. He thoroughly enjoyed working with clients and, like Mattie, loved Options and was matching the right yacht and best crew with the customer. He had trained himself to use Nautical Options and was going to demonstrate the app in several power point presentations during the show. He was a quick learner and surprisingly articulate with customers. He represented Lux Charters well.

Charles was pleased with Mattie's arrangement and thought Ned had real promise. He had been afraid that Ned would miss being part of a crew and day-to-day life at sea, but he seemed to have settled in nicely. He claimed that he did not regret his decision to leave Captain Llanos and *Liquidity* for a land job. And he was making more money than he had ever thought possible. He claimed that he had never been happier, and he took a genuine interest in the daily operations of the company.

Charles was busy with his wedding plans and helping Brenda arrange her move from her little townhouse to his spacious home. Before she moved in, he gave her carte blanche and an unlimited budget to make any changes she wanted to his house. He wanted his place to become her home with her own personal touches. She supervised the painting of a few rooms, bought a new master bedroom set, lovely bamboo sheets, and expensive plush towels. She picked out wallpaper for the powder rooms. Charles was pleased with the results and thought everything she suggested was both an improvement and beautiful. He was so in love with her that Brenda could have painted everything purple with red stripes, and he would probably have been wildly enthusiastic about it. He was truly in love and not at all ashamed to show it.

Brenda was anxious to become Mrs. Charles Cord. She had been by herself for so many years and yearned to be a part of a happily married couple. She and Charles decided to marry on the first Saturday in October in the back yard by the pool with only family and a few close friends. They both thought they were too old for a big fussy affair. They wanted a simple ceremony with champagne, caviar, and cake...and no presents.

They had everything they wanted. Mattie had agreed to stand up for her mother, and Charles' closest friend and his golf partner, Len, would be his best man. The couple planned to take a ten-day honeymoon to France after the boat show, returning in time to host a big Thanksgiving dinner… the first in Brenda's new home.

For turkey day, they had already invited Mattie and Evan, Cam and Mary, Sky and Carolyn, and Casey and Ned. Charles had included two of his single buddies from the yacht club and Len, his best man. All had eagerly accepted the invitation. Brenda invited her best girlfriend from work and Mattie's best friend, Linda and her husband, Ted. It was going to be an interesting and lively group, but that was what Thanksgiving was all about…good friends, family, and food. The Cooper family had accepted the invitation but insisted Mary be permitted to bring a pasta side dish and the pies. Brenda, thankful for the help, agreed.

Mattie had promised that Evan would attend. He had not been able to meet any of Mattie's family, as his original two-weeks in L.A. after their Mediterranean cruise turned into two months. Evan apologized profusely to Mattie and stated sadly that unless things changed drastically, he did not think there was any way he could leave California. He had never been so busy, constantly struggling to handle one crisis after another. He put the production of *Miami Intrigues* on hold. His writers, the Hurds and the Peters, continued producing scripts in anticipation that the filming would resume by the year's end. But no one knew exactly when. It was a tense and unsettling time.

Mattie flew out to the west coast every two weeks to visit Evan for a few days, but Evan was not himself. He was worried, distracted, and could not spend much time with her. He was always running from one problem to another, rushing at a frenetic pace. Mattie was worried about him. Evan was exhausted and many nights he was too tired to sleep, tossing and turning in bed until dawn. He was over-worked and exhausted. The Hollywood film community was in complete turmoil with no resolution in sight. It was a terrible time and tempers flared.

CHAPTER 60

The wedding of Brenda and Charles was understated, and romantic. Brenda looked beautiful in a pale pink, floor-length gown, and Charles wore a suit with a matching pink shirt and handkerchief. They made a handsome couple and were about to cut their cake when Mattie's phone vibrated. She had silenced it during the ceremony. Agitated at the interruption, she reached for it and checked the caller I.D. It was a California area code but an unfamiliar number. She assumed it was another robot call and put the phone back in her pocket. She watched the cake cutting ceremony with Brenda feeding a bite of red velvet cake to Charles and visa versa. It was not until all the guests had had their cake and made toasts to the bride and groom that she remembered to check her phone again. There were three messages from the same unknown California number.

Mattie moved away from the group and pushed the redial button on her cell. Her call was immediately answered by a woman's unfamiliar but agitated voice. "Mattie? Is this Mattie Cartwright?"

"Yes," Mattie answered, becoming nervous. "What is this about? Who are you and how may I help you?"

"My name is Lauren Tate. We haven't met before, but I am one of the assistants at Mr. Stone's production company. Mr. Stone fell ill earlier today. I was with him at the time. He broke out in a sweat, had chest pains that he described as feeling like an elephant was sitting on top of him and he became very pale. I was frightened, and so was he. I called 911 and they sent an ambulance and took Mr. Stone to Cedars Sinai. I rode with him, and he gave me your number and asked that I call you."

"Oh my God. Is he all right?" Mattie started to tremble. "Please, is he okay?"

"I'm afraid we don't know yet. The doctors are running a lot of tests, EKGs, blood work and the like. I know Mr. Stones is quite concerned. He wants you to come to L.A. right away."

"Of course. I'll catch the first plane out and come directly to the hospital. Can I talk to Evan?"

"Not at the moment. He's surrounded by doctors and monitoring equipment. I'll keep you informed by text, but please get here quickly. He's very anxious, and I think you're being here will have a calming effect on him."

"Okay. Thanks for calling. Please tell him I love him, and I'm on my way."

Mattie went over to Charles and quickly explained the situation. "Don't tell Mom till all the guests have left. I don't want to ruin her wedding day. I'm going right to the airport now and I'll call you when I know something."

"Don't you need to pack a bag or something? Do you need money?"

"No, I'll be fine. I keep clothes at Evan's house. Please ask Mom to say a prayer for him." She kissed Charles quickly. "Welcome to the family."

Smiling bleakly, she ran for the front door.

CHAPTER 61

There was one nonstop flight to L.A. from Ft. Lauderdale, and it had already left by the time Mattie arrived at the airport. The airline staff advised her that she could catch a plane to Dallas in an hour and change to a connecting flight to L.A. arriving at 4:30 p.m. California time, or she could drive to Miami and fly on a nonstop flight from there later in the day that would land in L.A. at 8:00 p.m. Mattie was too upset to drive to Miami, so she booked herself on the flight to Dallas and went to the gate to wait.

She had an hour to kill before boarding so she called Ned and filled him in on everything that she knew about Evan's condition and asked him to take over her clients and monitor her business calls until she returned. She had no idea when that would be. She planned to stay in California indefinitely until Evan was out of the woods and recovering from whatever was happening to him.

Not knowing what else to do, she called her family physician. "My boyfriend, Evan has been taken by ambulance to a hospital in L.A.," she began without preamble when he answered the phone. "I have no idea what's wrong. I'm on my way to the hospital there now." She told him exactly what Lauren Tate had told her. "What can it be? Is he having a heart attack or a stroke?"

"I can't tell from that description Mattie, but I doubt he's having a stroke. The symptoms are very different. However, he might have suffered a mild heart attack or some kind of cardiac event. The hospital tests will give you the answers. There's nothing you can do at the moment except go out there and be supportive. From my experience in treating cardiac patients, they are always scared and the best thing you can do is to reassure them."

"I'll do my best," she said in a trembling voice. "Thanks for listening."

"No problem. I wish I could be of more help. Once you know something specific, call me back and I'll try to let you know what to expect. In the meantime, take care of yourself. We can't have you falling apart. Evan will need your strength. And Mattie, he's damn lucky to have you. Hang in there."

"I will, thanks. They're calling for me to board. Bye."

Many hours later, after two long flights, she landed at LAX and grabbed a taxi to Cedars Sinai Hospital. Running into the lobby of the hospital, she went immediately to the information desk. "I'm looking for Evan Stone," she blurted out. "I think he's had a heart attack so he's probably on the cardiac floor."

"Excuse me, Mattie?" a short, middle-aged woman approached her. "I'm Lauren Tate. I've been waiting for you."

"How's Evan?" Mattie asked anxiously ignoring the introduction.

"He's going to be fine," the assistant assured her. "The doctors have determined that he did not have a heart attack, but they found a blockage in a major coronary artery. He's in the Cath Lab now undergoing an angioplasty procedure."

"What's that?" Mattie had only minimal medical knowledge. "Is it serious?"

"As I understand it, it's when the doctor threads a tube called a catheter through Evan's coronary artery and inserts dye. When he finds the blockage, he will inflate a balloon to open the blocked vessel and put in a stent…it's kind of like a bridge, to keep the artery open. Then Evan will have to stay in the hospital for 24 – 48 hours so he can be monitored, and he'll be put on a regime of medicines. According to his doctors, if everything goes as expected, his prognosis is very good. He will be fully awake after the procedure, and you can be with him. But remember, I am giving you secondhand information. You need to talk to his physicians yourself."

"Oh, that's wonderful news." Mattie started to sob with relief. "Thank you so much, Lauren. I hope I haven't been too rude. I've been so worried and frightened."

"I can imagine." She said sympathetically. "He gave our whole staff quite a fright. We have noticed how worn down and stressed he's been with all of the studio problems and the damn actor's strike. It was just too much for him to handle, I guess. I hope you can convince him to take a step back and take care of himself. Hopefully, this incident has scared some sense into him. He's been working night and day, and obviously it's taken its toll on his health."

"I'll do my best," Mattie promised. "Can we go somewhere to be near Evan?"

"Yes, there's a waiting room right off the Cath Lab. Let's go there."

Lauren led her to the room with numerous ugly green upholstered armchairs and three-year-old magazines lined up on a big square table. Soon a young doctor in blue scrubs came to speak with hem.

"Mr. Stone came through the procedure well. He's being taken to a private room on the cardiac floor where he will be monitored. You may go there now," he said cheerfully. "He's been asking for Mattie Cartwright."

"That's me." Mattie stood up and followed the doctor's directions to Evan's room.

Lauren went with her but stopped outside the doorway. "I'll give you two some privacy," she smiled. "Mr. Stone needs time with you alone, Mattie, and he knows how to reach me if he needs anything. I'll see you both in the morning."

"Thank you again," Mattie said gratefully.

She pulled out her compact and applied fresh lipstick and ran a brush through her hair. She did not want Evan to see her looking so disheveled and worried. Taking a deep breath and putting on a fake smile, she pushed open the door and walked into his room.

CHAPTER 62

Evan was lying on the bed surrounded by beeping machines with an IV dripping into his arm. His eyes were closed, and his complexion was pale. He was so still that Mattie wasn't sure if he was awake or asleep. She walked up to him quietly and whispered, "Hello, darling, it's Mattie. I'm here."

He opened his eyes at the sound of her sweet voice and smiled weakly. "Hi, honey."

"You gave us all quite a scare, but the doctors say you're going to be fine. How are you feeling?" She bent over him and tenderly took his hand in hers. Stroking it gently, she noticed the bandages on his arm and the EKG leads attached to his chest.

"I feel very tired," he answered in a soft voice. "But I don't feel any symptoms now...no chest pressure or nausea...no sweats. The doctors said the procedure went perfectly and the stent they put in me is working as it should."

Mattie could see the simple effort of speaking with her was taking its toll on him. "But I'm so thankful to be alive. I really thought my time was up. And, you know, honestly, it wasn't the fear of death that bothered me so much, but the thought of never seeing you again. Oh Mattie,

I love you so much. Being apart so much because of our businesses has been crazy. We have to rethink this lifestyle of ours. This separation could literally have killed me."

"Hush," she kissed him tenderly on his forehead. "Don't waste your energy talking now. I'm not going anywhere, and we have all the time in the world to make any changes that we need to. Just rest darling. Please try to sleep. I'll be right here by your side."

She pulled up a lounge chair as close to the bed as possible and took a seat, barely daring to breathe. She was flooded with loving emotions and tears leaked unrestricted from her eyes. As she watched him sleep, she was acutely aware that she could have lost him today…could have arrived after it was too late. Life was so fragile. She kept her eyes focused on the machine behind him that was measuring his heart rate and blood pressure. It was frightening and reassuring at the same time.

Eventually she fell into a troubled sleep and awoke a few minutes later when a nurse came into the room to check on Evan and give him his meds.

"Dinner will be coming around in a while," the nurse said, cheerfully looking at Evan. "We want you to sit up and begin to get nutrition back into your body."

"I'm not hungry," Evan answered, "but I'll try to eat. Do I have any dietary restrictions?"

"The doctors will be doing their rounds in the morning and will go over everything with you then. But you will be on a low cholesterol diet and a nutritionist will work with you to create a dietary plan. In the meantime, try to relax and rest. Your body has had a shock today and you need to give it time to reboot."

"Like a computer?" he joked. "Do I need the *Geek Squad*?" At least he had not lost his sense of humor. "Mattie, you've had a long day too."

He suddenly was aware that she was still in her maid of honor dress, and that his health scare might have ruined the wedding of Brenda and Charles. "I'm so sorry that this happened, and especially when it did. I hope Lauren's call to you did not disrupt the wedding. Were Brenda and Charles able to get married?"

"Yes, they are very much married, and the ceremony was beautiful. They are very happy, and I only missed the bouquet toss," she smiled. "Mom and Charles send their best wishes to you for a speedy recovery."

He looked at her again thoughtfully. "Why don't you go to the house? Take a shower and change your clothes. You'll feel much better. Poor thing, you've been in those clothes for too many hours."

"No," she said firmly. "I'm not leaving. Maybe someone could bring me a change of clothing and I'll shower here. I'm not leaving this hospital until I take you home."

Evan began looking around the room. "Where's my cell?" he asked the nurse. "I need to make a call."

The nurse went to the closet and brought him a clear plastic bag. "Your phone, wallet, and watch are in here." She handed the bag to him. He dialed Barney, his houseman, giving orders for him to bring his pajamas, a robe, and a change of clothes to the hospital. Then he handed the phone to Mattie. She listed the things she needed, and Barney promised to be there with everything within the hour.

The nurse left them alone, but it felt like every few minutes someone came into the room to take Evan's blood pressure, check his temperature or to collect a blood sample. Mattie wanted to complain that Evan needed his rest, but she knew that he was receiving excellent care. He finally fell back asleep, but Mattie was agitated. She was trying to think how they could resolve their bi-coastal lifestyle. It obviously wasn't working. She wondered if she should give up working at Lux and move to L.A. *or* could Evan relocate his production company permanently to Miami? All she knew for certain was that she would not be separated from him again. He was her world now. There were so many things to discuss and decide, but it all had to wait until he was better. She moved closer to his bedside and reassured herself that he was sleeping peacefully. Then she crept out of the room silently and stood in the hallway to call her mother and Charles.

"Mom," she began. "Evan had a blocked coronary artery and the doctors put in a stent. He'll be in the hospital for a day or two, and then he'll be recuperating at home. I'm going to stay with him here, so please tell Charles not to expect me back at work anytime soon. I know this is very inconvenient with the boat show coming up and the launching of *Nautical Options,* but I simply can't leave him."

"I understand, dear. Don't worry about anything on this end. Just take care of yourself and Evan." Brenda motioned to Charles who was waiting anxiously to hear Mattie's news. She put her phone on speaker mode and Mattie explained the situation again to Charles. He assured her that he could handle the boat show and the launch of her app and not to worry. Ned was a big help, and they could manage without her for as long as needed. Mattie hung up gratefully and returned to Evan's room to wait for Barney and their clean clothes.

It had been a long and exhausting day that could have ended so differently. She said a silent prayer of thanks to God for sparing Evan's life. Then she sat back in the chair to watch Evan sleep.

CHAPTER 63

The nurses brought a cot into Evan's room and Mattie spent the night restlessly napping beside him, checking his breathing every few hours to make sure he was still alive. She knew she was being silly, but she could not help herself. She was terrified that he might die in his sleep.

In the morning, a constant stream of doctors and nurses paraded through Evan's room – two physical therapists, a nutritionist, his own physician, and several cardiologists. Together they presented Evan with a protocol he was to follow diligently. It involved an exercise regimen, a strict diet, a schedule of medicines, and routine doctors' visits.

Evan asked all the questions he could think of: when could he have sex? when could he return to work? Could he drink alcohol and if so, how much and how often? Mattie took careful notes and wrote down all of the doctors' instructions and their phone numbers in case of an emergency. They spent that day in the hospital while Evan underwent another round of tests and a sonogram of his heart. He was released the next afternoon, and Barney drove them to Evan's Brentwood home where he was to begin his rehabilitation and make some important life decisions. They were both so happy to be out of the hospital and grateful for Evan's second chance at a healthy life.

Back in Ft. Lauderdale, Charles and Brenda settled comfortably into their new life together as husband and wife. They decided to postpone their European honeymoon until the spring because of Mattie's sudden absence from Lux Charters. Charles was busier than ever, but he did not mind. He had Brenda to come home to each night.

Back in L.A., Mattie settled Evan comfortably on the sofa in his bedroom and left the television remote by his side. She left the room to arrange for dinner in bed and to call her mother and Charles.

"There is no way that I can be back in time to work the boat show," she said in a grim voice. "I know that this will be a burden on everyone, but I have no choice."

"It's okay," Charles insisted. "I've already spoken to Linda and Ned. Between the three of us we will take care of your clients. Ned has your notes about which yachts to show which clients, and he can always talk to you by phone if he has any questions. He's going to present your *Nautical Options* app in several slide show presentations on the first and last day of the show, so don't worry. It will get great exposure. We have everything covered. You just take care of yourself and Evan."

Mattie apologized again. She knew the bind she was putting Charles and Lux Charters in, but Evan's health came first. She was fixated on getting him well. It was her main priority now.

Secretly, Charles suspected that Mattie had already chosen being with Evan over her job at Lux Charters. He did not blame her and sincerely wanted for her to be happy. He tried to have a positive attitude; however, he had to make contingency plans. Besides taking their honeymoon trip, he and Brenda had planned to travel extensively and enjoy their lives on different continents. Now with Mattie probably going to be out of the office, he needed to find someone to run Lux in his absence. He was not willing to put his life with Brenda on hold. They had wasted too many years already. He needed a succession plan.

Ned was proving to be remarkably resourceful, and his clients loved him, but he still lacked enough experience to even be considered as a candidate to take over running the company. Charles needed to find a new temporary CEO. That meant he was going to have to raid his competition and bring in someone seasoned from another chartering company. He began making phone calls to his contacts in Miami, Palm Beach, Delray, and the Keys.

The new person had to be familiar with Florida mega yachts and their crews. The individual had to be ready to step into the new job immediately, if Mattie decided to say in California permanently or simply retire to be with Evan. Ned had been thrilled when Charles suggested that in a few years he may be ready to take on an executive position in the company, but it was way too soon now. Additionally, the interim CEO had to understand that the job was not permanent. Charles needed to hire someone who would be happy to relinquish the position when a new CEO was appointed. An older candidate desiring to retire in a few years would be a perfect choice.

Ned was working excruciatingly long hours. Casey was trying to be understanding. Nonetheless, she missed their times together and she was bored simply waiting around for when he was free. She decided the best way to be with him was to help him out at Lux. Every day after her classes, she drove from Coral Gables to Ft. Lauderdale and pitched in with the filing, answering the phones, and anything else she could do to be helpful. Charles was amused by her tenacity and watched them from his office. He could not help but smile. They reminded him of himself and Mattie so many years ago, when he first started to mentor her. He had a good feeling about Casey and Ned and thought that, in time, they might be the perfect candidates to run the business, but not yet. For now, he needed to put a new CEO in place. He had set up a list of candidates to interview, beginning the week after the boat show and was hoping for the best.

CHAPTER 64

Mattie and Evan spent the next few days carefully following his doctor's orders, relaxing by his pool, and discussing the pros and cons of where to live. Mattie was adamant that wherever it was, their new home would have a gym specifically designed for his exercise protocol: a treadmill, an elliptical machine, and a Peloton bicycle. And the property must have a heated pool so he could swim laps every day. She planned to also work out on her yoga mat, and with free weights, and stability balls. They were both into healthy living now and had temporarily stopped drinking except for one glass of wine with dinner.

After hours of discussion, they finally arrived at a decision. Evan would put his Brentwood home on the market as soon as possible, and they would move to the Miami area. There they would buy a new home with deep water docking space for their own yacht. No more chartering. Evan wanted his own boat with a permanent captain and crew.

Evan gave Mattie a budget of forty million dollars to purchase and furnish a boat of her choice. She was elated about the prospect and planned to outfit their boat for their new lifestyle with their personal good health in mind. They would continue to entertain friends and family lavishly onboard and would offer their guests the same luxuries as a charter provided, but with health-conscious options for meals and exercise programs. They did not want Evan's cardiac incident to control their lives, but they wanted to make sensible choices and take care of themselves, their families, and friends.

Evan had long conversations and strategy sessions with his staff who visited the house regularly, and he made plans to relocate his production company to Miami. He was very generous with his employees and offered substantial raises and relocation expenses to any who were willing to follow him to Florida. He promised to give sizable severance pay and excellent references to those wishing to remain in L.A.

He and Mattie were excited about the prospect of starting over in a new town with *Miami Intrigues* as the cornerstone of his company. Evan had outlined a script for a comedy that he wanted to pitch to Netflix. His writers had come up with two other workable ideas for new television series to be shot in the Florida Keys. When asked, the Hurds and the Peters jumped at the chance to move to Miami and were looking forward to the tax benefits of living in Florida. Everything was falling into place nicely. Evan was getting stronger by the day; his color had returned, and he felt as healthy as ever. Mattie was anxious to get back to her mother and Charles and to begin house and yacht hunting. Their future was looking bright, but there were so many details to attend to before they could leave L.A.

CHAPTER 65

Mattie called Charles every day during the boat show to check in with him and to keep a written tally of the charters that had been successfully negotiated. She was happy to be by Evan's side in California and help him with arranging the move to Miami, but she missed the excitement which the boat show always generated. Ned had done stellar work as her assistant and earned several impressive commissions for himself. She was very thankful and proud of him. Lux Charters as a whole had a profitable showing but not as lucrative as the previous year when Mattie had been there.

Ned had kept his promise to take Sky, Casey, and Carolyn on board several mega yachts before the show officially opened. Casey was proud to be by his side and could not help but mischievously point out to Carolyn and Sky the hot tub on *Liquidity* where she and Ned first began to fall for each other.

In L.A., the housing market was vibrant, and Evan's home sold within two weeks for over the asking price. Mattie and Evan were thrilled but had hoped for more time to organize their transition to Florida. The new buyers were eager to move in and asked for a thirty-day possession.

Mattie worked with Evan's household staff to separate furniture and personal things to be donated to charity or put in storage until she and Evan found a new home and knew what they would want to take to Miami. With Lauren's help, Mattie supervised everything. By mid-November, the movers had come and gone, and the house was ready for the new owners.

Mattie and Evan moved to a bungalow in the Beverly Hills Hotel for a few days while he took care of the paperwork and final details of transferring his production company to Florida. He sat for hours at a large conference table with four company attorneys and signed document after document until his hand cramped from the effort. After the last paper was signed and notarized, he went to the office for the last time and personally said goodbye and thank you to all the employees who were staying in L.A. Most had already found other jobs in the industry. Evan choked up, and Mattie tried not to cry. It was a sentimental departure. The end of an important time and the beginning of another.

Holding hands and trying to keep their emotions in check, they left the building and walked slowly to Evan's car. The city of Miami, a new production company, a new home, a new yacht, and a new life together lay ahead...only a plane ride away.

CHAPTER 66

Before she checked out of the hotel, Mattie called her mother. "Is the invitation for Thanksgiving dinner still on the table?" she asked hopefully.

"Of course," Brenda answered happily. "Does this mean we can expect you and Evan? I had no idea you could wrap things up that quickly in California."

"Neither did we, but yes, Mom. Everything's done at this end, and we'll be flying back to Ft Lauderdale on the red eye this evening. We're flying first class, so the seats make into beds. Otherwise, we'd wait for another flight. But this way, we'll be well rested when we arrive."

"That's wonderful news, honey. Do you want to stay here with Charles and me, or will you camp out at your condo?"

"My place until we find a house. I'll tell you all about everything when we see you. There is so much to tell you and Charles, and I have to figure some things out about Lux Charters going forward. Can the four of us have dinner tomorrow night?"

"Of course, be here at 7:00. Charles and I cannot wait to see you and hear all about your plans. You've been pretty mysterious about them."

"I know. I'm sorry. We've had so much to do with selling the house and closing his production company here and starting a new one in Miami. And Evan's been working with me in the evenings on ideas for expanding *Nautical Options* to service other businesses, even television and film entities We have been so busy that I haven't had a minute to fill you in. We will tomorrow. I promise."

"By the way," Brenda said cautiously before hanging up. "We didn't know if you'd be here for Thanksgiving, and we didn't want to be by ourselves, so we've already invited quite an eclectic crowd. The more the merrier. Charles has invited a few friends and so have I. In addition, the whole Cooper family is coming...Cam, Mary, Casey & Ned. You know Casey goes nowhere without him nowadays. They are like Siamese twins, joined at the hip. It's very sweet, and Charles has come to rely on Ned a great deal. He has a good head on his shoulder. And of course, Sky and his girlfriend, Carolyn, will be here. I hope that doesn't upset you."

"Not in the least. I'll be happy to see them all. I am so thrilled with my life with Evan, and I want to introduce him to everyone." She smiled from ear to ear because she really meant it. She had never been as happy and wanted the world to know it. The painful hurts and secrets of the past were definitely behind her. She said goodbye to Brenda and tucked her phone back into her purse.

Evan came up to her wearing a mischievous smile. "We have several hours to kill before we have to be at LAX for our flight back East. Let's leave the bags here at the hotel and take one last leisurely stroll around Rodeo Drive."

"That's a great idea. It's gorgeous out and we can use the exercise before the long plane ride."

Evan arranged for a limo and slipped the driver a piece of paper with an address written on it. "Please drop us there," he said smiling slyly.

"What are we doing here?" Mattie asked innocently, when the limo stopped curbside in front of the Harry Winston Jeweler building with its distinctive ornate, double glass doors.

"Well," he smiled wistfully. "I was hoping we'd arrive in Florida with a ring on your finger and we could announce our engagement at Thanksgiving in front of your whole family and friends. What do you think? Is that too pushy? I know this is not the most romantic proposal, in the back seat of a limo. I could try to kneel here on the car floor, but it'll be a tight fit. I'm not sure there's room but..."

"But nothing," she grinned and threw herself into his arms. "Yes! Yes! Yes! I thought you'd never ask. Yes, I will marry you, and the sooner the better."

CHAPTER 67

From the moment the plane from L.A. landed in Ft. Lauderdale, Mattie and Evan's lives were a whirlwind of activity. They celebrated "turkey day" with Charles, Brenda, and all their guests and family. The newlyweds, Mr. and Mrs. Charles Cord, outdid themselves preparing the delicious meal and decorating the table with gourds and colorful fall flowers. Mary brought side dishes of Lasagna, Penne alla vodka, and four kinds of pies in a cooler from Tampa. Mattie proudly introduced Evan to everyone, showed off her seven-carat diamond ring and received heartfelt congratulations.

Sky took Mattie aside and told her how happy he was that she was starting a new life with Evan and that he wished her the best, always. He said how impressed he was by Evan and hoped he would be the wonderful husband Mattie deserved. Evan had heard a lot about Sky through Mattie and found Sky to be a genuinely nice person. He asked if Sky would consider becoming his internist. Laughing good-naturedly, he said that he had heard a rumor that Sky was an excellent physician, and he wanted to put it to the test.

"Carolyn and I have an announcement of our own," Sky announced proudly taking her hand. "Two days ago, Carolyn took a home pregnancy test and discovered that we are expecting. We called Mom and Dad right away to share the good news and to ask them if we could get married in their back garden right after the first of the year."

Sky was ecstatic that he was going to be marrying Carolyn and having a baby. They had already decided that Casey was going to be Carolyn's maid of honor and Cam was going to give the bride away since Carolyn had no family still living. Mary and Cam were thrilled at the prospect of becoming grandparents.

"That's wonderful news," Brenda said happily. "There are certainly a lot of things we all have to be thankful for today. Happy Thanksgiving everybody. Let's drink to love, marriage and babies."

Sky was beaming with happiness and pride, and when he thought no one was looking, lovingly patted Carolyn's stomach and kissed her.

"That's the most wonderful news," Mattie beamed as she hugged Carolyn. "I guess I'm going to be an aunt in a few months. I can't wait."

CHAPTER 68

Mattie took several weeks, but finally found the perfect home for their needs. It was a two-story Mediterranean style house with a separate guest house, an infinity pool, and a tennis court located on a large point lot on the intracoastal waterway. There was a large space along one side of the seawall for the new 165-foot yacht they commissioned to be built in Italy, patterned after *Liquidity* but with their own special touches and modifications. The yacht would be delivered in about eleven months. Mattie and Evan decided to call her *Mattie's Choice*. Evan approached Mercer Llanos and offered him the full-time job as his captain on *Mattie's Choice*. Captain Llanos agreed to leave his beloved *Liquidity* and become the Stone's full-time captain when their new yacht was finished. He also volunteered to marry the couple onboard when the yacht set sail on her maiden voyage from Ft. Lauderdale. Mattie and Evan were delighted and accepted his offer. A wedding at sea seemed perfect for the couple who had fallen in love on a cruise in the Mediterranean.

Mattie informed Charles that she was retiring from working in his chartering business. She assured him that she would always be only a phone call away if she was ever needed. She knew that Charles had hired a competent temporary CEO for the next two years to run the company.

She explained to Charles and Brenda that she wanted to devote herself to running the new company that she and Evan had founded, *Stone Enterprises*. Its primary mission was to expand her *Nautical Options* app to reach a broader audience. She asked Charles to release her from any "do not compete" stipulations and to assign the patent to her exclusively. He agreed on the spot, with no hesitation. It had been Mattie's idea from the beginning, and he felt no ownership of the app. Besides, he wanted to retire and travel with Brenda, not invest his time and more money in a new startup company with all the ensuing headaches.

Evan had put together a group of investors and a distinguished board of directors – one of which was Dr. Tony Grant, who would help guide the project along. The new umbrella company, *Stone Enterprises*, would continue to match yachts with prospective purchasers and charterers. However, it would also match travelers with hotels, restaurants, cultural events, and leisure activities around the world. Mattie would be working from a home office in her new house. The potential was enormous, and Evan was talking about taking the company public in a year or two. Dr. Tony wanted to explore the possibility of the new app getting involved with telehealth, especially for people traveling on ships worldwide.

Evan's Miami production company was on the cusp of becoming a mega success story. He had scripts and plans for producing feature films, animated series, game shows, podcasts, and television reality shows. Nine new series were in production for the following television season. *Miami Intrigues* still boasted the largest weekly audiences and had a huge fan base. *The Wall Street Journal* recently reported that a deal worth about $ 800 million for a buy-out from a private equity group was likely in the works.

In spite of all the busy activities, Evan and Mattie never lost sight of his cardiologist's advice. They maintained a reasonable, but not over-loaded, schedule. When they weren't working, they played tennis or golf, chartered boats or worked out in their home gym. They frequently trav-eled and visited friends around the country and the world. Their life was full and happy…only one thing was missing – a child.

Mattie and Evan kept trying to conceive, but she did not get preg-nant, although they had fun trying. Frustrated, they eventually consulted a fertility specialist who, after putting them both through arduous testing, announced that there was no medical reason that they could not have a baby. The doctor told them to relax, and a pregnancy might happen in time. However, after another year, Mattie remained barren. She finally gave up hope of conceiving a child of her own, and she and Evan, after long heart to heart discussions, started exploring adoption possibilities. It should have been easy. They would make excellent parents but at Evan's age of almost fifty, the agencies were a little more cautious about placing an infant in his care.

Once Charles found a new interim manager, Charles stepped away from Lux Charters as its full time CEO. The new one, along with Ned and Linda, handled the day-to-day workings of Lux Charters and com-municated with Charles as needed when he was not riding an elephant in South Africa or snorkeling in the Great Barrier reef. If Charles was unreachable, and there was a problem, they called Mattie. Linda pros-pered and became Lux's number one salesperson and office manager. Ned became her personal assistant, but he was also free to handle his own deals. Casey worked with Linda as a salaried employee, learning the business. She still wanted to cruise on yachts but was content to work as a saleswoman chartering them as long as she could be by Ned's side.

Lux Charters continued to thrive, and by using Mattie's app, it was able to expand to thirty brokers and became the largest chartering company in the United States. Lux was making plans to open satellite offices in Nice, France and Monte Carlo, Monaco the following year. Business prospects were exciting.

Sky and Carolyn had a baby girl seven months after they married, and two years later, a boy. Cam and Mary were ecstatic and loving grandparents and Casey and Mattie fawned all over their niece and nephew. But Mattie still hungered for a baby of her own.

Several months after her nephew was born, one morning, she felt ill at breakfast and began throwing up. The morning sickness lasted nonstop for seven months. Her pregnancy was difficult, and her beautiful slim figure became bloated and cumbersome. Her ankles were swollen, and her feet hurt all the time. She moaned and complained about how fat and ugly she looked, but Evan thought she was still the most beautiful woman he had ever seen. He adored her more each day and showered her with gifts, and gifts for their baby. They decided to be surprised by the sex of their infant, so the nursery was elaborately decorated in yellow and white. They also refused to consider names until the baby was born.

After an arduous labor, Mattie delivered a healthy, eight-pound baby boy, Charles Evan Stone, forever called "Charlie." All the misery of her childless years and difficult pregnancy were forgotten. She felt the wonderous love of a mother for her child, and for the first time *truly understood* completely what Brenda had done so many years ago…that a loving and devoted mother would do *anything* to protect her child.

Mattie finally had the family she had always wanted: a child of her own, a loving brother and sister, and the husband she adored. She had been truly blessed. Hurtful secrets of the past had been dealt with and buried forever.

Sunny skies, smooth seas, bottles of formula and piles of dirty diapers lay ahead...with joy.

ACKNOWDGEMENTS

My utmost gratitude to my husband, Bart, for his infinite patience and editing skills. He spent countless hours reviewing this manuscript, tightening up the prose, and correcting inaccuracies. The story flows more smoothly because of his input. His help has been invaluable.

My sincere thanks to photographers Lauren Petrella and David Cartee. I am very unphotogenic, but somehow, they used their superb talents with the camera and made me look presentable. Their photo is on my *website, Peggychernowbooks.com,* and on the back cover of *Secrets.*

Secrets would never have made it to market if not for my terrific publisher, Stephanie Denton at Monkedia. She guided me through every facet of the process and helped design the book's cover. Her patience in answering my questions and addressing my concerns has never wavered. Thank you for your professionalism and friendship.

And kudos to Hunter Schmitt, my amazing granddaughter, for her thoughtful and accurate proof reading of this manuscript.

And finally, thank you to all my readers. Your time is valuable, and I appreciate you giving some of it to spend with the characters I've created on the pages of this and my other novels. I hope I don't disappoint you.